THE RHEA JENSEN SERIES

BOOK 6

SHERALYN PRATT

WICKED SASSY
SALT LAKE CITY, UTAH

ISBN: 978-0-9743331-9-9

Cover Art: Angela Olsen Baxter
Cover design © 2016 Sheralyn Pratt
Published by Wicked Sassy
Salt Lake City, Utah

Printed in the United States of America

10 9 8 7 6 5 4 3 2 1

Destiny is no matter of chance;
it is a matter of choice.

—William Jennings Brian

PROLOGUE

Elliott Church might personify everything I hated about Los Angeles, but the man had a gorgeous home.

Well, mansion, really.

As a valet pulled my car out of the roundabout in front of the main entrance, I tried to wrap my head around the fact that I was standing in front of a private investigator's home and not some Hollywood bigwig's.

The estate sat on five acres of prime Hollywood property, all meticulously maintained. A lifetime of seeing properties through my father's expert landscaping eyes had me picking up the details of exactly how much care Elliott put into every bush and blossom he kept hidden behind stone walls, imported trees, fifteen-foot hedges.

Good fences made good neighbors in Elliott's world, it seemed.

Based on the soiree visible through the windows as I moved up the front walkway, Elliott's world also included swanky parties with the elite. Part of me wondered if Elliott agreed to meet me at his home on purpose just to show off a little. He'd offered me a job about a week and a half before, reassuring me that we could make each other rich. I'd said no thanks. His response had been to smile and tell me to look him up when I reconsidered.

I hadn't reconsidered, but I'd woken up that morning to circumstances that required the man's unique brand of help. Immediately.

As I walked through the front entrance, scanning for Elliott's face in a crowd of men in fine suits and women sporting elegant designs from the likes of Jason Wu, Dolce & Gabbana, and Zac Posen, a woman in a cobalt blue dress approached me.

"Miss Jensen," she said, her tone not a question but a greeting. She knew who I was. "I'll escort you to Elliott's office. He will be right with you."

I nodded and started to respond until my escort turned away and started walking. She led me across the main lobby—yes, the home had a lobby—past a sitting room full of pretentious sophisticates who acknowledged no one but each other, and through a doorway leading down to a lower level.

The house must have had some serious insulation going on , because the moment I hit the bottom level, all upstairs sound disappeared. I could no longer hear party noises or even the sound of footsteps from above. The unnatural silence amplified otherwise inaudible sounds—the swish of fabric brushing as we walked, the soft click of a door lock popping open as Ms. Cobalt passed some invisible threshold—as she led me to an office with a color scheme that looked like it had been inspired by a cologne box.

"Elliott will be right with you. Feel free to have a seat," the woman said before leaving the room.

I didn't sit. I was too anxious to sit.

I'd screwed up. I wasn't used to screwing up, but somehow I'd screwed up in every important way possible in the past few weeks.

My first mistake had been assuming that a shy girl from

Alabama needed to change to thrive in Los Angeles—that she needed to harness her natural beauty to her advantage.

It's what I'd always done; it had worked for me. It should have worked for Kay, too.

It hadn't.

It had backfired in the most catastrophic ways possible. I still didn't understand how everything had gone so very wrong in Kay's life since I befriended her, only that I had to undo as much of the damage as possible.

To do that, I needed to find where Kay had run away to and, to do that, I needed someone like Elliott Church to put me on the top of his priority list.

He'd agreed to see me within four hours of me calling him on a weekend, so that was a good start. Now I just needed him to take the job and help me clean up an uncleanable mess.

Good intentions, man…I'd never offered them to anyone before meeting Kay and I never would again. If someone wanted something from me from now on, they needed to ask. End of story. If my experience with Kay had taught me one thing, it was that potential could not be rushed or forced. It must come into its own, at its own pace.

I could support people, sure; but bad things happened when you dragged people to your personal finish line at a pace you set for them. It was like forcing a flower to bloom, leaving bruised and broken petals where all the good intentions had been focused on pulling things open.

Another mistake had been leaving Kay with the wolves she thought to be friends. I'd known better; she hadn't. But I'd figured seeing the wolves for who they were was a lesson she needed to learn firsthand—that they'd show their colors by saying nice things to her face while crucifying her behind her back.

You know, the usual petty, mean girl fare.

I'd never imagine that the sorority sisters asking her to pledge to their house would hand her a drink laced with Ketamine and deliver her to the fraternity boys as a...what? A gift? An offering? A sacrifice?

I still hadn't wrapped my head around that part—how in the world one girl, not to mention several in cahoots—could treat another girl that way. But whatever their motives, based on the findings of medical professionals, it was likely that Kay had been raped by all the freshman fraternity initiates.

So yes, Kay had learned that those sorority girls were not her friends in one of the most horrifying ways possible.

And I was the friend who had left Kay with them at the party.

The next in my long list of mistakes had been trying to manage the aftermath of what had happened like a case worker. Kay had needed a friend. She'd needed a shoulder to cry on and someone to listen to her, not someone focused on the nuts and bolts of making sure the business end of dealing with all the trauma was all accounted for.

As it turned out, for all my efforts, I hadn't known what I was doing. I hadn't even documented anything real-time. It hadn't felt respectful, and I'd figured the hospital and the police officers had all the evidence needed for a criminal case. Not once while everything was playing out did I imagine that all the evidence would all go missing within the first week and that the criminal investigation into Kay's rape would go inactive.

That part wasn't my fault, but I should have thought to make copies of everything and taken pictures as backup.

I should have. I hadn't. Now there was nothing.

I didn't blame Kay for dropping out of college and catching a plane home after finding out there would be no investigation. All her wounds were still fresh, and the taunting on campus had been unreal—almost as if the frat boys knew they were untouchable. They'd spit insults at her on campus, spray painted her dorm door, and even given her little spanks as she passed by.

The administration didn't care. Campus police didn't care. Not enough evidence, they said. Guys will be guys, they said. Hypersensitive girls will be hypersensitive girls, they said. Never mind that these same guys had drugged and raped Kay as part of pledge week and a case had been opened to investigate them.

"Allegedly," the administration liked to remind me. Innocent until proven guilty and all that.

So, yes, in the face of everything, I understood why Kay had run home. But I also knew that going home meant giving up on her dream of having an education and career. Going home meant getting married at eighteen and living the farm life.

There was nothing wrong with that except I knew for a fact that Kay didn't want that for herself. She wanted to be an investigative reporter. She wanted to live in a big city and take vacations around the world. She didn't even really want to date yet, not to mention get married and start having kids.

Yet she'd fled to a home where that was the only future for her.

Kay didn't want the rural life, and I needed to remind her that one party and a handful of frat boys didn't have to change her life forever. She could still be all the things she'd dreamed for herself, and I'd help her get there—at her own pace this time.

My thoughts had me nervously pacing plush cream carpet as I waited for Elliott to join me. I glanced over items in display cases to give myself something to do, not recognizing anything I saw, but sensing that the keepsakes were rare. It seemed Elliott had a thing for collecting ancient tools and sculptures. On impulse, I glanced behind one of the cases to check to see if it had an alarm system and wasn't surprised to see it did. Elliott Church didn't strike me as the trusting type.

I continued to look around, noticing that the objects in the room weren't the only things with a security system. The single bookcase in the room had the exact design I'd seen in a catalog my dad had picked up when he'd been toying with the idea of creating a panic room in his home. He'd opted to skip that investment, but I'd glanced through the catalog and once my eyes saw an image, my brain had the habit of memorizing it.

I was about to go knock on the wall behind the bookcase to see if I could tell where the safe room ended when near-silent steps came up behind me and a familiar voice spoke.

"Miss Jensen," Elliott said, that salesman smile of his greeting me as I turned to face him. "I had a feeling I'd be seeing you again soon."

"Mr. Church," I said, trying not to sound too rushed. "I want to hire you. I need you to find someone for me. Today."

"Is that so?" His lips pursed with interest even as he played coy. "I don't know if you're going to like my price."

"I have money," I said with a little more attitude than I usually threw around. "Unless your rates are ridiculous. Then I'll go somewhere else."

Elliott took a seat at his desk and leaned back in his chair, overtly studying me. "Last time we spoke, I offered you a job."

That was a bit of a curve ball, but I went with it. "I remember."

"I don't do that often, for your information, Miss Jensen. But you have some very impressive test results that tell me that we could be invaluable to each other."

"You mentioned that, but I'm pretty sure I'm not interested in becoming a private investigator."

"How do you know?" he challenged. "Have you tried it?"

He had me there. "Obviously not."

A smirk pulled one corner of his mouth. "Wouldn't you like to know how I'm going to find your friend with just a few keystrokes? Wouldn't you like to be able to do that?"

Obviously, yes. I was willing to drop a huge chunk of change for that particular skill at the moment. But just because I needed a car repair didn't mean I wanted to become a mechanic.

"I'd rather just pay you." Reaching into my pocket, I held out a paper to him. "This is her name and social security number. I know she lives in Alabama, but I have no idea where."

He smiled, reaching out for the paper. "See? You're already resourceful."

"Can you help me?"

He smiled at me as he leaned across his desk. "That's what I've been trying to tell you since the day we met, Miss Jensen. We are both in a position to help each other."

Man, the guy just wasn't giving up, which was a weird mix of flattering and creepy. "I'm eighteen, Mr. Church. I'm more interested in earning my degree and having a little fun than I am in starting a career in your industry. I'm sorry, but I'm not interested in accepting your offer."

"That's too bad," he said thoughtfully.

"Maybe in a few years—"

"It's too bad," he added. "Because you don't really have a choice."

That brought me up short. "What?"

"I *will* help you, Rhea. And you will work for me."

I grew still, refusing to let him see the flash of fear that passed through me at his words. "Uh, excuse me?"

He pushed a few buttons on his keyboard and a large wall-screen lit up behind him with a list of video files ready to be selected.

"I'm sure you heard about the fraternity house fire last night," he said lightly.

His words hit me like a punch in the gut.

He knew about last night…or, at least, he knew enough to fish for hints from me.

I forced myself to stay calm. "Who hasn't? That was insane. It was a miracle no one was hurt."

Elliott nodded. "Wasn't it? Small blessings."

He double-clicked on the top file on the list and a player opened, showing a still-standing frat house from the view of a camera somewhere across the street. The timestamp was just a few minutes before the fire started. I knew because I knew what time the fire started. I'd been there.

I hadn't planned on being there; I'd just caught Ben and the rest of my band on their way out and refused to stay behind. They had been dead set on burning the frat house down to send the message that the fraternity was indeed touchable. All sorts of strings might be being pulled in the fraternity's favor following Kay's rape in their house, but consequences could come through unofficial channels, too.

That had been the conclusion the guys in my band had come to; and in the heat of the moment, I'd been seeing the same shade of red.

My main goal in going along was to make sure they didn't do anything stupid to get themselves caught or start the fire in a way that screamed arson. It had to look like an accident, and the house had to be empty. My friends hadn't planned for me to be there, but I had been.

And Elliott knew it. I could see it on his face.

Across from me, Elliott pointed to two folders from his desk before pressing play on the screen. "The question now is, which version of events will be filed with the police?"

On the large screen, five hooded figures ran out of the frat house and scattered—three larger figures, one medium, and one smaller. From there the screen turned into six quadrants, each one showing a black-clad figure's progress as they raced through several decoy miles to return to the same rendezvous point on screen six: Ben's house.

Elliott said nothing as the video played out. He just watched me watching it.

"Gosh," he said after the last black-clad figure disappeared into Ben's place. "I wonder who burned down the frat house, Rhea. Any ideas?"

I looked at Elliott, meeting his gaze head on. "You want me to believe that my friends were involved with that?"

His lips curved up in amusement. "Your friends?"

I shrugged. "We both know that footage is fake."

A quick bark of a laugh escaped him as he clapped his hands together. "You are an excellent liar when you put your mind to it, Rhea. And please know I mean that as a compliment."

I shook my head. "You honestly want me to believe that's real?"

That confident smile of his returned to his face. "Oh, you know it's real, Rhea. Just like one of these investigative reports is real and one of them reads exactly how you want it to read."

Crap.

Crap, crap, crap.

He knew.

Last night still felt like a surreal dream, but it didn't change the fact that it had definitely happened. The frat house was a pile of ashes because Ben, Isaac, Danny, Aaron, and I had lit the thing up like a bonfire. There wasn't a single part of me that regretted turning the house and everything inside of it into a charred husk. And the investigation into the fire should read that it was an electrical fire because it had been. A faulty wire with no accelerants. No sign of arson. Those were the facts.

At least they were without all of this video surveillance footage.

"You've put me in a very awkward position, Rhea," Elliott said, not sounding at all put out. He was just fine with the position he was in.

"Is that so?"

He nodded. "Because, you see, while I am fully willing to protect my own, I have no such loyalties to people outside of my circle. And if you choose not to work for me…"

He let the threat hang out there, unfinished.

"All I see are black shadows, Mr. Church. I'm not sure why you're showing me all of this."

"And still the poker face," he said with a satisfied sigh before gesturing around the room. "Look around, Rhea. Look how I live. Look at who I am. Look at all those people up there. Those are my clients."

That was impressive. I couldn't lie about that, but that didn't mean I wanted to join Elliott's life—especially under the pressure of blackmail. "I'm eighteen, Mr. Church. I'm a kid. I don't belong in this world yet."

"Wrong," he said quickly. "I wish I could have gotten my hands on you ten years ago—fifteen years ago, even."

Well, that wasn't creepy at all.

"This *is* your world, Rhea, and we don't have any more years for you to waste." He shook his head. "You have no idea how many strings I'm pulling just to get you in the door, but it's my job to know a good investment when I see one. It's my job to see you and everything you are before you see it yourself, and I'm afraid that I just can't have you twiddling away your college years doing stupid teenage things. It's time to get you on track to who you were born to be."

"Which is…?" I drawled.

He smiled. "You have to join my team to find out."

The room fell silent as we stared at each other until Elliott pushed both the folders my direction. "So, tell me, Rhea, which report gets filed with the police? Are you in my inner circle and on your way to help your friend in Alabama, or are you and your band mates about to go on trial for arson? It's your move."

He had me. He knew it, and I knew it. One stupid night and one stupid decision were about to change the rest of my life.

I didn't say anything, but Elliott saw my decision on my face.

"Welcome to Church Investigations, Rhea. I know we're not starting out on the best foot, but you'll understand why I'm fighting so hard for you soon enough. Also, given enough time, you're going to start liking me." He smiled then—a kind smile replacing the hard, unflinching gaze that had been there only a moment before. "Now, let's find your friend, shall we?"

CHAPTER 1

7 Years Later
March 17ᵗʰ, 3:15 a.m.

Slipping out of Ty's arms shouldn't have made my heart ache, but things felt different when you didn't know if you were doing them for the last time.

My husband was a snuggler. I would never have imagined that to be something I liked in a mate. Personal space was kind of a thing with me, but something about Ty had always made me lean in rather than step back.

I'd fought loving him—I really had—but even if the past few months were all I ever got with him, giving in and becoming Mrs. Ty Kimball had been worth it. For me, at least.

Time would tell if he'd feel the same.

Once I slid out of his arms, I stayed facing Ty on the bed, letting my eyes trace over his features as he slept.

Would this be the last time I saw him like this?

No. It wouldn't be the last time. It couldn't be. I would make sure of that.

In a short span of time, Ty had become the center of my world. My soul mate. My training partner. My anchor to the world I hoped existed. I'd told him everything I could about my situation without endangering his life right along with mine, but he had yet to wrap his head around how much trouble I was in and who I was in trouble with.

Some things, if not seen with one's own eyes, sound like hyperbole when explained.

Ty had tried to understand. He really had. But he still didn't get that there was a devil out there who believed he owned my life—body and soul. I hadn't known I'd been making a deal with the devil in Elliott's office seven years ago, but hindsight was 20/20. I'd been naïve when it came to who my boss was and why we had the clients we did. Today was the day I learned just how deep the pit beneath my feet descended.

I knew enough to be scared. The group I'd been working for through Elliott called themselves The Fours, and they could end my physical life on a whim and erase my digital life with a keystroke. They'd already proven that much. I could buy a house with cash and they could show up an hour later and say, *No, you didn't,* and take it right out from underneath me. It was a world where the lowest level bodyguards were elite super soldiers who could outrun me or outfight me just as easily as they could shoot me from a mile away.

I'd tried to communicate all this to Ty over the past few months without outright saying it. There were ears and eyes on every wall, not to mention what all the cell phones and electronic equipment around the world picked up. I could never assume privacy. Recent experiences had taught me that everything I said and did was being monitored, without exceptions. That being the case, I'd done my best to share with Ty that today could end very badly.

Like, really badly…in a permanent way.

He, of course, downplayed my worries in an effort to soothe me and to urge me not to push so hard in my training. His mind was thinking long term—about how my intense training could impact me over time—whereas I'd only been thinking up until today…surviving today. There was no long term if I didn't make it past whatever gauntlet the day would bring.

One final job awaited me—likely one that came with repercussions attached, like prison or death. Either way, I was about to find out. Today was the day I found out if I'd done enough to prepare over the past few months to win amnesty from The Fours…yet all I wanted to do was stay in bed, slide back into Ty's embrace, and live out the rest of my life in the high-security suite I'd secured for a total of three days from the richest and most paranoid conspiracy theorist I knew.

Some homes had a safe room, but my associate was a bit next level in creating safe zones. He had safe suites in every city he did business. You could hit the walls of this particular hotel room with a wrecking ball, and the wrecking ball would bounce. That was only the beginning of the security features. The suite had dedicated cameras and surveillance looking out, but nothing could look in. That was important, as were all the other features that turned an unassuming floor of a hotel into a stronghold.

It was the safest place I could find for the people I loved to stay while I turned myself over to The Fours. Was it overkill? Maybe. Hopefully.

Time would tell.

My body didn't want to move from the bed, and the debate between a shower and ten more minutes with Ty disappeared when his eyes blinked open and focused on me. His hand came up to push some stray hair out of my face. "Hey there."

"Hey, yourself."

No, there would definitely be no shower for me on what might be the last day of my life—just a quick rinse off before getting into my usual jogging clothes.

The Fours instructions were for me to be standing outside on the northeast street corner at 4:00 a.m. sharp. Pre-dawn. The world would be asleep, and that was for the best. The people I was meeting up with operated in the dark and killed anyone who happened to see a shadow move.

I didn't need any witnesses when they picked me up.

Ty watched from the bed as I stepped out of the bathroom in my running clothes.

"Let me walk you out," he said.

I shook my head. "We've talked about this. It should just be me. You don't walk out the door for any reason today."

Without another word, he rose from the bed and walked over to me, his lips pressing against mine as his hands slid up my arms. When we broke apart, I leaned against his chest and inhaled. Not everyone smelled good in the morning, but Ty did.

"How do we make this day not happen?" he asked softly. "How do I steal you away?"

"You don't," I said against his chest. "You can't. Never blame yourself for that."

"I know," he whispered. "You've said as much a hundred times."

We stood like that for maybe a minute. There was nothing left to say. The only thing left was to live the day out and see what the world looked like for us at this same time tomorrow.

"I need to go," I said when the clock changed from 3:44 to 3:45. Being late was not an option.

"Yeah," he said, his voice cracking on the word. Only then did I feel the heat of his tears seeping through my shirt. "I love you."

"I love you, too," I said. "More than words."

I stepped away just enough to give us the angle for one last kiss, and man, did Ty make the most of it. When it took us one step closer back towards the bed, I pulled away.

"I have to go."

"I know."

I didn't hesitate this time. I went straight for the door, not looking back as I stepped through to find a small group of people waiting for me in the main hall.

Dahl and Kay stood side-by-side, looking like they wanted to lean into each other, but had collectively opted for the wall behind them instead. My breath caught at the sight of them—not expecting, but glad, to see them.

Dahl's proposal a few weeks before hadn't been met with the response he'd been hoping for, and the two had been on a break since. Feelings hadn't changed on either side, but avoiding physical contact seemed to be an unspoken rule between them ever since. I couldn't help but hope they'd get over that sooner rather than later. Kay deserved a man like Dahl in her life.

Next to them stood my dad, his gaunt expression the culmination of more than one night's lost sleep. I'd told my father as much as I could about everything, but he still didn't understand. All he knew was that he couldn't talk me out of what I was about to do and that there was the possibility he might not see me again.

What parent could accept that kind of news regarding any child, not to mention his only child?

My throat clenched at the unexpected trio waiting for me, emotion hitting me before I quickly blinked it back.

I tried for a smile. "I thought we said all our goodbyes last night."

Kay shook her head. "If you think any of us are going to miss giving you one more goodbye hug, you're insane."

And I would be insane not to accept those hugs.

Kay was the first to step in, wrapping me in those elegant arms of hers and holding me tight enough against her that I could hear the rapid thumping of her heart.

"Do what you need to do to come back tonight," she said fiercely. "Whatever it takes. Do it."

I nodded against her. "I'll do my best."

She was reluctant to let me go but stepped to the side when I reached out for Dahl. Our hug was more of a bro-hug.

"If anyone can make it through this, it's you," he said.

"Thanks," I said, stepping back. "You know what to do here. None of you leave this suite all day. No matter what."

"Understood," he said with a militant nod.

I reached out and squeezed his hand. "I mean it. No exceptions. No matter what the lure, none of you leave."

Dahl's nod was a silent vow that allowed everything else to remain unspoken. I could trust him…or if nothing else, I could trust the fact that while he liked and respected me, he loved Kay. Even if they were on a break, he loved her. Given a choice, he'd save her life over mine and that made him perfect for my needs.

Dahl was the only person I knew who seemed to sense how bad things could go today. He'd come to me privately and let me know he wanted to be on hand to watch out for Ty, Kay, and my dad. It was an offer I couldn't—and didn't—refuse. The fact that he wanted to go back to his soldier days to watch over them was the best thing I could have asked for. It only made it better that I hadn't had to ask. Dahl wanted to do this as much as I wanted him to, and in doing so, he was giving me the peace of mind to focus on whatever The Fours threw my way.

There was no way to repay him for that. But if I made it through the day, I would try.

Dahl and I shared a quick nod of understanding before I stepped away and turned to my dad.

"Don't," I said when I saw him blinking back tears. Unable to look at him, I hugged him. He held on tight.

"I'm scared," he said.

"Me, too," I whispered back. "But I'll do everything I can, okay?"

I felt him nod against my cheek as Ty's hand rested on my shoulder. "It's 3:54."

I pressed a kiss to my dad's cheek and stepped away. "I can't be late."

"Okay," my dad said.

Turning to get one last look at the people most important to me, I gave them all quick nod. "See you all on the other side." Other side of the day or other side of the veil, I wasn't sure. Either way, it all started with me getting to the start point in five minutes.

I moved to the front door, hearing Ty's steps trail me. When I reached it, I turned, threaded my fingers through Ty's, and gave him one last kiss.

"Don't walk out this door for anything," I said before stepping away, shutting the door between us, and walking to the main elevator.

I was officially out of the safe zone.

My eyes glanced to the camera in the elevator, fairly certain that somehow The Fours could see me through its eye. I had no idea how that was possible, only that it was the only explanation for how they seemed to know all things at all times.

Somehow they were dialed in. Somehow they had eyes and ears everywhere, like an omniscient god.

God.

I'd been an agnostic nearly all my life, but for the past year I'd been trying to believe in something bigger…in a plan. God's plan. There were still things I was trying to wrap my head around, like faith: things hoped for, but not seen. Nothing was more counterintuitive to me than faith, but I did like prayer. I liked the process of it. I liked how it forced me to be honest.

When I did pray, I was rarely formal about it. But if you wanted God or the universe or whatever might be watching over life to give you something, it made sense to make those wants known. These days I shared my will silently, though, in case The Fours were listening as well.

Please keep them safe, I said in my mind as the elevator made the journey to ground level. *I have no idea what today will bring, but I pray no one will be harmed. I pray no one will be killed. Whatever lies ahead of me today, help me see a way through it that allows me to return to my life and my family and friends. If that is remotely possible, please let me take the path that harms none and leads home.*

The elevator doors opened, drawing my attention back to the present as I stepped out. The hotel's early morning skeleton crew gave me a passing glance as I walked through the hotel lobby and out the front door. Automatic doors opened for me, leading me to the roundabout entrance. No valet. Not too many people checking in at four in the morning, apparently.

I turned to the right, moving away from the hotel and down the sidewalk, reaching the corner at 3:59 a.m. I was right on time and the street was empty…for about thirty more seconds. Then a black Escalade approached and stopped in front of me.

Without hesitation, a man stepped out of the vehicle on my side while two enforcers got out on the opposite door. The non-enforcer handed me a capped vial.

"You know what to do."

I did. There was no need to ask questions or make a scene. This ended the same way no matter what I did, so I took the cap off the vial and drank the liquid in one shot.

The enforcers stepped in on either side of me, hooking their arms under mine as they walked me to the car.

"You have a big day ahead of you, Ms. Jensen," the man said. "It's time to get started."

My last name is Kimball now, I thought to myself but said nothing. These guys didn't care that I was married.

They didn't care about me at all.

By the third step, my feet faltered beneath me. Halos and sparks filled my vision a moment before my body drooped as if I were somehow melting. One moment I was noting that there was a fourth person waiting for me in the back seat of the SUV with a syringe in his hand, and the next moment everything faded to black.

CHAPTER 2

Tension snapped through my body, forcing my eyes open. Instinct had me covering my nose to try to block the ammonia catalyzing my return to consciousness. When an adrenaline shot hit my system a moment later, I shot up off my back, somehow landing on my feet as the air around me cleared back into breathable oxygen in record time.

All my senses came back online at once, swirling and spinning incoherently for a moment as I got my bearings.

Large room—warehouse big—and empty. Multiple commercial airplanes could park in the space around me, but there were none in sight today. Today the hangar housed only two large, transparent cube cages. I was in one of them, and a man built like a pitbull stood in the next cube over.

I noted that, unlike me, my neighbor didn't look the slightest bit disoriented. He looked like he'd danced this dance before—his trained eyes assessing the space with unblinking thoroughness—even as I fought the vertigo of switching from drugged-out to fully wired in the blink of an eye.

Where had the adrenaline shot come from? I was alone in the space. There was no one to administer the injection and nothing in the space to inject me with.

A quick personal inventory revealed that a new wristband had appeared on my wrist, its face dark for the moment. I pushed the buttons on the edge of the face with no reaction—neither from the watch nor from nerve endings where my right hand brushed up against my left wrist. I was completely numb, but only around my wrist. I could feel my hand just fine. Odd.

Before I could figure out what that was about, the human pitbull started rapping lightly on his cube with his knuckle. He cocked his head to the side as if listening for something. I heard nothing, but I saw the look he sent me.

We were not friends. I could tell that much through the glass, but I also got the sense that he knew who I was. He didn't have the look of someone taking stock of another person for the first time. He had more of the look of a fighter at a weigh-in—the look of a man who had studied his opponent in videos and was now seeing them for the first time in person, confident that he was going to win.

He knew me, but I didn't know him.

Advantage: Pitbull.

My neighbor was tall, thick, and muscled. Not useless pretty muscles either. He had muscles like Ty…muscles that were trained to routinely do what few people ever even tried. I watched as he walked, noting that he didn't move like a man burdened under his own weight. He was a foot taller than me and at least a hundred pounds heavier, yet he moved with the ease of a man half his size.

All things being equal, I was looking at a man who could kill me, and I had a sinking feeling that was exactly what he was supposed to do.

Don't make assumptions, I reminded myself. *Take everything in. Watch your environment.*

Not that there was much to watch. The warehouse consisted of four walls, a ceiling, support beams, and a floor so polished I could practically see my reflection on the ground.

I looked around to see what else I might be missing when a male voice sounded out from a speaker overhead.

"In times of old, gladiators were placed in a coliseum to fight to the death for the entertainment of the elite," the voice declared. *"It's been said that high-impact modern sports have taken the place of ancient coliseum games—football, MMA, rugby—but this is untrue. True gladiators still exist; only the coliseum has changed."*

The pitbull and I locked eyes. Yep, we were enemies. No doubt about it now.

"Victory to the winner, and ignominy to the defeated," the voice declared as if he expected a room full of people to cheer in response. Who knew? Maybe that's exactly what happened wherever he was in the world. *"Freedom isn't free; it must be earned. And one of you is about to do the earning."*

A world atlas the size of a football field appeared on the far wall with colored dots scattered across it.

"Around the world, the elite have reviewed your profiles and made their wagers as to which of you will be victorious. With $12.3 billion in the pot to start and unrestricted side-betting through the end of today's bout, know that people around the globe will be watching your battle very closely. This is important for you to know for two reasons: first, know that you cannot run. There is not a place on this earth we won't find you. And for every day we don't find you, we will execute someone you love until we do."

A new type of vertigo washed over me as the man's words registered. I'd known The Fours were a powerful organization, but the sight of thousands of dots across all the continents was more than I had imagined in even my most paranoid moments. I expected a presence in the US, of course. But not everywhere.

"Second," the voice continued. *"Once a gladiator is victorious over his opponent, each of these dots will turn either green or red. Green dots will be benefactors offering sanctuary or*

employment to the victor. Red dots will signify individuals who were displeased with your performance and have contributed to the bounty of the assassin who sees you dead first. Be aware that these assassins are already in play and allowed to track you throughout the day, but will only be unleashed at midnight."

This little welcome orientation was pretty much everything I'd been hoping I wouldn't hear. Deep down, was I surprised to hear it? No. But after weeks of talking to Ty and Kay, I'd allowed myself to hope that maybe The Fours just wanted a final job out of me or something. I'd let my mind wish for something I knew wasn't possible while pushing the biggest question of the day to the back of my mind: Could I kill to stay alive?

Police officers and members of the military had to answer this question every day, but their circumstances were different. They took oaths to act in the public good, whereas Mr. Pitbull and I were being asked to commit premeditated murder in the name of entertaining the elite.

Could I really do that?

"Your gladiator match lasts until midnight," the man continued. *"There are no rules, only a winner. All requests for assistance from gladiators will be denied, and any interference from internal sources to influence the day's events will be met with capital punishment. There is simply too much money involved to allow for anything but a zero-tolerance policy."*

Right. Because money. That's what was important here.

"You now have twenty minutes to study your opponent," the voice said as one of the glass walls of my cube lit up like up like a computer screen, showing me a digital folder on what was apparently a touchscreen. The folder was labeled with a name: Anton Petrov. *"At least one of you will die today. The information you focus on in the next twenty minutes will likely determine your fate."*

The pitbull was already tapping the folder on his wall, opening a carousel of files all about me. I stepped forward and did the same, blinking in surprise when my wall flooded with folders. I wouldn't be able to get through this volume in a day, not to mention twenty minutes.

Without wasting time, I started tapping open the files and filtering them into three piles: Required Reading, Read if I Have Time, and Irrelevant.

"Impress us, gladiators," the voice mocked. *"We trained you, which means we know what you can do. It also means that you know what we can do. You will be tracked. You will be watched. We see everything. We hear everything. If you cheat or try to change the rules of the game, you both will lose."*

I half-listened as I focused in on the folders. Anton's training history? That was required reading. His family history? If I had time. Known associates? Required. Cognitive aptitude tests? Required. Work history? Required. Financial history? Required.

Crap. Was there anything in the folder I didn't need to get my eyes on?

A glance at my opponent convinced me of the worst; he wasn't seeing my files for the first time. His movements weren't manic like mine. He seemed to be simply scrolling through my carousel of files to see if there was anything new he hadn't seen before.

How was that fair?

Feeling the time crunch, I opted to take a peek at his training.

To call it extensive would be an understatement. Anton Petrov had received eight black belts before I'd ever taken a class on how to kick. His styles ranged from Kung Fu to Systema. The man was well rounded. He had every skill I had, plus at least a dozen I didn't, and five I'd never heard of. It was almost superhuman.

Feeling a bit panicked, I selected his aptitude tests. Spatial abilities? Basically perfect. Abstract and mechanical reasoning? Pretty much the same. He dipped slightly on verbal ability and a little bit more on numerical aptitude. His lowest score was in fault diagnosis.

Great. Just great. I was dealing with a man who was used to having other people think for him. Whoever he was, he was accustomed to taking orders and that wasn't good for me at all.

"Fifteen minutes remain," the voice said over the speakers. *"When your time is up, you will each be returned to the city and your wristbands will be activated. Again, you have until midnight to track and claim victory over your opponent while thousands of the most powerful men in the world watch you with extreme interest. Why?"*

The giant atlas on the wall was replaced with the schematics of a bomb.

"Tonight, this bomb is going to be the loser's co-star in a domestic terrorist attack. Kill your opponent before midnight, and you will earn the honor of not being named as the terrorist responsible for the attack in tomorrow morning's news. Whichever of you does die first, know this bomb and its impact will be your legacy in history books. Your ignominy. Around the world, you will be known as the terrorist who plotted one of the most heartless attacks of this century."

My brain froze up as it processed the threat. My mother was from the Middle East and Anton Petrov's father was Russian. It was like we were prepackaged terrorists built for media consumption. Put either of our faces up and mention our pedigree and nearly anyone would buy the "homegrown terrorist" story.

And that, of course, was exactly why The Fours had chosen us to face off against each other. No matter who won, they won. They'd had six months to set all this up, and they weren't going to waste a moment of all that effort. They would have their games and they would eat cake, too.

"Also know that if both of you are still alive at midnight, you will jointly be blamed for the attack and hunted not only by our vast resources but by every law enforcement officer around the

world."

I listened to their insane conditions with one ear as I continued to absorb as much information as I could from Anton's files.

He had gone to all private schools, none of which I'd ever heard of. His class list seemed to be a schizophrenic mix of centuries. Fencing. Computer Science. Socratic Method. French. Chinese. Broadsword. Classic Literature. Debate. Computer Programming. Arabic. Assassin Protocols. Meditation. World Religions. Cultural Customs. Munitions and Weapons.

Where had this guy gone to school? The Hogwarts for bodyguards? From everything I could see, he'd been trained to understand and blend into environments around the world since he was five years old. All I could hope was that "the city" we'd be returned to was Los Angeles, and not some exotic city that only one of us knew how to navigate. Because it looked like Anton Petrov could be dropped on any continent and still be able to navigate quite comfortably.

The more I read, the harder it was to keep my spirits high. My opponent was a machine. He'd been born and bred to kill on command. Now he was being told to kill me. If I didn't want him to succeed, I had to kill him.

But I didn't want to kill him.

I didn't want to kill at all. I'd just prayed in an elevator that no one would die before the end of the day. A prayer like that meant nothing if I was willing to pull the first trigger on someone myself.

But the game had just changed in a big way. Could I kill to save the people I loved from seeing me branded a terrorist?

I didn't know, and it was past time to make a decision. Anton Petrov had already made his decision. I could see it in his eyes. He was coming for me and he had no intention of dying in ignominy. He'd killed before and he could do it again, which changed the question I needed to ask myself to: Could I kill in self-defense and live with it?

Yes. If Anton Petrov came at me and forced my hand, I was pretty sure I could, and I had just under thirteen minutes to find a way. Because, at the moment, this was all looking like a very one-sided fight.

Tapping on a folder of Known Associates, I flipped through the profiles of several military and private security individuals. All formidable. All men I never wanted to meet in an alley—especially the one man on the list that I actually knew.

Mark Weston.

My heart sank when I saw his name on Anton's list of mentors. I tried not to falter as his profile popped up, but I definitely had a deer-in-the-headlights moment.

Mark Weston had taught me 80% of what I used in the field. He was the personification of a diehard militant with no work-life balance. There were survivalists, there were conspiracy theorists, and then there was Mark. He was a category all his own.

Even worse, Mark knew my every weakness and had exploited them all firsthand when he'd try to train them out of me back during my first year with Elliott. True, I hadn't seen the man in years, but that really didn't mean anything. Mark knew me like very few did.

And Anton Petrov knew Mark.

No wonder Anton looked so confident. He had every reason to be.

I continued to look through folders as quickly as I could, taking mental pictures of the information more than actually reading what I saw while Anton took a more relaxed approach.

At about the eight-minute mark, a dull ache started building underneath my wristband. It didn't stem from my skin—I still couldn't feel that—but from within my wrist itself. When I rubbed at the pain, I noticed that the band didn't move. It was tempting to look down and figure out why, but I needed to wait until the countdown clock was done ticking before poking around the band because so far my only advantages against my opponent were that I was smaller, faster, and could blend into a crowd easier.

Anton beat me at everything else. Literally.

When the countdown clock hit zero, I still had three folders to go. It didn't matter. The glass wall in front of me stopped being a screen and returned to looking like nothing more than a pane of glass. At the same time, the face of my new accessory lit up on my wrist.

"Your wristband tracks your locations with a ten-second time delay, just to keep things interesting," the same man explained. *"The three other modes on the watch will be activated for the victor. But know that we have real-time feedback on your vital signs at all times and that removing that band will not remove our ability to track you. You drank your tracking device earlier this morning, and it's currently swimming throughout your entire body."*

I flexed my hand as I listened, annoyed at the dull ache that was growing inside my wrist. I was just raising my hand to get a closer look at the situation when the voice explained it. *"You may have noticed that your new wristbands are bolted through your wrist to prevent removal. Tampering with or removing the device is forbidden, and constitutes immediate forfeiture. Remove the band and an immediate bounty of $1 million dollars will be placed on your head. And, as previously mentioned, bounty hunters will be in place to collect immediately."*

Slipping my finger under the band, I felt the post that anchored it in place. It had been pushed through the gap where my radius and ulna bones came together at the wrist, either side of the post firmly fixed to the band as if it were all one piece.

No wonder my wrist was starting to ache. The cooler metal inside me now would take some getting used to.

"The rules are simple," the man said. *"One of you dies before midnight and becomes a terrorist. The other lives and is given until*

midnight to make it to safe ground. If you make it, you will have sanctuary…if you can reach it."

His light and breezy tone almost convinced me that this was a dream. A bad, bad dream. If only I could wake myself up.

"Get ready to fight for your lives, gladiators. Because the next time you wake up, the battle to the death will begin. One of you will live through the day, and the other will live in infamy. And it all starts now."

A hiss coming up from the floor tipped me off to the fact that gas was being pumped into the cage. There was no way to avoid it, so I followed Anton's lead and laid down to avoid any injury that might occur from collapsing.

As the world went black once again, one thought was clear in my mind: I was glad I'd given everyone that extra hug because today would almost certainly be the last day of my life.

CHAPTER 3

The rocking motion of my head against a hard surface brought me back to awareness. It took me a second to realize that I was lying on my back and a large hand was smacking me awake.

"Rise and shine, little girl," a man said. "Time to pay the piper."

I opened my eyes—or thought I did. The world was still black. It took a couple of beats to realize I had a blindfold on.

"Wakey-wakey," another voice cooed. "It's time to get on your feet and get moving."

"She's awake," the first voice said. "Respiration and heart rate are rising to normal. Body temperature also rising."

The next slap against my face was much harder.

"Yep," the guy said. "She felt that. She's good to go."

"Up you go!"

A van door rolled open off to my right letting in the noises of what sounded like a crowded area. I was awake enough to remove the blindfold, but hands gripped my wrists before I could reach my face, dragging me to the van's door. I felt the sun hit my skin a moment before my legs were pushed out of the van. The two men dragged me out and placed me on the curb before pulling the blindfold off me.

Sunlight blinded me and my eyes squinted to adjust to daylight as the van door shut and I heard the engine pull away. I didn't worry about the van. I would never see it again. I had other things to worry about.

Things like: where was I?

My eyes were still adjusting when Iron Man came into focus—not a poster or a picture, but…Iron Man. I blinked, unsure that I was actually seeing what I was seeing until I shielded my eyes with my hand and got a better look at everything.

The Dolby Theater in Hollywood. That's where they'd dropped me.

Tourists milled around me, moving in that halting fashion people used on vacation. No one seemed to notice or care that I'd just been unceremoniously dropped off by a van. Selfies and finding celebrity stars on the walk of fame were on most people's minds as I looked around at one of the most tourist-infested parts of LA.

Darth Vader posed for pictures about fifty feet off to my left, as did Sponge Bob, The Flash, and a giant leprechaun—a reminder that it was St. Patrick's Day.

I'd totally forgotten to wear green.

Around me, everyone was taking in the sights, smiling for a camera, or frowning as they chose the best Instagram filter for their images while I stood frozen. No one seemed to notice me any more than was necessary to walk around me, yet I knew thousands of eyes were watching. My life—and death—had just become their game, and whatever happened next was my first move. Bets were no doubt being placed at that very moment. Would I go north? South? East? West? No matter what I chose, someone would win and someone would lose. That's how these men entertained themselves, and there was no way not to play along.

Get on a Greyhound and run away? Someone won.

Stay where I was and take a tourist hostage? Someone won.

Run to a news station and try to preemptively clear my name? Someone won.

Turn myself in to the police in an effort to seek protection? Well, no one would really win if I did that because it would be idiocy. Yet I had to make a move before Anton Petrov found me or all these tourists would witness the ending of my life right where the Oscar red carpet had been laid out last month.

Odds might be overwhelming that I'd die sometime in the near future, but I had my pride. Going out on the Hollywood Walk of Fame was not an option.

Glancing at the display on my wristband, I took note of Anton's location and mentally mapped the dot in my mind. He was at the Griffith Observatory—four miles away—and moving my way. *Don't forget the ten-second delay*, I reminded myself. As he drew closer, that time lag would grow more and more important.

A tourist backing up to get a shot of the main arch crashed into the side of me, bringing my attention back to the present.

"Hey, watch where you're going," the guy barked, looking at me like I was the one who bumped into him.

I had no response and didn't move, even though it was clear the guy thought I should. Taking a step meant picking a direction and picking a direction meant having a purpose. I didn't want to be on the Walk of Fame when Anton caught up with me, but was there any place I did want to be?

The man who bumped into me found his shot about five feet to my left as I scratched under the new band on my left wrist and tried to wrap my brain around my situation.

Thanks to the wristband, I knew how The Fours were getting audio but they had to have a camera somewhere on me too. My eye would make the most sense—so they could see what I saw—but I couldn't feel anything. No implant. No lens. Nothing unusual.

So how were the men who were betting seeing what I was seeing? There weren't enough cameras in LA to track me everywhere I went in the city, nor was every location hospitable to broadcasting signals for a live feed. Yet they had to have a way to do all that to play this game of theirs.

Or did they?

There was no time to stand around and figure it all out. I needed to move and think at the same time. I knew that, yet my feet were paralyzed by one core thought: *They want to turn me into a terrorist.*

There had been so much to process back in that glass box that the weight of that particular fate hadn't really settled in.

The Fours were 100% prepared to attach my face to a terrorist attack.

The trickle-down implications of that turned my feet into lead while making the rest of me unsteady. Yes, dying a terrorist would be a horrible legacy and haunt Ty and my father for the rest of their lives, but my mind got over those aspects pretty quickly as I thought of my mother's side of the family overseas.

I had an American father, but my mother was Persian. When she was eighteen, she had talked her father into letting her attend college in the United States. My grandfather was Zoroastrian—one of those religions you don't hear about much when the media talks about the Middle East. He was a good man who had respected his daughter, insisted on her education, and accepted her desire to explore a future in the western world.

The average American doesn't understand the difference between a Persian and an Arab, or a Muslim and a Zoroastrian, but those differences had been the gateway to my mother receiving religious asylum in the United States before she met and married my father.

All of my mom's family still lived overseas.

If I died a terrorist…

I couldn't even finish that thought.

My mother may have passed on years ago, but she had made

me into who I was and had always been open to discussing my racial heritage and what it did and did not mean.

People will look at you and see what they need to see to support their world view, she had often told me. *What they see is not a reflection of you, but of them. Their labels and the cages they wish to put you in have nothing to do with you. Those labels are just a window into how they navigate the world. Always remember that when people try to force you to accept their beliefs of you.*

I had leaned on that advice pretty much daily over the years.

As far as prejudice went, my life hadn't been that bad. My ambiguous coloring had some assuming I was of Latin descent and spoke Spanish. Others saw me as a tan white girl thanks to my pale, blue eyes, while people with Middle Eastern backgrounds often saw me for what I was—the product of an interracial couple. For some, this was not a problem; to others, I was impure. I'd never really gone out of my way to care what people thought one way or the other.

But now, after a lifetime of letting other people's preconceptions of me be their problem, The Fours were forcing a label onto me in a way I couldn't ignore. Their labeling of me would have worldwide implications.

What happened today didn't just impact me and my legacy. It would impact an entire demographic. My mom had been raised among Muslims, and I was a first-generation American on her side. It wouldn't matter that there were no Muslims in my family line. No one hearing about an attack would look that hard at that little fact once they saw the news. My skin tone plus the words *Middle East* would be all The Fours needed to plant a runaway story few would question about Muslim extremism.

I could already see the news headlines in my mind's eye, and none of them were good.

Today I couldn't pretend that labels didn't matter. They mattered a whole lot. The people closest to me might know the truth, but no one would listen to them—especially not the politicians looking to capitalize on the tragedy.

Never let a good crisis go to waste. That was one of the Ten Commandments of politics, and if I took the fall for today's bombing there would be a whole lot of politicians capitalizing on twenty-four-hour news stations.

As much as I loved and respected my mom, today her counsel to me didn't count. Today I was my mother's daughter. Today I was Persian; and by American education standards, that made me Arab since my mother's home country was 95% Muslim. The Fours would prop me up as a product of Islam, and that mattered. It really, really mattered. And after a lifetime of picking and choosing what those labels meant to me, I didn't know the full weight of what being my mother's daughter really meant.

Did it mean sport-killing a man I'd only seen once so that he could bear the weight of the fate I sought to shield myself from? After looking at his profile, I wasn't even sure that was possible. But if I did get a shot, could I really take it just to push the blame onto Russia?

The part of me who picked her own labels and values knew the answer to that question. No. I couldn't.

But the part of me that was accepting the new labels that would be used in news stories with their accompanying definitions was still processing the question. It was still trying to think its way around murder, but given the stakes, it wasn't giving the idea a hard "no" either.

"Think and move at the same time, Rhea," I muttered to myself, wondering if all The Fours were hearing my little pep talk. Probably.

Note to self: Stop talking, start moving. Don't run—not yet. You need resources.

It was time to get practical and start making moves that— while questionable—didn't leave me morally paralyzed.

Whoever placed the side bet that picking pockets to get money would be my first item of business was about to hit their first jackpot for the day. I had money stashed around the city, but all the locations were too far away. And while I wasn't planning on spending money, I didn't want to have my hands tied by the lack of it, either. Today would be a bad day to have an overachieving retail employee chase me down for shoplifting.

Glancing around the walkway, I targeted men with visible outlines in their back pockets, taking half the bills I found before slipping the wallets back where they belonged. The first three guys put just under $100 in my hand, which wasn't anything that was going to change my day. I was about to chuck the idea of risking another pickpocket when I spotted a Japanese tourist with a beautiful woman.

Hating that I was profiling, but also knowing I was right, I brushed passed the man. He had a money clip, not a wallet, which made things a bit more cumbersome. Still, I unclipped the bills, swiped several, then put the clip back where it belonged.

$1,200. That was better.

I now had money in my pocket, but I was flying blind as I moved up Hollywood Boulevard. Anton was already three miles away and headed my way fast.

And to think, all I would have had to do to avoid all of this was not *quit my job with Elliott,* I couldn't help but think. I might have died of old age having never heard about The Fours or knowing that they were providing my training and funding my paycheck.

But I had quit my job, and for some reason, The Fours had found that move threatening enough to think death was a reasonable severance package.

I still didn't understand any of their logic, but I'd been around the block enough to know that anyone who played by the rules was setting themselves up to lose. I needed to stop and think—to process everything that had just been thrown at me. I needed a plan just as much as I needed an opponent who wasn't currently averaging six-minute miles on a crash-course to me.

I was faster than Anton, so I could put a dent in that distance when I was ready, but my speed would only help me so much in a city full of alternate forms of transportation. His current pace showed that he was definitely using a vehicle. If I didn't move, he'd be on top of me in nine minutes.

I needed to run.

I needed to think.

I needed a way to do both.

Anton was coming at me from the northeast, so I headed west to buy a little time. I needed to take us both to a place that wasn't vehicle friendly. If he'd been trained by The Fours, then he knew how to turn a car into a weapon, just like I did. Starting a battle like that in the middle of a city would not end well for spectators. Maybe Anton and I had a 99% chance of dying today, but that didn't mean we needed to take anyone else with us.

But where could we go?

The sad truth was that my chances of succeeding against Anton went up exponentially if I kept us in the city. I was a petite, "tan" girl in Los Angeles. I could change my appearance any number of ways and blend in. Anton, however, would remain a six-foot-three, thickly muscled brute. Blending into a large group was much less of an option for him. He was far too militant and imposing to fit into casual scenery.

Strategically speaking, I should keep him in crowded areas where I could easily see him while he was forced to search for me in a sea of similarly sized girls.

A mall. That's where I needed to go, and I needed new clothes while I was there. Anton knew what I was wearing, which meant step one was changing my appearance…then changing it again and again between run-ins. So…clothes. I needed clothes and the Beverly Center Mall was just under four miles away. At this time of day, it would take me about as long to get there on foot as by taxi, so I set off at a run.

All the chauvinistic betters who had wagered that the girl in the game was about to drop everything and go shopping with stolen cash were about to get their first win of the day.

CHAPTER 4

H&M was my best shot at one-stop shopping for different looks to swap out throughout the day. I knew my size and the basic looks I was looking for, which meant I got in and out of the store with three new outfits in thirteen minutes. One glance at my wristband on the way out showed that Anton was less than two miles away.

He'd moved into an area that had slowed his pace, but he was still *way* too close. I had to move…but to where? Yes, staying in the city was good for me; it was just bad for everyone around me.

Decisions, decisions.

Not only did I need to make one to know which direction to turn as I stepped out of the mall, but I also needed to know what outfit to put on next.

I felt a split second of annoyance at the realization that I hadn't considered the fact I might be dying in the clothes I'd just bought. Not that it made a difference. Not really…or it shouldn't have. But the fact that my brain started mentally revisiting the racks to search for something more acceptable got a sigh out of me.

There was a 100% chance that Anton wasn't debating his wardrobe choice at the moment, which was yet another of his many advantages over me. His head was in the game. He was ready for this, which meant he had a Plan A and a multitude of Plan Bs, if A didn't pan out.

I had no plan. I only had a question: How did a fish win a game of fish-in-a-barrel when the human on the other side of the gun was an expert marksman with unlimited ammo? Hiding seemed like my only option, but thanks to our tainted blood, I couldn't do that. Anton knew my exact location, accurate to the inch, minus a ten-second delay and not accounting for altitude. Multi-level buildings gave me an advantage, as did crowds. Facing off in nature would be a bad choice. Based on his profile, the man had been training outside since he was a toddler, whereas I'd spent a few months poking around the outskirts of Los Angeles once upon seven-ish years ago. If I was a fish in a barrel in the city, outside of the city I was a lost rabbit without a burrow facing off against a panther.

At least I knew Los Angeles. I'd grown up here. I'd gone to college here, whereas Anton had been raised and trained on the East coast. I had no doubt that he'd done recon on the sites where he wanted to corner me, but there was no way he knew the city better than I did.

A nervous tickle on the back of my neck urged me not to trust that assumption. The man was a trained bodyguard and assassin. Before today, his job had been to protect very powerful people in cities around the world. He may not be a man who knew everything about everything in LA, but he was a man who knew what he needed to know to win in LA.

Never assume the advantage.

Mark Weston had warned me of that over and over again. The only thing Mark trusted in was the fact that nothing and nobody were truly trustworthy. Everyone and everything would fail you at some point; if you weren't prepared for things to go south, or for your opponent to be smarter, then you deserved what you got.

Well, one thing was for certain: Anton Petrov was way more

prepared for today than I was. He'd known who I was and been able to plan, whereas I was still debating outfits and unsure as to whether I really could pull a trigger.

Even worse, I didn't even know if I preferred to be a fish in a barrel—where other fish might get hurt—or a rabbit in the woods.

What a mess. What an absolute and utter mess.

With the thousand questions swirling in my mind at that moment, there were only a few I could answer with confidence and one of them was whether or not I should have a gun.

Yes. Absolutely. With Anton, I needed a gun.

Even if I wasn't sure I could pull the trigger yet, I needed one in my hand. Luckily for me, this was one of the few fronts where I was actually prepared. I'd hidden three guns around the city, just in case, and left one other as an emergency backup with a street dealer. He would be a last resort, obviously. But one of the guns, hidden behind a loose brick of a building, was only about four blocks away. It was possible someone had found it and stolen it already.

I was about to find out.

CHAPTER 5

Accessing the hiding spot containing a .38 semi-automatic and the utility wristband I usually wore in the field required moving a dumpster. But the sticky effort paid off when I removed a brick out of the wall, reached into the gap, and found both items where I'd left them.

My hand instinctively went for the wristband first since it contained the lock picking set and other tools I habitually used in the field. I was so used to wearing a wristband on the job that the one The Fours had surgically implanted onto me at some point that morning actually felt quite normal. It was going to be weird wearing my usual band on the opposite arm, but I'd get over it.

I pulled out the gun next, checking the magazine—full—with a bullet in the chamber. Everything appeared to be the same as the last time I'd handled the gun, although that didn't really count for anything. If the gun had been tampered with, I wouldn't know until I pulled the trigger.

If I pulled the trigger.

In the meantime, at least I had the physical presence of a gun. That was worth something. It also picked out my next outfit for me since I needed a waistband that would hold the gun in place.

Getting changed took about thirty seconds, after which I tossed my morning clothes into the dumpster before checking in with the tracker.

Anton was 1.8 miles away to the east of me and holding. Why had he stopped? I wasn't sure. There wasn't really a huge tactical advantage in keeping his distance, which meant the move was likely intended to stop me from moving east as I made my next move. Which, of course, made me want to go east…eventually. I couldn't right away. He was literally sitting there waiting for me, but when I had an opening it was good to know he liked having the east at his back.

I'd give Anton his wish, for the moment. I'd let him push if only to see where all the pushing pointed us. Knowing where he wanted to be might give me a clue as to what he ultimately wanted to do.

Glancing south, Cedars-Sinai Medical Center caught my eye above the throng of bodies coming and going on the sidewalk. On the street, cars moved along at the expected stop-and-go crawl. The hospital was the same direction I'd just come from, but it also felt like the right choice as far as a next move. Anton might be trying to herd me west toward the ocean, but being surrounded by the lunch crowd from the mall and the hospital made sense. The noon-time crowd, plus the mall, plus the tourists, plus the hospital made south the more congested choice, which would force Anton to ditch any vehicle he might be using. Congestion meant the ability to move faster on foot than in a car, which played into one of my few advantages. I was faster than Anton both on foot and on a bike, and I unquestionably had more endurance.

LA traffic might suck 365 days out of the year, but today that fact was my best friend. I had to keep the man on his feet and his heart pumping as much as possible. Tired people screwed up. That was just how physiology worked.

This realization was my first glimmer of hope as I jogged in the direction of the mall and hospital with my shopping bag still in hand and my .38 covered by a light hoodie. I needed to keep my eyes open for a backpack to free up my hands.

Anton waited about thirty seconds before his dot started following mine. He was coming my way, and he was coming fast.

Man, I really needed to choose where I wanted him to find me, or everything was going to go down in a very public setting.

I considered taking cover in the hospital. I could pick a floor and give myself some time to think. Or maybe go back to the mall. That had more exit points, but it was also more exposed…and it would be easy to restrict exit points in the hospital.

Don't go there, a little voice whispered in the back of my mind and I trusted it. My primal brain didn't want to touch the hospital or the mall. I'd just made a point of getting in and out of the mall in record time, and I needed to trust that impulse. But every location had pros and cons—mostly cons.

Still, I had to pick one of them.

My mind kept jumping to the Arts District as an option. It would be busy with deliveries this time of day, but there were abandoned buildings where collateral damage would have minimal impact. Areas like the beach could also work, but the Santa Monica area seemed to be the direction Anton was pushing me, which made me not like it as much.

As I approached the mall, a strip of russet orange cloth caught my eye—a sniper's flag hanging from a light pole like it belonged there. It didn't. Even worse? I knew that shade of orange. The color had been imprinted onto my memory through a series of traumatic events linked to one man.

Mark Weston.

I hadn't seen the man for years, and suddenly he was everywhere. And if there was one thing I knew about Mark, it was that no one saw him unless he wanted to be seen.

I almost missed a step as I tried to wrap my head around why Mark would be announcing himself. He had always told me that if ever the day came when I was on the run, he and other men like him would be the ones in pursuit. Hanging sniper flags in open view was his way of telling me he was in play. Any other color and I wouldn't have known who put it there, but russet orange? Placed so conspicuously?

Mark wanted me to know he was out there.

Anton was bad for me, but Mark was the guy who trained guys like Anton to be bad for me. Mark was just like Anton, only faster, stronger, and more experienced. Getting on Mark's bad side or on the bad side of his employer ended exactly one way. And, apparently, Mark was one of the bounty hunters on the scene who stood ready to collect at the end of the day.

Not good. Supremely not good.

My stomach turned as I processed the development. The Fours had certainly seen Mark place the flag, even if it was just under the assumption that he was going to use it as a wind gauge for a distance shot. They likely wouldn't know he used that color exclusively throughout our training together.

But why make the flag so obvious and in the color I would know? Was he taunting me, or messaging me? The first option was immature and the second would get him killed.

Neither option made sense for his militant personality.

Mark had told me story after story of people he'd hunted down over his career and how they'd all failed to elude him. Half of my training with Mark had involved him proving he could find me and end me at any time. More than once, he'd told me to be careful who I crossed or the next time wouldn't be a drill.

I'd freaked out at the time, of course. I'd gone to Elliott and demanded an explanation for the extreme methods, but Elliott had laughed them off and blamed Mark's intensity on PTSD. In the face of each concern, he had encouraged me to learn what I could from Mark without allowing his delusions to become my paranoia. And, despite everything, teenage me had ignored my instincts and done as Elliott instructed.

What an idiot.

Nearly everything wrong with my life came down to the fact that once upon a time I had listened to, been coerced by, and/or eventually trusted Elliott Church. Without that man in my life, this day would be going very, very differently. Without Elliott, I'd probably be the lead singer in a band, juggling an on-again, off-again relationship with my unfaithful lead guitarist. We'd probably be on tour somewhere, just starting to wake up after a late night of partying hard.

Or maybe I would have scrapped the band even without Elliott's influence and gone on to get a Master's degree in something I cared about. Even making six figures or more a year with Elliott, it had always irked me that I only had a Bachelor's degree under my belt. That was my mom's side of the family coming through. Education was huge for them. My mom had chosen raising me over having a career, but she'd always been proud to be educated and would have wanted the same for me.

Would I have gotten an MBA? Or maybe a Master's degree or PhD relating to social justice?

If Elliott Church had never visited my entry-level Communication course at UCLA and administered a little aptitude test, and if I'd never walked into his office after Kay ran away and asked for his help, what would I have done with my life?

The part of my mind that didn't want to accept the reality of my current situation was obsessed with this line of thought—me in some alternate reality, living out some other life. In the meantime, I was just about to walk under Mark's russet flag while Anton was 1.6 miles away and closing in.

Scattered thoughts were not serving me, but processing my current reality had my brain seeking diverting thoughts without my permission.

I had to stop letting it do that. I had to focus.

Fact: Mark was in play and he wanted me to know it.

Fact: Mark had trained me for months and trained Anton for years.

It seemed pretty clear where his loyalty would lie, especially since Mark had never been onboard with training a female. All the same, my training had me recognizing the russet flag and looking for a secondary marker as I moved within range of the cloth.

Mark left visible flags to communicate rendezvous points. Anyone passing by could see the flags, but few would see the secondary markers Mark placed, not to mention know what they were looking at if they did see them. Two rocks pointing to the north would mean the next marker was one mile to the south or three broken branches on the east side of a plant would mean the next marker was 150 yards to the west.

Everything was always a misdirect with Mark. You had to know his code or his breadcrumbs were useless to you, but the fact that there were two dimes lying on the ground under the flag was exactly the type of thing he'd do. Not that he'd put his faith into loose change on the sidewalk. Someone could kick it or pick it up, which would make it a useless communication tool.

To prove to myself that the dimes were nothing more than a coincidence, I kicked at one as I passed by. It didn't budge. It was glued to the sidewalk.

This development took me completely by surprise even as I forced myself to keep walking forward as if nothing was amiss.

Eyes forward and feet moving at the same speed, my mind raced over the possibility that the dimes might actually mean something. The noses of the coins had been pointing behind me, which meant that if it was an actual message it was pointing me in the direction I was already walking. Two coins worth ten cents each. If the coins weren't there randomly, that meant the distance was their value halved—ten miles—down the street I was walking on.

That would put me in the Arts District, which was at the top of my personal list of places to go. Heading that direction was a good choice whether Mark was directing me there or not.

But was he? Was I seeing things? Hoping for things that weren't there?

The only way to know was to head to the Arts District.

CHAPTER 6

A $200 bike and a $10 backpack from a pawn shop had me pedaling past stop-and-go traffic toward the Arts District. Traveling ten miles on surface roads in Los Angeles took a minimum of forty minutes by car on a good day. I could definitely beat that time on a bike.

Biking it turned out to be the right move because two miles into my ride my tracker showed Anton 2.8 miles behind me. I was gaining ground, which boded well for getting my bearings before facing off with my own personal pitbull.

Moving into the Arts District opened up my options exponentially. Most of the areas would be busy with mid-day business, but there were a few empty buildings, the rail tracks, the Los Angeles River, all with the bonus of industrial backdrops. My small size and speed would still be assets and, if I was savvy, tourists would be safe from our antics.

By the time I approached the ten-mile point from where I'd spotted the dimes, I'd half-way talked myself out of the coins being anything more than a coincidence that pointed me in a decent direction. That was until I saw another russet sniper flag hanging off one of the lights on The Geffen building.

One russet flag was random; a dime beneath it was potentially a coincidence. But a second flag ten miles away from the original point of origin? That was design.

For some unknown reason, Mark was talking to me.

My heart raced in my chest, not from the exercise, but from the realization that I was about to see yet another message from my former mentor—a message he'd risked his life to put in place, no matter his motives. Anything that influenced the outcome of bets would be met with capital punishment. That's what Mr. Overhead Voice had said that morning, and I was certain Mark wasn't an exception.

I was still half a block away from the russet flag when I realized I had to ditch the bike. The alternative was to pass the next breadcrumb at fifteen miles per hour or so and chance needing to take a second pass. Couldn't do that.

Slowing down, I swung my right leg over the seat and coasted to the nearest stop point to stow the bike. It would be nice if no one stole it, but I couldn't worry about that. My first priority was to live long enough to maybe need the bike again later.

Stashing my ride by The Geffen's full parking lot, I started down Alameda Street on foot. I was careful not to give the russet cloth a second glance as my eyes searched for rocks or sticks or coins or anything pointing where to go next.

There was nothing.

Not a single bread crumb, unless you counted the black-and-white bumpersticker someone had stuck on the wall for *Film Downtown*, a business that managed filming properties all around the city.

I felt a bit of panic as I walked under the russet flag, my eyes searching a bit more blatantly even as I refused to slow my pace. But all my covert tactics were for nothing; the space was clean. No rocks. No sticks. No trash. Nothing. Just that business sticker.

Maybe I was wrong about the whole Mark sending messages to me thing. Maybe he was just mapping out where his sniper flags were…which would be stupid.

I kept walking down the sidewalk with purpose in my step as I tried to process this new development. The dimes indicating ten miles had definitely been a marker. I was sure of that. It had pointed the right direction and there had been a flag right where there should have been one…just no secondary marker telling me where to go next.

A glance at my wristband showed that Anton was 3.1 miles behind me. I flexed my hand as I did the mental math of how much time that gave me. The dull ache of the metal post that held the band in place on my wrist wasn't so dull after thirty minutes on a bike. I needed to be careful not to put too much pressure on the joint moving forward. A little ache was fine but hampered function definitely was not. I needed my hand firing on all cylinders.

My feet kept moving as I moved my thoughts away from aches and pains and back to the business at hand. It was good to be out of downtown, but the area was still populated with tourists and the lunch crowd moving to and fro. As I approached a group of people standing in front of the Japanese-American Museum, I felt myself falter.

Where should I go next? Keep going straight? Turn on 1st? If so, which direction? Mark wasn't telling me, so that meant I needed to start picking directions myself.

Left made sense. Right or backward put me on a crash course with Anton; left and forward took me deeper into the district where I was more likely to find abandoned space.

Toying with the idea of going left as I approached the intersection, I noticed yet another *Film Downtown* sticker on the pole. Beneath it was a second sticker, one of those Equality stickers that someone had hung vertically. They were the only stickers, not only on that particular pole but on every other pole in sight.

I thought back to the *Film Downtown* sticker behind me on

The Geffen building. It had been the only one in sight too, right under the sniper flag. And now I had the same sticker a few feet away with what could possibly be argued as a secondary marker— a sticker someone had hung sideways so that it looked more like the Roman numeral two, rather than the equal sign it was.

Two…that could mean something. But two what? Two streets? Two miles? Or were the two lines like sticks and he really meant one? In either case, which direction? And were we talking blocks or miles?

There was no protocol for this. I felt the urge to curse under my breath before remembering that my wristband gave all my spectators audio. I'd headed down here with purpose and I had to keep on moving with purpose not to raise any eyebrows.

Anton was now three miles away. He was catching up and would continue to do so for as long as I kept up to a leisurely stroll and did things like stopping at intersections to wait for a light.

The lights were blinking that it was safe to cross left, but I needed a moment to think so I waited to cross straight.

Looking around at the other poles, I noted that they were all clean. No stickers. No ads. No street art stickers. The absence of all of those things meant that the neighborhood was actively cleaning them up and that *Film Downtown* might actually get a complaining phone call for their vandalism after they were discovered and scraped off.

You know Mark put them there, I thought as the light changed. *Just own it and figure out what it means.*

There were just too many options. Yet as I crossed the street, keeping pace with the rest of the pedestrians around me, it hit me that I'd just crossed 1st Street and I was headed for 2nd Street.

Two…2nd. And half of two was one…and 2nd Street was one street away. The clue worked on two levels.

Yes, it was a stretch, but it was also my best guess and I didn't have time to come up with a second-best guess.

Quickening my pace, I pulled ahead of the herd and pushed for 2nd Street, half forgetting that I wasn't really sure I trusted Mark's motives in any of this. In the moment, my need to figure out the puzzle was overriding the cautious part of my brain, especially when I approached 2nd Street and spotted yet another sticker on the no right turn sign.

Left. Mark wanted me to go left.

So I did, noting that Anton had somehow hit a burst of speed and was now only 2.6 miles behind me. My window was closing and I picked up my pace to see where this little Easter egg hunt was leading.

I went a block. Then another block. Then another before getting a little nervous that I was stringing a series of coincidences together into a wild goose chase. The river and tracks would be coming up soon, and I was debating whether to head into that terrain when I saw another sign. This time it wasn't a sticker, it was a sign on a two-story grey brick building. A series of large floor-to-ceiling windows lined the top story.

This had to be it.

I stopped in front of a loading garage big enough to allow most film trucks to back in and unload equipment. The loading door was closed, but a paper was taped to it. From a distance, I could see it was a notice of filming. Instinct told me to go take a closer look at it, so I did. Allegedly, the location was reserved for a movie called *The Hunted* that was arriving to film at 4:00 p.m.

Of even more interest was a note at the bottom of the notice which read: *All audio/visual equipment must be provided by leasee. No cameras or other equipment on site. Wifi requires password.*

There was no reason for that additional note, and it certainly wasn't a standard disclosure. The note was for me, telling me that the interior of the building was clean of cameras but activity could still be monitored through the wifi waves. The Fours still had audio through my wristband and could monitor movements within the building, but there were no actual cameras broadcasting out.

This was as private as things were going to get in downtown Los Angeles, reducing the incentive for either Anton or me to make a kill move. It would be a stupid move to kill off-camera the very first time we met when we were being judged based on our entertainment value. Ending the "game" so quickly off screen wouldn't earn the survivor many green lights when it came time send out the assassins.

No. Killing inside the building was a bad, bad strategy, which meant it was a great place to feel Anton out.

Maybe Mark had led me here, or maybe it was just a series of delusionally strung-together coincidences, but I was rolling with it.

Anton was 2.3 miles away. Close, but not so close that I didn't have time to scout the building before going in. A walk to the corner revealed that the building was a city block long moving north and south and very much occupied. The side being rented out for filming was likely the property management company capitalizing on property that needed to be fixed up for tenants but worked perfectly as a rundown filming location.

I doubled back to where the sign hung over the loading dock and took a look down the alley between the building and the new construction rising up next to it. It was big enough to park some cars and house a dumpster. I glanced at the window above the dumpster and noted that in a pinch it might make for an emergency exit.

Anton was 1.8 miles away and seemed to have found a steady pace. It was time to head in.

Picking the lock with my tools took just a beat longer than using an actual key, then I was in.

I heard nothing. No talking, no footsteps or other ambient sounds. The space was abandoned.

Moving quickly through each area, I searched for the space

that gave me the best tactical advantage—dismissing the main level and heading up to the second floor.

As far as filming locations went, this one was pretty solid. Neutral colors, distressed floors and walls, high ceilings. Those floor-to-ceiling windows were the real selling point, though. Great natural light…if you were there to film a movie.

I wasn't.

Setting up in the room with the street-facing windows wasn't a good option, in case any guns went off, so I moved back in the space until I was in the room over the alley with the dumpster. Only the new build of the construction site next door was visible through the room's windows, and no one seemed to be working in that area.

The good news? It was perfect for a fight.

The bad news? There was absolutely nowhere to hide.

There was one door, four walls, one ceiling, and a wall of windows over an alley with a dumpster in it. That was it. Also, Anton was less than a mile away now, which meant I had five minutes—tops—before he was on top of me.

Adrenaline started kicking into my system at the realization. It all seemed so surreal now. A guy I'd seen once in my life in a glass box was allegedly about to walk into this room and try to kill me. Or maybe he'd climb up into that construction site and try to shoot me from afar.

Both options seemed ridiculous—like some bad movie, not my actual life. But the dot on my watch was moving closer and closer. Anton was en route, and I was standing in the room where we would once again come face-to-face.

This was it. This was where Anton and I would find out how this all played out. It might not feel real yet, but my gut told me it would all feel very real in about four minutes.

CHAPTER 7

My body quivered from excess adrenaline and my hands sweat as I waited for Anton to appear. To keep my hands as dry as possible, I tucked the .38 in my waistband and dragged my sweaty palms back and forth along my pants. All my senses felt sharpened, but I knew many of my current reactions were counterproductive. There was a difference between being over-stimulated by every little thing around you and being hyper-focused on the relevant.

Anton was a city block away, and I was solidly in the category of being over-stimulated by both the relevant and the irrelevant. I could hear everything around me—a man speaking loudly on the sidewalk, water flowing through the pipes in the walls, nail guns popping out nails at the construction site next door—none of which were things I needed to be paying attention to.

Forcing myself to ignore the distractions, I focused on the dot on my watch. Nausea washed over me as I realized I possibly had eight seconds before things got real.

Based on speed and direction, Anton was on the roof. I should have predicted that. Of course he wouldn't come at me from the street level where I could shoot him walking in.

Drying my hand on my pants one last time, I pulled the .38

from my waistband. I had mere moments to pick where I wanted to be in the room when he arrived. The ten-second lag worked both ways. Whether he dropped in through one of the windows and sprayed me with glass or just took aim at me through the roof, I did not want to be where he thought I was.

He probably has equipment that allows him to see exactly where you are without the watch, my mind whispered. *Ever thought of that, genius?*

No. I hadn't. Not until that very moment.

Get away from the windows, instinct told me, and I didn't fight it. Nor did I fight it when that same instinct drew me into a position next to the door. With the ten-second delay, our trackers were useless now. I was down to my five senses and instincts.

A second wave of adrenaline surged and my body tried to pressure me into panting for breath, but I kept the inhales and exhales slow and silent as I strained to hear footfalls above me. Nothing. Anton couldn't be more than fifty feet away, and yet I had no evidence that he was really there.

Get close to the wall. The instinct was so strong that it felt like an audible command. I heeded it before it even occurred to me to question it, pressing my back into the wall with the only door into the room inches to my left and all the windows in the room straight ahead. Unless Anton came bursting through the wall behind me like the Kool-Aid Man, I'd theoretically have a split second to see him and react.

A third wave of adrenaline caught me off guard, making me feel each heartbeat like a kick drum against my temples as my breathing grew more shallow. My palms were magically wet again and even my eyeballs seemed to be sweating. I gave several rapid blinks, trying to clear my vision as I forced air deeper into my lungs. This was no time to get lightheaded.

A second passed...then another, but my sense of time was off at this point. My brain saw everything in snapshots rather than in one fluid stream. Life was suddenly playing out in hiccups of perception, and I didn't know the difference between eight seconds and eighteen seconds.

"Breathe," I whispered to myself just a gun whipped around the corner of the door to my left. He knew exactly where I was.

Training had me stepping toward the motion, blocking Anton's forearm so that his gun pointed over my shoulder when he appeared around the corner. When we came face-to-face, my gun was aimed at his head and his was pointed over my shoulder.

I had the shot.

It happened so fast, it felt like a dream…a dream of my gun pointed squarely at a man's face that some rich dudes wanted dead.

I don't know who was more surprised: me or Anton.

In either case, the moment of mental hesitation that followed somehow ended with me twisting my gun around, aiming the butt of my gun at his groin, and hammering it into the target. There was no protective cup beneath those jeans. I felt it in the strike and saw it Anton's face as I brought the butt of the gun back up to hit him right above the elbow and again on the back of the hand. I might be tiny compared to Anton, but hitting those three spots didn't require superior strength to be effective. When my strike to the back of his hand had his muscles spasming in reflex, I stripped the gun and stomped on the back of his knee.

Anton's knees hit the concrete floor with a painful clack right as I pressed my gun into his head. Again.

I had him. I absolutely had him. All I had to do was pull the trigger.

Our eyes met and I saw the stunned realization in his eyes that he had come to the same conclusion as me. It lasted for a second. Then two.

Pulling the trigger would be so easy. I'd done it thousands of times with paper targets at the other end. But could I live with myself if I did it this time—with a man on the other side?

At my feet, Anton saw my hesitation and silently raised a finger to point to his jacket pocket.

If his intention had been for me to hesitate even longer, it worked. I nodded before thinking about it, allowing him to reach into his pocket and pull out a strip of paper. He opened it, holding it out for me to read.

If you'd rather fight our common enemy and not each other, follow me. And go under, not over.

Anton used my moment of concentrating on the paper to make his move, clearing my gun in one smooth motion before reclaiming his own with a brute force that almost pulled my shoulder out of joint. Face-to-face and gun-to-gun, we both leveled our pieces at each other with our fingers on the trigger.

Despite the invitation on his little paper, the look in Anton's eyes as we squared off told me he didn't trust me, and I definitely didn't trust him. Two guns a twitch away from firing said as much. Then something shifted in his eyes.

Windows, he mouthed.

He wanted us to move back into the range of witnesses on the other side of the windows? If so, I wasn't going to let him keep his gun for that.

Then his eyes glanced down at his belt. *No more ball shots.*

I actually smiled right before kicking the gun out of his hands.

The man was lightning quick, moving to the side and clearing my hands and gripping my arms to slam me into the wall before stripping my gun and tossing it across the room. When he threw me in the direction of the windows I went with it. Our audience needed to be distracted away from analyzing the silence that had just occurred between us.

I barely had my feet under me when Anton was on top of me again, this time aiming a fist the size of a kettle bell right at my face. I moved, letting him punch out the window behind me while I rammed my fist into his stomach. It was like punching a clothed statue, stunning me a moment before his bleeding fist crashed across my face.

He could have hit me harder. I realized that even as I staggered to the side, fighting for balance. Anton was all but on top of me, so I went with it—rolling onto my back and using his forward momentum to launch him over me with my legs.

He rolled out of my throw, rising back up to his feet before I did.

Distance was my friend. I had to stay out of range and try to get hits in without being hit back or grabbed. Yet moving away wasn't an option when he lunged in. I was still on my back so when I saw his upper body coming at me, I horse-kicked my feet up—aiming right for his face. It wasn't a pretty move, but it landed and forced his hands to catch his own weight instead of grabbing for me.

I popped onto my feet, spotting my gun on the other side of the room. I needed it—even for a fake fight. Anton was just too strong and good. I'd never faced off against someone as fast as him. Not even Mark. I might land a shot in here and there, but no one would buy me holding my own against this guy much longer.

"You fight dirty," he said, marking the first words between us.

"I kind of have to," I replied.

He smirked, taking the comment for the compliment it was. "I feel like I'm fighting a really cunning chihuahua. Crushing you seems cruel, but" —he held up the hand that had gone through the window, blood streaming off it— "I don't want to deal with your little nips either."

Little nips? I'd just done better than a few nips, thank you very much.

"Careful what you call me," I warned. "You don't want your legacy to be death by chihuahua, do you?"

"Fair point," he said, stepping to put his back to the windows while holding up two fingers. I wasn't sure what he meant. "Or it would be if you had even the slightest chance of winning in all of this."

His eyes glanced over his left shoulder to the row of windows behind him. Was I supposed to understand what that meant?

"How do you want to go out?" he asked ominously. "I see you thinking about your gun, but if you get yours then I get mine, and we both know your trigger finger is a bit reluctant."

It was, although maybe it would loosen up in the heat of the moment.

"Or maybe I could choke you out or toss you out a window," he offered.

A one-story drop onto cement? There was every chance that would cripple me while leaving me alive and aware for whatever came next. No, thank you.

Anton mouthed *dumpster* and I finally realized that he was saying it was located under the second window from the far wall. He wanted me to let him throw me out the window and down into the dumpster?

Not happening. Not a chance. If he felt so good about that plan then he could take the ride.

"If anyone is going out a window, that would be you," I replied, to which he raised an eyebrow and laughed.

"Color me impressed if you actually pull that off."

Guard up, I circled him. "Well, pick your color then, because it's about to be applied."

He moved first—lightning quick. I was able to bat the fist targeting my face off course a moment before it made contact, but his front kick landed before I even saw it coming. It hit me like a horizontal stomp to the abdomen and would have knocked someone Anton's size off balance. But I was not Anton's size, so it literally picked me up off my feet and launched me backwards. I had to scramble my feet beneath me to keep myself upright, running in reverse until my back slammed into the wall.

He smiled again. "It's like kicking a beach ball. There's barely enough of you to take the hit. You just fly away."

Oh, I'd taken the kick, all right. I couldn't let him see that, though. One sign of weakness and he would throw me out the window and down into the dumpster. His idea, his ride. I was sticking to that stance. Whatever miracle I needed to pull off to make it happen, Anton was the one taking the fall off this second floor.

Think strategic, I thought. *He's never fought someone as small as you before. Use that.*

Mark had always been quick to point out the weaknesses of my size and sex, but one thing he had mentioned over and over is that smaller people were smaller targets. Getting effective hits in was harder if you guarded well.

Yes, Anton could overpower me. Two of his black belts were in jiu-jitsu and judo. If I let him get his hands on me he could throw me around like a rag doll, break any bone he wanted, and choke me out until the world turned black for yet another time that day. I needed to be small, only allow ineffective hits, and give him nothing to grab onto. If anyone was going to be grabbing anyone, I needed to be the one grabbing him.

After all, tiny people could still lock the joints of big people.

And the bigger they were, the harder they fell.

In the time it took me to settle into that approach, Anton had moved to his fallen gun and was reaching to pick it up.

I was out of time.

"Don't worry," he said. "I'm not going to shoot you in here where no one can watch me. That was good planning on your part, leading me here where our audience can't properly watch a finale."

He was talking to The Fours more than me, rationalizing the fact that my heart was still beating even though he had a clear shot.

"So let's get you back outside, shall we?" he said, holstering the gun at his side to free up his hands.

It was dumpster time for one of us, and it needed to happen fast.

Stay small, I coached myself, moving away from the wall. *Stay centered.*

Anton watched my every move, allowing me to line up with the second window before going on the offensive again. I was expecting fast and I got it, but this time I had a plan. When his punch flew in, so did I, stepping forward and to the side of his fist. I felt the wind of his strike brush past my face as I drove a single-knuckle punch right into his sternum, earning a surprised grunt from him.

Now that I was in, I stayed in, flipping the blades of my hands out in a peek-a-boo motion to force his arms to the side and set him up for the drive back.

I aimed for pain points and moved fast, using my strikes to draw focus as I lured Anton out of balance. He stepped back, trying to gain the space he needed to hit or even elbow me back, but I moved in, forcing him to deal with my hands until I got him where I wanted him. With my right foot checked behind his left heel and Anton's back lined up with the second window, I brought my hands in and pushed.

The look on his face told me he hadn't been expecting that. It also told me that his loss of balance was genuine. But I also saw the moment when he could have regained his balance but chose not to. Instead, I watched him glance to the side to gauge the distance to the window and brace himself for the hit.

He was going to take the fall. He didn't need to, but he was going to.

The moment before his back hit the window, Anton locked eyes with me and mouthed, *Follow me.* Then his back hit the glass and he tumbled out of the room backward, leaving a shattered pane in his wake.

Staring at the broken window, it occurred to me if Anton had landed on any of that glass, he might be in trouble. Knowing there was only one way to find out, I moved toward the window, picking up my gun along the way and aiming it out the window as I glanced down.

He wasn't in the dumpster.

Movement to my left showed Anton running down the alley. I leveled my gun at him as he ran toward the sidewalk, my finger on the trigger, but hesitating like it always did.

As if sensing my gaze, Anton glanced over his shoulder and up at me. He kept his feet at a full run as he raised his gun and pulled the trigger. Pure instinct had me taking cover an instant before a bullet lodged itself in the window frame and sprayed me with a light shower of tiny splinters.

He'd shot at me—really shot at me. The bullet had hit right at chest level exactly where I'd been standing. If I hadn't moved…

He had to make it look real, part of me rationalized even as the rest of me crashed down from the adrenaline rush, allowing logic to filter back into my thoughts.

I'd had him.

I'd. Had. Him.

Twice.

The realization of what I'd had in my hands, only to let it slip through again, hit me like a sucker punch to the stomach.

Forget about The Fours and their need to be entertained; victory could have been mine just now. Two times I could have pulled the trigger and ended all this. It could be over. Done. But I'd hesitated and hadn't even tried to pull the trigger on a man who had no problem taking a kill shot at me even after claiming to raise a white flag.

What had I done?

I wasn't going to get that chance again—not with a man as skilled as Anton. He wouldn't make the mistake of underestimating me twice. That had been my one shot, and I'd fully botched it. No one to blame but myself.

My hands shook and my stomach lurched as I stood framed by the jagged window. Across the way, one of the construction guys eyed me.

"Everything okay over there?" he called out.

No. Nothing was okay. Not a single thing.

I stepped away from the window, not saying a word to the man, and waiting until I was out of his sight before pitching a fit that consisted of slamming the heel of my hand into the wall over and over as I accepted that I'd just thrown away my one shot to end the day alive.

What had I been thinking?

My legs jittered beneath me, barely holding me up. I leaned against the wall and slid down into a squat, one hand pressing into the wall and the other holding my useless gun as I replayed the events of the past few minutes again and again in my mind.

Two opportunities for me to kill Anton, followed by dozens of chances for him to do the same, topped with an offer to allegedly join forces.

Yeah. Right.

What in the world did Anton Petrov have to gain by joining forces with me? In his world, the ways he benefitted if I survived the day included a short list of zero perks. There was no reason for him to want me alive. And yet...I hadn't killed him and he hadn't killed me back.

That was a fact.

I understood what had stopped me from pulling the trigger, but I had no idea what had stopped a trained assassin from not killing me in return. The closest thing I had to an explanation for that was an invitation to some sales pitch in the place of his choosing and the directions to "go under, not over"...whatever that meant.

Anton was either leading me to a glamorous death that would earn him serious fans among The Fours, or making a sincere offer.

I closed my eyes, searching my gut instinct for an answer as to whether or not I should follow this man. All I felt were tiny splinters across the right side of my body and the shaky sensation that followed a good adrenaline surge.

"C'mon," I whispered to myself. "What's the next move here?"

The only thing I could think to do was follow Anton. It made no logical sense to trust him, yet it felt right. So, for better or worse, I did the stupid thing and let my enemy lead me to the destination of his choosing.

CHAPTER 8

I'd been right about Anton wanting to push me west. I'd even been right about the destination.

I didn't need to see the Ferris wheel on the Santa Monica pier to know where we'd be meeting next. He'd stopped right near the shoreline at the pier—not directly under the Ferris wheel, but definitely within a stone's throw of it.

We were right back in the same environment I'd tried to get us out of. The pier would be packed with people. St. Patrick's Day wasn't a top-tier holiday—it was barely a holiday at all in most people's books—but it was still an excuse to dress up and leave the house. There would be more people riding rides and playing games on a pier than on a typical weekday.

Why was Anton putting us both back in the middle of a crowd?

Street vendors along the beach peddled four-leaf greenery, and I debated grabbing something festive in an effort to blend in. But no. I was not going to die wearing a headband that made it look like I had four-leaf Care Bear ears on the top of my head. I could just see the crime scene photos leaked online in my mind's eyes with some sort of headline like: *Middle Eastern Terrorist Tries to Blend in on Whitest Holiday Ever.*

Dead or alive, it was just a bad look. Attire in the field should be tactical, yes, but I had my limits.

No St. Patrick's paraphernalia for me.

I walked until I reached the grass adjacent to the beach and had a chance to survey the space ahead. The message to "*go under, not over*" made a lot more sense as I looked at the pier and saw the choice of walking onto it or under it. The underbelly of the pier wasn't really somewhere you went on purpose. It was gross and cluttered with support beams that made swimming a treacherous affair. It was easy to get pushed around and scraped up if you were less than savvy. So avoiding the area came naturally to the 99% of people with a good sense of self-preservation.

Yet instinct told me that was where Anton and I would end up—among the barnacle-covered support beams.

I paused on the threshold between grass and the beach sand leading to the pier, taking mental pictures of my surroundings. Nothing stood out as atypical or staged. Tourists on rental bikes pedaled along the Ocean Front Walk while others walked, ran, or showed off their might on the beach's fitness equipment. Two surfers had ventured into the ocean. They floated a good distance off of the shore on boards, watching the horizon for signs their dedication would pay off in the form of a sweet ride.

Ocean water in the area averaged out at about 57 degrees Fahrenheit in March. Those guys had to be feeling the cold, but it wasn't stopping them from hanging out beyond the break and waiting for a decent wave while everyone else stuck to dry land where the warm sun and cool breeze were a pleasant combination.

According to my wristband, Anton was only a few hundred yards ahead of me. The dot showed him right on the dock. Or under it.

If I was really going to blindly do as I was asked by Anton's instructions, I needed to give my audience a show that made going under the pier look more like a tactical approach and not a planned meet up.

Step 1: Get there.

Luckily for me, the beach was far from empty and a group of teens was heading my way. Tucking my thumbs into the shoulder straps of the new backpack, I waited for the teens to cross my position, then fell into step with them as they headed toward the pier. They were younger than me, yes, but I was short enough to blend in as we made our way to the pier.

The thought that Anton might try to shoot me in the group tickled in the back of my mind, but I pushed the thought away. Anton hadn't dragged me 17 miles away just to shoot me on the beach. He had a plan, and it kicked off when I stepped under that pier.

Besides, there was no tactically secure spot to set up a shot. Dozens would see someone with a rifle on the pier. Taking a shot in these conditions exposed him, and would make it next to impossible for him to make a getaway.

The teens were safe, and I was safe until I stepped into the dank shade of the pier.

You're an idiot, a voice in the back of my head warned. *You're walking onto a stage Anton has set just for you. It's a trap, and you're walking right into it.*

All true. The increasingly graphic worst-case scenarios popping into my head with each step were all feasible. Yes, the pier could be rigged to blow and he could just be waiting to take me out with everyone else. Yes, he might knock me out and tie me to a post and let the tide kill me. Both of those options and a dozen others were totally feasible.

Yet I kept walking until two of the teens ahead of me threaded their fingers together and pulled away from the group. The girl's playful giggle as she went up on her toes to kiss the guy was the warning that kept me from walking right into them. Keeping things as casual as I could, I moved around the couple and caught back up to the main group as I debated the merits of bringing a gun onto the pier.

I could only see the harm in it.

Was I glad I'd had the .38 in my hand during our last meet up? Definitely. But we'd been alone with no witnesses.

Witnesses changed everything.

Cameras covered the pier and there were hundreds of cell phones to pick up both the audio and video of anything Anton and I did. Whatever happened up top would have hundreds of human and digital witnesses, and I didn't want a single one of them to catch sight of me with a gun. I had to ditch it, and what better place than under the pier?

Okay, so now I had firm motive for heading under the pier. Good for me. At least I'd look like I was doing something logical when I died. Bonus points.

The teenagers around me all started pulling their phones out and taking selfies. Of course they were. What was the point of a teenager going to the Santa Monica pier if they didn't alert everyone on social media of how cool it was to be them right then?

Well, their selfish motives were clashing with my selfish motives at the moment, because them stopping to take selfies meant I was about to lose my cover altogether. Great.

Twenty steps later, they were all grouped in a selfie pod and I was a lone wolf lurking in the background of their shot as I continued down the pathway—totally exposed.

Even though I'd convinced my mind that I was safe until I moved under the pier, my instincts hadn't gotten the memo and were pretty much freaking out. The stupidest ideas started feeling smart—like stealing a car and driving away.

What in the world would that accomplish?

Nothing. Literally nothing.

Whatever destiny I had involved going under—not over—and that's what I was going to do...even if my instincts screamed that I had better odds running into the ocean, stealing one of those surf boards, and paddling my way to Hawaii.

It's amazing how survival instincts could attach hope to acts of insanity. Truly. But seeing as how stealing cars and surf boards were off my list of legitimate options, I was sticking with Plan A.

I glanced at my band to see if Anton had moved since I arrived. He hadn't. He was in position and holding…waiting for me to walk into his lair.

Seriously? my inner voice chided. *You're doing this?!?*

Yes. I was doing this. I was walking into the lion's den for the simple fact that the lion hadn't eaten me when we'd met outside of the den. Given that one circumstance had nothing to do with the other pretty much made me an idiot when it came to the logic of it all, but I couldn't think of any other move. I had zero mental preparation for any of this. My only option was to follow my gut and wing it.

And my gut told me to hear Anton out.

It was either that or paddle to Hawaii. And it wasn't like my gut had the worst track record. The last time I'd ignored my gut I'd let Ty talk me into marrying him, even knowing that today was coming. Did I regret being with him these past months? On a personal level, no. But had my gut instinct been right that marrying me would cause him great pain?

Yes.

Objectively speaking, Ty's life would have been better if I had broken things off and moved back to Los Angeles without looking back. His heart would have been broken, as would have mine, but it would have insulated him from most of this.

Six months ago, my gut had told me today would be irredeemably bad, and I'd married Ty anyway. Now that same voice was telling me that Anton really did want to talk to me before he killed me, so I was going to trust that…even if it killed me. There was a 99% chance I was dying today anyway; might as well go out following my internal compass.

Resigning myself to that decision and telling my survival instincts to take a hike, I stepped onto the beach, my shoes sinking into the sand with each step that took me to the underside of the pier. The air was cooler and damper in its shadow, with the sound of the surf and seagulls mixing with the sounds of good times above me.

Removing my backpack, I wadded it up to be as small as possible while my eyes searched for a place to stow it—or at least I hoped that's what it looked like I was doing. In truth, I was looking for Anton—the guy who easily could have shot me by now, but hadn't. He either wanted to talk to me, or he simply had a very glamorous death planned for me to impress The Fours.

Whatever the case, I was right where he wanted me.

Let the games begin.

As of ten seconds ago, Anton had been 70 feet ahead of me at my one o'clock. That put him at the dead center of the pier, right at the shoreline, which didn't match what my eyes were seeing on the shore level. Not unless he was hugging the underside of the pier like Spider-man.

My eyes darted up—fully accepting the possibility he was capable of such a feat while also looking for security cameras and a place to tuck my bag. The underbelly of the pier didn't leave much room for hiding a bag, not to mention a grown man. And I didn't see a man, which meant Anton had to be above me on the topside of the pier.

A chilly mist from the surf tickled against the back of my neck as I realized I'd have to dig a shallow hole to hide the bag. There really wasn't another option. The ocean lapped lightly against the shoreline as I counted off the posts to where I knelt in the sand and burrowed in. I didn't go deep, just enough to cover the bag with a pile before standing and checking Anton's position on my band and noting that our dots were only about ten meters from each other as of ten seconds ago. I was basically standing right under him.

At least that's what I thought until I was tackled like a linebacker from behind.

Anton was not above me. He was on top of me.

We both hit the edge of the ocean with a splash and I gasped as frigid water washed over me. The shock of it had me fighting to get out of the cold as Anton's hand snaked up to grab my hair. Once he had a solid grip on a huge chunk of hair, he stood, dragging me to deeper water.

"Your profile says you can hold your breath for five minutes," he sneered. "How about we put that to the test?"

Instinct told me to struggle, but the thinking part of my brain heard a courtesy warning in his words. We were going under and I needed to get a serious breath in my lungs before we did.

"How about death by drowning?" he said, the water now to his chest while my feet touched nothing below me, even when I pointed my toes. "I hear it's quite peaceful."

One big breath was all I got before he used his grip on my hair to push me face-first into the water. Was he planning on holding me like this for five minutes? It didn't make sense. Not one bit, so while my body clenched defensively against the cold, my mind did its best to assess my situation.

My hands and feet were both unrestrained as Anton held me face-down. That wasn't the kind of thing a trained assassin did by mistake, which meant he hadn't. He was leaving me room to defend myself on purpose...because we had an audience to perform for.

Given our positions, Anton had to be expecting defensive action from me, so I gave it to him—mule kicking him in the chest and using his solid frame to push myself under the water.

He let me go. To an outside eye, it might look like the force of my kick got him to release me, but no. My small legs were no match for his tree trunk of a chest—especially with me kicking through the water to get to him. When his hand released, it had nothing to do with my kick. He was playing along.

Some of my hair stayed in Anton's hand as I escaped, jerking my head back as I swam away from him. I was out of his reach, but only barely so, with the water level above my head but below his chin.

To get distance between us, I dove deeper underwater, moving down and away from Anton. A glance back in the murky water showed his outline right behind me. He snagged my ankle as I swam, dragging me back far enough to grab my forearm. Then his murky form pointed out to deeper waters like he wanted us to move that direction.

He wanted me to…what? Follow him?

He clamped a hand around my wrist and again pointed out to sea. Not knowing what else to do, I nodded, indicating I wouldn't fight him if he went that way. He responded by moving toward the post off to his right and diving down to its base, dragging me after him. He seemed to be looking for something on the ocean floor, a task made harder by the fact that he only had one free hand to search with. Even still, it was only a matter of seconds before he unearthed a looped end of a rope, slid his hand through it, and made a sound that sent a wave of air bubbles up to the surface. An instant later, the rope grew taut, rising up out of the sand and pulling us out to sea.

The polluted water barely allowed me to see Anton an arm's length ahead, but more than once I spotted one of the supporting beams of the pier just in time to avoid scraping against it. But when I wasn't dodging obstacles, I forced my body to stay calm and conserve oxygen. I could hold my breath for five minutes, yes, but I'd never done so in water this cold. It was different, and I'd already burned enough oxygen in our struggle to feel the need to gasp for air building in my lungs.

I had no idea how long this drag out to sea was going to last, and the need to breathe was like an insistent hiccup that required my full attention to suppress. Once we moved beyond the pier, I only moved two more times to pressurize my ears. Under typical circumstances I would guess we were about thirty feet underwater, but the temperature might have impacted pressurization as much as it impacted my ability to hold my breath. All I knew was that it had been around a minute since we'd gone under when my lungs demanded air if I didn't want the world to turn black.

Static apnea in a swimming pool was different than fighting for your life in the ocean during March before dropping thirty feet below the surface. Five minutes wasn't going to happen today. Not under these conditions.

I didn't see the submerged upside-down boat Anton was aiming for until we nearly ran into it. When the rope tried to drag us into its helm, Anton pressed his feet into the lip to give himself the leverage to guide us under the hull, rather than into it. His move whipped us under the rail and when we reached the other side, I found air again. It was pitch dark and freezing cold in the hull, but the rope had dragged us right to an air pocket the size of a yacht.

Anton broke the surface an instant after me, gasping for air. I couldn't see him, but I could hear how hungry his lungs were for oxygen. I aimed for a little more decorum as I felt around the dark space for something to hold onto so I wouldn't have to tread water.

"They can't hear or see us here," Anton said once he had control over his breathing. "Their frequency can't go through this hull, but we need to hurry. We've got four minutes, tops."

"For what?" I asked, finally finding something to take my weight so I could focus on Anton.

"To decide if we want to work together," he said right before a light flickered on from a cell phone he had inside a plastic bag. It was nothing more than a flashlight app that made the screen glow, but it lit up the space between us well enough for me to watch him and the little clouds our exhales made in the air between us.

"Work together?" I asked. "To what end?"

He studied me as if rethinking what he wanted to say. "As soon as I learned today was going to happen, I found out who you were—"

"How?" I interrupted.

"Connections. Doesn't matter," he said. "Point is, I've known almost everything there is to know about you since back in October. And when I saw Mark had once been your trainer, I went to him to ask about beating you."

That didn't sound good. At all. I'd never been Mark's favorite. He'd made that clear. His training wasn't for girls and his gym was *Men Only*.

"You know what he told me?" Anton said, pulling me from my thoughts.

I shook my head.

"He told me to think very carefully about taking you out—that if I wanted to live, I'd find a way around it."

That made no sense. "Why would he say that?"

His eyes regarded me as if mentally weighing something. "Because he was telling me that if I killed you, he would make it his business to kill me."

"Not likely," I tried to joke as an involuntary shiver up my body from the cold. "He probably meant something else."

"No. He meant what he meant. But he was also sending me another message that took me a little while to confirm."

"Which was?" I prompted.

"That the moment I kill you, I'm a dead man no matter what. That's what he was telling me—that in all the years and all the times The Fours have had people face off in gauntlets like this, exactly none of the players has lived to walk away."

That...actually made sense.

"The bounty hunters aren't on hand just in case one of us lives past midnight," he said. "They're here to kill us no matter what. There's a guaranteed payday at the end of all this, which is why so many showed up. Definite money plus a head-to-head competition in front of the richest men in the world? The bounty hunters are the ones auditioning for jobs right now, not us. We die no matter what. That bomb goes off no matter what. And just like there are bets on how the first person dies, there are bets on how many die and are injured by the bomb, and which bounty hunter kills the victor and how. It's all a rigged game, Rhea. That's what Mark was telling me that day."

There was no reason for me to trust a single word coming out of Anton's mouth, and yet…it all made terrible sense. It *felt* true, and Anton must have seen his words were getting through to me because he kept talking.

"We both know what these guys are capable of, Rhea. They can create videos showing us doing whatever they want us to do and pump it right into the media machine they own and operate. They can kill us, they can frame us, and do pretty much anything else they want with us. Our only hope of not giving them exactly what they want is to work together."

I wanted him to be telling the truth, which meant I had to assume he wasn't. I had to feel him out, which was hard when your near-numb body was starting to tremor to generate the heat necessary to avoid hypothermia.

Still, I gave it a go. "Work together? Or do you just need a fall guy and this is your way or luring me into position to take that fall?"

Anton frowned. "I've had six months to watch you, Rhea. I know who you are and believe I can trust you. I also understand that you don't share this advantage. Trust me, I would have loved to have this conversation months ago so you would have time to process it, but there literally wasn't an opportunity. We were being watched so closely. I could bring information in for me, but there was no way to connect with you. They would have caught anything I did."

I believed that. He couldn't have reached out and I had no doubt that he'd wanted to earn my trust months ago. Doing so would have been very smart of him.

But that made him smart, not innocent.

He held out the glowing phone between us. "There's a video on here that I got for you."

Despite being suspicious, I reached out to take the phone. "What is it?"

"The worst video you will probably watch in your life," he replied, his face more in the dark now that I held the phone. "When you watch it, I think you'll quickly piece together the history of how you got to be here. And I'm hoping that even if you don't trust me after you see it, you'll be pissed off enough to help me with my plan."

"Which is?"

His eyes grew very serious. "We're going to stop that bomb tonight and we're going to survive."

My body shifted from tremoring to shaking, my teeth chattering as I gripped the phone in a numb hand to keep the light between us. "How?"

"First I need to know you're in," he said firmly. "And I'm going to be nice and not make you choose in the next ninety seconds." He pointed to the phone. "I'm going to let you watch the video first."

"Okay," I hedged. "But do you know what kind of attack they're planning for tonight?"

"I have people on it," he said, but I could read between the lines. He didn't know.

"We can't stop something if we don't know when or where it's happening," I said.

"That is true," Anton said. "But I have people. Once things start moving, I'll know who, when, and where. Then we can act. But it will be on the fly, and you can bet that safeguards will be in place to make stopping the bomb nearly impossible. If we collaborate then we have a shot at stopping it and living to fight another day. If we don't work together, we both die. Period. If nothing else, at midnight all the bounty hunters race to impress their world-wide audience by being the one to deliver our heads on a platter. The bounties will stay good until we're dead, whether that's seconds or years from the moment they're offered."

My unwitting reply was the clattering of my teeth as my entire body spasmed against the cold.

"For what it's worth, I'm really sorry you got sucked into this, Rhea," he said. "I was born into this world and broke an oath. That's what landed me here. But you were lured and coerced. You'll understand once you watch the video. It's why I'm extending my exit plan to include you. You're a good person, plus you have skills we can use to stop the attack. In addition, killing you increases the attention placed on me until midnight, while not killing you leaves you as a lingering threat. Bringing you onto the team is not only the right thing to do, it's strategically smart." His blue lips gave a little chatter as he shrugged. "So here we are."

An alarm went off on the phone I was holding and I knew without being told that it was our cue to head back to the surface.

"If you're in, go to the Third Street Promenade and find the Queen of Hearts," he said, pushing off his handhold to float to the side of the boat. "And don't forget that the more entertaining we are, the more distracted our audience will be and the slower they'll be to see a curveball when we throw it. So be entertaining. For both our sakes. Keep moving. Keep things interesting."

I held up the phone. "How do I watch this without them seeing?"

Anton took a few breaths to prep himself for the return to the surface. "Use the included headphones in some place like an empty bathroom, where there are no cameras and no other cell phones or equipment. Do that, and The Fours will have no idea what you're seeing while you sit on the toilet."

"How do you know this?"

He hesitated. "I know people who are on the betting side of all this so I know what The Fours are seeing and hearing."

I felt my eyebrows shoot up in surprise. "They're filling you in as we go?"

He nodded and I'm certain my mouth fell open in surprise despite my freezing state. He had people watching me and filling him in on everything I was doing real-time? That was an insane advantage on top of all his other advantages.

I didn't even know how to process that.

"This is a serious offer I'm making, Rhea," he said, interrupting my shock. "I'm really sorry for the video I've chosen to show you to make you choose my side, but I need you to see that we're each other's best chances. The Fours may be richer than God and have the world as their joystick, but not a single one of them can do what you and I can do. If this is our last day on earth, I say we go out on our own terms, not like puppets."

Well, he was certainly pushing the right buttons there, but we were both too cold for me to get a read on his sincerity.

"We're out of time, Rhea," he said, his skin growing pale even though he wasn't shaking like I was. "I'm going to swim up to the surface and head south. You go north and keep that phone out of sight."

With that, Anton took one breath and disappeared under the water, leaving me alone with the cell phone. I pointed the light down to the water beneath and caught his legs just before they disappeared on the other side of the boat.

He could have killed me. Again. He hadn't. Instead, he'd given me a phone and claimed that its contents would convince me that

we were on the same team.
It was time to find out if he was right.

CHAPTER 9

By the time I broke through the ocean's surface, my body wasn't fully cooperating with me anymore. Thanks to the cold, my fingers were curled into little perma-claws I could no longer straighten at will. My lungs cramped against my inhale and my knees felt permanently bent as they fought to pull up into an instinctive fetal position to hold in heat. I was guessing the water was about 54 degrees at the surface—tops—but it had been much, much colder down where Anton and I had our chat, and I was feeling it.

The two diehard surfers were floating on their boards about twenty feet away from where I was doing my best to tread water. Teeth chattering and muscles clamping, I eyed the surfers first then the much more distant shore. I could definitely make it to the surfers, but swimming to the shore on my own would take a lot out of me.

When in doubt, be interesting. That seemed to be the unofficial motto of the day, which gave the excuse to overcome my ego to the point that I no longer felt I needed to prove that I could swim to the shore. In asking for a ride back to shore, I was *choosing* not to prove how strong I was in the name of making all the rich authoritarians who didn't predict I'd surf back to land lose money.

A worthy cause.

Neither of the surfers noticed my approach. They were too busy scouting for something surf-worthy on the horizon when I came up behind them.

"What's up?" I said to get their attention, but it really didn't come out right. My voice cut in and out as I spoke—like my vocal cords had gotten cold enough to shiver or something. But whether they understood or not, the two guys heard me and turned.

"Dude," the guy closest to me said, glancing back at the shoreline behind us. "A riptide get you or something?"

"Or something," I said, treading water as my chin tremored with the cold. "Think I could get a lift back to shore?"

The two guys glanced at each other then off into the horizon.

"Today's weak," the farthest one said. "I'll take her in."

Thank heaven. With every moment that passed, I was getting less confident about my ability to make it to the shore on my own.

The guy paddled around to me. "Aren't you freezing?"

"T-t-totally," I said, reaching out a frozen hand so he could pull me up onto the board. That was when he saw I was in clothes.

"Whoa. Did you fall off a boat?" His eyes narrowed. "Are you legal?"

"I'm legal," I replied, pulling myself onto the board. "But my boat did decide that it was done with the whole floating thing."

He laughed, which was good for me. "Well, then, you're lucky we're out here. Climb on up."

I did not need to be asked twice.

Seconds later, I was on the board, teeth clacking together loud enough for both guys to hear.

"Dude, how long have you been out here?" the guy on the other board asked.

"Not long," I said. "It's just freezing."

He shook his head and looked at his friend. "Get her out of here, man."

My guy laid down on his board and glanced back at me. "Not to be totally pervy, but I think the only way this will work is if you lay on top of me. You don't look too coordinated right now and I don't trust you not to fall or throw us off balance."

He had a point, which I only proved as I fumbled and faltered my way into laying on his back and gripping my fisted hands onto his body suit.

"Hold on," the guy said. "I'll see what we can find to ride in all this chop."

There wasn't much to work with, but my guy was good and in short order a wave barely bigger than our flattened bodies was carrying us to the shore. My surfer planked his body up on his hands with me on top of him and adjusted his weight to make sure we stayed in the sweet spot all the way until the tip of the board hit sand.

"Okay, stowaway," the guy joked. "End of the line."

Stand. I had to stand now, which I did with a bit of caution. "Thank you."

It was embarrassing how hard my teeth cracked together as I shivered through those words. It was enough to get the guy to stand up and help me to my feet. "You going to be okay? You're freakin' blue right now, babe."

"I'm good," I said, not because I knew it was true, but because it had to be the truth. Unless he had a hypothermia blanket in his back pocket, there was really nothing he could do for me.

"I have a hypothermia blanket in my car if you want me to grab it for you."

Well, whaddayaknow. Still shaking, I looked under the pier. "I have a bag over there. I can pay you for it."

"Nah," he said, picking up his board. "I'll be right back. It's all yours."

The chilly breeze on my clothes made me want to tip over in the sand and give up the will to live. I wanted to strip off my soggy shirt so badly, but that would make the outline of the phone tucked into my pants clear for any camera within range to see that I was carrying something I shouldn't be. I needed to wait just a little longer to change, but in the meantime, I did manage to get some blood flowing as I lurched over to grab my bag. No one had stolen it in the past several minutes, which felt a bit lucky.

I had a change of clothes; I had a gun; I had money. If only a sauna would magically appear in front of me, I'd be all set.

"I got the blanket!" my surfer called out from the side of the pier.

It wasn't a sauna, but it was a start.

CHAPTER 10

If you walk into a hotel with enough confidence, no one questions you—even when you look like a half-drowned rat who just crawled out of the wrong side of the ocean. The ruse works even better if you've stolen a keycard off of a guest before walking in. Bonus points if you picked the hotel because you know right where the pool and hot tub are.

I had no swimsuit, but luckily my underwear was close enough to not earn me too many looks as I rinsed the salt off in the locker room to start, followed by three minutes in the 70-degree pool to stabilize me a bit before spending five minutes in the 104-degree hot tub to feel genuinely warm again. I didn't have time to indulge any more than that, but those ten minutes were enough to give me the use of my extremities again and to make my wrist with the post going through it feel less like a block of ice. Whatever the material The Fours had used to secure the wristband, it got hot and cold like a frying pan. Not good.

The salt that had covered me minutes before I walked into the hotel was replaced by chlorine as I got out of the hot tub and went for my bag. Lotion and new underwear. That's what I was missing, but I was definitely not in a position to be picky. I needed to get changed, get alone, and watch Anton's contraband video. The man had studied me for six months and believed he'd handed me a video clip that would lure me into joining Team Anton?

Well, it was time to see how well the man knew me.

The entrances into the hotel bathrooms did not lock from the inside, so I settled on only changing and tossing my ocean-drenched clothes in the trash on my way out. The hypothermia blanket went into my bag. Just in case.

I glanced at the mirror before exiting the bathroom. Wet hair and utter lack of makeup aside, I now looked like a typical, on-trend, twenty-something tourist as I walked back across the lobby and left the same way I'd arrived.

Privacy. I needed privacy and a door with a lock. While my eyes searched for that, my mind mulled over all the developments I had yet to process since meeting with Anton.

All the talk about Mark Weston advocating for me made no sense, but the revelation that neither Anton nor I would get out of this alive felt right. I believed that part. The bigger reveal was that Anton had friends on the betting side of all this.

That was huge.

It meant that once the bets were laid out about the bomb attack later, Anton was in a position to have that information relayed to him. If I made sure I was in the same room as him when he got the info, that would put us on even-ish footing to make our move. Although we couldn't really do anything unless we took off our wristbands, and doing that was an instant death sentence. Yet removing the wristbands would be necessary if Anton was serious about stopping the attack. We couldn't have our locations broadcasted while simultaneously sabotaging a near omnipotent enemy.

Too many things would have to go perfectly for any collaboration between Anton and me to have any remotely positive outcome. Even with Anton's eyes on the inside, it was still all a nearly impossible proposition that only got off the ground if our wristbands came off.

But I'd cross that bridge when I came to it because the truth was that there was only one choice for me: The best path to protect my mom's family and avoid leaving Ty the widower of an accused terrorist.

There were worse things than dying. I hadn't known that for sure twelve hours ago, but I was certain now. Losing me was not the worst thing that could happen to Ty. He could lose me, be branded a coconspirator, *and* spend the next several years being investigated by the FBI as the public crucified him for any alleged complicity in my "actions." My mom's side of the family could also be investigated and banned from traveling to the United States.

None of those outcomes were options, but it was the outcome I was looking at if Anton really had all the resources and intel that he claimed he had and I chose to fight him anyway.

I glanced at my wristband as I walked toward the bathrooms at Santa Monica Place, noting that Anton was giving me space. He was 1.5 miles away and pretty much staying there. Maybe he was warming up too. Whatever he was doing, I hoped it was interesting enough to distract from the fact that I was about to go into a bathroom and stay there for a while.

The mall bathroom wasn't empty, but there wasn't a line so I walked right into the farthest available stall and took a seat. Opening my bag, I pulled out Anton's phone and started peeling off the multiple layers of sealed plastic waterproofing the device and the headphones. Anton had clearly planned to deliver this to me underwater in advance. Not a drop of water could have gotten through any one of the layers, not to mention the three he'd used. Plus, he'd put a small piece of fabric against the touchscreen so he could still operate it through the plastic while we were underwater.

He said he'd been planning this for six months, and I was starting to believe him. While I had been training myself into oblivion, Anton had been researching and plotting right under the nose of The Fours.

But how? Who were his contacts, and how had he kept everything under the radar?

Once I had all the plastic off, I tucked all the packaging away in a sanitary napkin dispenser before bringing the screen to life. It was empty save for one file icon. It was pretty obvious what I was supposed to do.

Don't forget that he gave this to you to manipulate you, I told myself. *Whatever it is, take it with a grain of salt.*

I didn't have time for much more of a pep talk than that. The clock was ticking, and I was dealing with people who knew exactly how long I spent in the bathroom. Not long. Disappearing into a bathroom stall for minutes on end would raise flags in some of the spectators.

Pushing my last hesitations to the side, I plugged in the earbuds and clicked on the icon. A video popped up and started auto-playing. The image was dark, so I didn't recognize the location at first. I only saw torches and heard the hubbub of a group of people talking. Decade-old music played in the background, and all I could really make out in the video was a bar stocked with alcohol on the far wall and silhouettes standing in front of it.

On the screen, a menu prompt appeared and showed me someone manually brightening the picture. Without me doing anything, the person who had made this video for me brightened up the image and increased the contrast. Dark silhouettes became people—guys—all standing around one focal point. I couldn't see what held their attention, but there were about thirty teenage guys and they were all gathered around the same focal point.

Color-correcting prompts continued to appear, showing me how the image was being adjusted to bring the images out of the shadows until I saw a man in a hood facing the group.

Subtitles appeared on the screen as muffled voice started

talking.

Tonight we initiate the willing. Those who wish to prove themselves worthy to join our ranks over the next four years take their first steps tonight.

Several of the boys on the screen raised their arms in a gesture I couldn't make out.

May we be worthy, appeared in the subtitle area as the boys said the words aloud in unison. I heard the words, but without the subtitles I wouldn't have been completely sure what they were saying.

What in the world was I watching?

The man in the hood spoke again. *Each of you will prove your dedication in full view of a camera tonight. You will do this, not only knowing that you are above other men, but that you are entering a brotherhood that protects its faithful.*

The guys replied in a chorus. *That we may be worthy.*

Okay, this was weird. Top-to-bottom weird. Had Anton uploaded the wrong video? Because none of this was lighting a fire under me. Given everything I was looking at that day, I didn't care about The Fours little initiation ceremony, or whatever this was. It was dark. It was weird. It was narcissistic and full of entitlement. None of this was a big truth bomb that was really opening my eyes to anything I hadn't already figured out.

I glanced down at the progress bar, noting that the video was forty-five minutes long. I definitely didn't have that much time to sit in a bathroom stall staring at a screen.

The hooded man on the tiny screen looked toward the camera that had taken the footage I was watching, gesturing in its direction. Computer lines appeared over his shadowed face, mapping it.

Confirmed Identity: Elliott Church appeared on the screen, grabbing my full attention.

Elliott? In a room full of frat boys? It was plausible. He had come to my class at UCLA. That's where he had recruited me, so why wouldn't he have recruited other freshman at the same time?

I paused the video, taking a screenshot of the hooded man's face and zooming in. It was Elliott. All the features lined up, including the scar above his upper lip.

A little more curious now, I pressed play on the video again, watching as all of the new initiates walked up to the camera, introduced themselves, and told the camera it was their honor to pledge their loyalty to a fraternity I remembered all too well from my college days. It was the fraternity that had hosted the party where I'd left Kay with her new "friends" all those years ago…the frat house I'd helped burn down.

But this couldn't be a video from that same night. It couldn't be…even though the song choice was right for the year. Still, it couldn't be from that night. At least that's what I told myself until the frat brothers onscreen stepped back to reveal the object of the felony pledge.

Kay. Eighteen-year-old Kay, her unconscious body hanging from shackled wrists. Her feet touched the ground, but that was irrelevant since she was drugged into oblivion and couldn't have stood if she wanted to.

My breath stopped in my throat as I realized what I was looking at and what the next forty-five minutes of video would show. I pressed stop on the screen, my hands shaking as I realization dropped on me like a cinder block.

Not only had Kay been gang raped all those years ago, but The Fours had taped it all as blackmail to any initiate who might get cold feet down the line. It wasn't an unusual tactic for secret societies. Guaranteeing you had everything you needed to destroy someone before raising them up was a great way to ensure fealty. Pride and self-preservation were powerful things, but…this?

My hands grew unsteady as I stared at the paused picture, previously disjointed puzzle pieces from my past falling together in an instant.

I knew how my old boss thought. I was more than familiar with Elliott's passion for killing two, three, or even four birds with one stone.

He had planned this. He'd chosen Kay. She hadn't been some random, convenient girl grabbed from a party. She'd been chosen—probably the same day Elliott first made me a job offer and I'd refused with the grace of an overconfident teenager. Elliott had needed a sacrifice and wanted my attention.

And in usual Elliott Church form, he'd gotten exactly what he wanted as efficiently as possible.

I have no idea how long I sat on that public toilet while the realization of what had really happened so many years ago settled in.

Elliott had handpicked Kay for the initiation of the freshman Fours, and he'd chosen her because of me. I'd refused his offer and he'd created a situation where he could have both the ceremonial lamb for his fraternity and my full attention.

And all that on-campus harassment and taunting that came at her afterward? The lost rape kit and evidence? That had been Elliott, too. He'd pushed and pushed until Kay ran away, somehow knowing—or guessing—that I would seek out his help and accept his terms to hunt her down. And lucky him, I'd doubled down on his leverage over me by joining the frat house burn-down party.

The whole idea that Elliott went through so much effort to get me on his payroll sounded too convoluted to be true, yet I'd worked with Elliott for years. I knew his mind. He was the king of getting dominoes to fall in his favor. When you worked with him, life was smooth. When you worked against him, your plans turned to confetti.

But...why me?

Seriously.

Why put that much effort in me based on a personality test I took with hundreds of other students in a 101 class? How could I have tested in a way that made me that special to him? He would have had to have studied me after I declined his initial offer. He would have had to perform surveillance and study it—realizing that even though I'd just met Kay, her situation and naiveté had me feeling more than the usual level of protectiveness over her.

Why hadn't he targeted Ben to get my attention? I'd been in love with him back then. All of my friends had been men, in fact. Girls and I had never jived that well, and Kay—

Even as I argued with myself over better targets Elliott could have used to get my attention, my mind came back to the obvious. Kay was female. It was as simple as that. I'd befriended her, she was female, and Elliott had needed a female. She'd literally been the only option.

It was good I was in a bathroom because I felt like puking all of a sudden. Everything made sense in the worst way and for the first time that day, I felt an unfettered willingness to kill someone.

I wanted Elliott Church dead.

If I was going to end this day as a named dead terrorist, well then, Elliott Church was going to be one of my nonsensical victims. He'd dragged me into all of this. Without him, I'd probably be signed to a record label and touring with Ben's band right then. Who knew what would have become of Kay. Maybe she still would have become a reporter; maybe she would have gone another way. But without Elliott, her freshman year at college wouldn't have broken her into a thousand pieces that still hadn't put themselves back together again.

Kay was a stunning woman in the prime of her life and she still couldn't let her guard down enough to let someone love her. She might have been unconscious that night back in our freshman year, but that didn't mean something inside her hadn't broken and never healed.

Elliott's selfishness and single-mindedness were not only

going to get me killed in a truly horrific fashion that day, but I now knew the promise that those I left behind would remain unharmed was an utter lie.

Elliott knew it. The Fours knew it. Anton knew it. And now I knew it.

The entire premise of the rules explained to me that morning served only as a system of control. They were going to do whatever they wanted and take whatever they wanted, no matter what I did. I had no control over any of that. I only had control over my own actions.

Shoving the phone back into my pocket, I flushed the toilet and pushed out of the bathroom stall.

Anton wanted his team to get a plus-one? Well, congratulations to him. He was going to get his wish. I just needed to make one stop first. And to do that, I needed a rope, a knife, and the quickest route to Elliott's office possible.

CHAPTER 11

Elliott knew I was coming his way, just like every other Four with a screen did. If I'd done things right, none of them knew *why* I was heading to Church Investigations, only that I was seeking out my old boss. That shred of ignorance on their part was likely the only reason I found Elliott sitting alone in that leather throne of his when I pushed through his office doors.

"Rhea," he said with that salesman smile of his. "I'm not sure what you're doing here. You know I'm not allowed to help you."

Help me? There was only one way he could help me.

Not trusting my voice, I sprinted across the twenty feet between me and his desk before vaulting over it. The look on his face shifted from smug to stunned as I kicked both feet straight into his chest, pushing his rolling chair into the wall with him in it. The kick had more flare than power, but it still served the purpose of backing him into the wall while I got my footing. I moved in for a more debilitating strike, but Elliott was quick. By the time I got my feet on the ground, he was standing too.

"Interesting," he said, circling away from me. "That's not exactly what I was expecting from you."

I tracked him with my eyes. "Well, now you know what to expect."

His eyes narrowed on me. "Shouldn't you be out fighting someone else?"

"Trust me. There is no one I'd rather be fighting right now than you."

He reached down to his watch and pressed a button on it. "I'm sorry, Rhea, but that's not an option. You have thirty seconds before I do Anton Petrov a favor and take you out myself."

It was a bluff. If the guy that morning had been telling the truth, there was $12 billion being wagered on how I died, and Elliott wasn't going to mess with that.

Still, I went with his threat.

"Well, the thirty seconds are going to be the worst of your life," I said before taking a swing. But Elliott was no novice. We'd both spent time training with Mark Weston—something that became apparent as his thick arm blocked my strike like I was a nerf bat, locking my elbow and using it to swing me into his desk.

Realizing I was about to be bent over his desk had me seeing red, and my eyes scanned for something to throw as my stomach slammed into the desk.

Coffee cup.

I had no idea if there was any coffee still in it, but that didn't stop me from snatching it off the desk with my free hand and hurling it at his face. My aim was as true as Elliott's instincts to protect his precious face. The hand locking my elbow moved up to bat the mug away from connecting, freeing my arm enough to slip free and let me land a strike to his sternum.

His eyes flared in both offense and surprise as the pain registered. My next shot would have been to the neck, but Elliott stopped it when he pushed me into the desk with such force that I ended up on my back on top of it. Unwilling to let him get his hands on me in that position, I back-rolled over the desk and stood to face him on the other side.

One of his eyes twitched in his pain and a hand pressed against his sternum as he eyed me from across the desk. He was in pain, yes, but not enough to give me an advantage. I needed to choose my next strike better if I wanted to get the upper hand.

"Why are you here, Rhea?" he asked, his voice cold. "I tried to save you from all this. I gave you everything. I cut you every break, and this is how you repay me?"

"You didn't save me from a thing. You dragged me into all this from the beginning."

He shook his head. "You came to me."

"After you and your fraternity set up my friend and raped her," I sneered. "You specifically chose Kay to get to me."

He blinked in surprise, waiting a few beats to reply. "Is that what you think?"

"That's what I *know*," I replied. "You designed it from the moment I took that stupid test of yours and declined your job offer. You decided you didn't like my answer, so you took a look at my life and designed a way for me to say yes."

He actually smiled. "Because the world revolves around you, Rhea? I don't think so." He gestured toward the door. "Now I suggest you leave. As much as I'd like to kill you myself at the moment, it would mean losing my bet and I'd rather not do that."

"Oh, you're going to lose your bet either way."

He straightened, dropping his hand away from his chest to stand with his usual overconfident posture. "You forget how well I know you."

"And you forget how very fine the line is between who I am and who I want to be," I shot back, feeling my body grow irrationally calm. My anger disappeared, as did my fear. Everything disappeared but facts.

This quality—this ability to go into a cold zone that I always tried to avoid—was probably one of the test results that had landed me on Elliott's radar all those years ago. In that moment, I felt certain of that. It was the reason he'd wanted me to train with

Mark—the reason he wanted me to learn how to kill while pretending the whole time that wasn't exactly what he was doing.

Looking back, I could see that he never wanted me to be a simple investigator. He'd been waiting for my personality profile to lure me into darker territory…he'd been waiting me out until I thought it was my idea to transition, then he could act like he was doing me a favor by letting me change my course.

He'd been grooming me the entire time.

Even before Elliott had walked into my life, I'd had trouble connecting like everyone else did. I'd always connected generally, rather than specifically. In the rare instances where I did connect specifically, it was fast and hard, like with Ty and Kay and Ben. But when I didn't connect, I saw people more as probabilities and aptitudes than individuals.

That attribute would have been imperative for the future Elliott planned for me.

Unfortunately for Elliott, I'd had good friends. Even worse for him, I'd gone so far as to try to find my moral compass through dipping my foot into religion, which had led me to Ty—the first person in my life I'd ever trusted with everything. Being with Ty had made me so much better a human being than I'd ever been without him.

But that better person was gone at the moment, and someone with the chill of a snake had taken her place. Cold, calculating, and completely willing to do the unthinkable.

As the chill settled in, I realized Elliott's office smelled vaguely of hand sanitizer. I hadn't noticed that before just like I hadn't noticed that despite the steely look in Elliott's eyes, his weight was shifted away from me.

He was afraid.

It had been over thirty seconds since he pushed his button, and…nothing. No one was coming, and that could only mean one thing.

"I wonder what the side bet is for what's going to happen next." I stepped forward. "I wonder what your friends think I'm going to do to you…what they think you'll do to me."

His eyes dropped to his computer monitor and I could tell by the flex of his jaw that I was right. Whatever happened next was officially part of a side bet.

I sent him a cold smile. "Time to be entertaining, Elliott. Smile for the camera."

This time I didn't launch over the desk, but used his guest chair as a stepping stool to get on top of it. Elliott moved in, going for my knees, but not before I kicked his computer monitor into his face. It hit him an instant before the cord jerked the screen back toward his desk while I aimed a second kick at his nose. He blocked it with one hand, the other reaching to pull my standing leg out from under me. I jumped, kicking at him with the leg he'd just been grabbing for. Again, it wasn't the strongest move, but it was enough to get him to recoil a bit while I got both feet firmly back on the ground.

The hair on the back of Elliott's hands grazed me with his next swing. His follow up was on point to crack me right in the face, but a small parry and shift of weight put me in the clear while leaving him exposed. As with Anton, I didn't shy away from the low blow, but to make sure it landed, I faked high first. The punch I aimed at his face was telegraphed and when Elliott's hands moved up to stop my hand from connecting to his face, I soccer kicked him right between the legs. A low oomph escaped him as he dropped to one knee. His left hand dropped to cover his injured bits while his right hand gripped onto the desk.

He was stunned, not defeated, and the part of my mind that had gone cold fought with the rest of me about what I should do next. If I was going to die today, a big part of me wanted to take Elliott with me. The world would be a better place without trash like him.

That's what my instinct told me.

Then there was the deliberate part of me that hadn't eaten meat in fifteen years because I didn't feel stealing life was right. If I wanted the privilege of living out my life to its natural end, who was I to rob someone or something else of that same privilege?

But if I wasn't going to exact revenge on Elliott for what he'd done to me and Kay, what was I doing in his office?

I kicked Elliott in the ribs while figuring that out. It was a defensive move to delay him coming at me again. It didn't stop him, though. He absorbed the kick with a grunt before pushing to his feet and lunging my way as best he could, given his current pain situation. I stepped out of the line of fire, this time taking out his left knee. I might not be sure if I wanted to face God as a murderer yet, but I had zero moral dilemma when it came to sending Elliott into surgery as I forced his leg to bend the wrong way.

Elliott fell to the ground, punching the carpet in frustration as he realized what I'd just done to him. His knee was done. It would take a surgeon to get it back into working order.

"I'm going to kill you," he hissed, his hand darting out to try to get a hold of my legs. I danced away, circling around the desk to grab the rope I'd brought in as I removed the knife from my boot. On the way back around the desk, I purposefully came full circle so I could get a look at his computer monitor. My earlier kick hadn't killed it, although the screen did have a blue hue to it now. But that didn't matter; the bets did.

"Huh," I mused, looking over the scoreboard on the screen. "You say you're going to kill me, but it looks like bets are heavy that I'll be the one killing you." I stayed out of his striking range as I looked over the other bets. "Second highest odds are that I'll do to you what you did to Kay, but those betters are forgetting that I'm doing my best to die with a soul."

The bets were changing by the millisecond, rising and falling in the ranks of likelihood. So many options. Maybe I didn't need to figure out what to do. I could just choose from a menu. Would that not entertain my elite audience? Me getting a peek behind their secret door and choosing a winner at random?

When Elliott used his good leg to lunge at me from the ground, I realized that I needed to tie him up, at a minimum. For safety reasons alone, I needed to put him out of play while I figured out how dark a soul I would be walking out the door with. Elliott might be down a leg, but he still had two fully functioning arms thicker than my thighs that I needed to contend with.

"Any part of you that touches me gets broken," I said, looping a slip knot around the ankle of his injured leg and pulling the line taut. He cried out at the pressure it put on his knee. "That's your reality now, Elliott."

"Big talk from a girl who is about to die," he hissed between pained breaths. His hands dropped down to protect his knee instinctively, and I used that moment to loop the rope around his neck and hog-tie him so that any movement aggravated his injured knee.

As I finished off the knot around his neck, I leaned forward and spoke into his ear. "Big talk from a man who just got beat up by a girl and has no one coming to his rescue."

"Well," he said, trying for composure. "We all know that you can't pull the trigger. No one's here to save me because I don't really need saving, do I?"

I hated that he was right. I may have been incensed and imagining all sorts of evil on my way over, but now that I was here, all the fantasy of revenge was stripped away. I could break a rapist's knee and hogtie him, but following the impulses of my imagination would lead me into the spot I'd promised I'd never go.

"Everyone else was right about you from the beginning, weren't they?" he said, sounding frustrated. "All the effort...all that money I poured into you really was a waste. You've always just been a bunch of potential that never was going to pan out.

Pathetic, really."

Was he trying to piss me off? If so, a gold star to him. It was working.

"If not killing people makes me pathetic, then I guess I'm guilty," I said, walking around to I could look him in the eyes. "At least I don't lie about cowardly things I've done to helpless girls in the past."

"Cowardly?" he scoffed. "I haven't done a cowardly thing in my life."

"Like raping unconscious teenagers?" I challenged, baiting him. I wanted to hear him say it. I wanted a confession. And while I wasn't ready to kill him anymore, I was willing to go pretty far to get that out of him. "Does that make you feel big and strong, Elliott? Stringing up helpless girls and showing your recruits how to violate the powerless? Is that step one of becoming a man of honor in The Fours?"

His lips flattened into a straight line. "You need to stop talking, naive little girl."

"Am I naive?" I challenged, getting close enough to bait him into grabbing at me. He did, and immediately regretted it when the motion cranked his knee. I stayed right where I was. "Have I said anything untrue?"

He forced himself to chuckle through his pain. "You're digging your own grave here, Rhea."

"I thought it was already dug. You have the press release ready and everything, don't you?"

He smiled. "Bet on it."

"So why not tell me the truth?" I said, pulling Anton's phone out of my pocket. "Or do I need to play a video for you to refresh your memory?"

That got a surprised blink out of him, and Elliott looked at the phone with a bit of concern.

"I wonder what the penalty is for allowing a female like to me to access your precious initiation tapes," I mused. "I wonder if the reason no one is in here helping you right now is because your bosses know that the leverage I have to keep my friends and family safe after I'm gone includes videos you made year after year with all your recruits, showing the self-incrimination of initiates to ensure their fealty to your cause. Do you think your brothers are upset to know that, Elliott?"

"You're lying."

I was bluffing, not lying. There was a difference.

"Am I?" I said softly, pulling up the video that was still paused at the same spot I'd left it back in the bathroom. "Shall we have a reminder of your recruits from my freshman year and what they did to my friend, based on your instructions?"

When his eyes met mine defiantly, calling my bluff, I pressed play.

"Who among you wishes to be found worthy?"

It was Elliott's voice, and the flare of his eyes told me he knew calling my bluff had been an accident.

"Who, Elliott?" I taunted. "Who will be the first of your recruits to incriminate himself on camera for you by raping my friend?"

"Stop!" he said, reaching for the phone and disregarding the pain in his knee for a moment.

"Say his name, or I'll let him say it," I said in a cold tone that came right from my heart.

"Darren Campos wishes to be found worthy," a voice on the video said.

"Darren Campos," I said over the continuing dialog. "Do you think he's watching us right now, Elliott? Do you think he appreciates how well you've guarded his secret—that you've let a 'naive little girl' get her hands on the same blackmail material you've lorded over him all these years?"

"You did *not* get that from me," he said vehemently.

"I didn't?" I said with a bit of innocent flair. "Then where did I get it, Elliott? Who else had access to it? Are you accusing one of your superiors of giving it to me?"

"Of course not!" he said, his usual cool making way for traces of panic.

"No? Then who else did you give this video to?"

"No one."

I let the video play, allowing the sounds and damning dialog to fill the silence between us as I looked him in the eye. "Then who gave it to me, Elliott? How did I get it, if not for your incompetence?"

"I don't know," he hissed. "But I will find out."

I sent him a dark smile. "We both know that's not going to happen, don't we."

He wanted to punch me so badly—no, that was an understatement. He wanted to kill me. It was written all over his face.

"You call me the coward," I sneered. "But you're the one who won't admit what you did, even as I play a video of you doing it. You missed your calling, Elliott. You should have been a politician."

"And you should have been the one I drugged that night," he shot back.

Now we were getting somewhere. "Because that's how you deal with women who are stronger than you? Of course, it is. An even playing field has never been your thing."

I felt the whiff of his next punch burn past me as he lashed out. His fist didn't touch me, but I definitely felt it.

In response, I pulled his leather throne over to me and sat in it as I faced off with him. "That's the terrifying thing in all of this, isn't it? That you weren't wrong about me—that I'm everything you thought I was. I mean, you're lying there on the floor calling me a wasted investment and a coward, but you just had the shit beat out of you by a girl half your size." I leaned forward, purposefully taunting him with my condescending posture. "I'm smarter than you—or at least smart enough to get all your blackmail material in my back pocket to protect the people I love if I happen to die today. Hurt anyone I love after killing me, and it's going to rain pain on The Fours. I promise you that."

"Not possible!"

I ignored his protest. "And while I'm not physically stronger than you, I just proved that I don't really need to be, didn't I?"

"Untie me, and let's find out."

"Untie yourself. Since when do you need a girl's help with anything?"

"I'm going to—"

"Kill me?" I offered. "I think we've established that you're not really up for that right now. What you're being slow to grasp is that I'm not leaving here until you admit what you did. And if you refuse to admit it, then I'm going to put this phone in front of one of your many cameras and let it play so that all your brothers can see how you've compromised them."

I hadn't planned a single bit of this before I walked through the door. I was flying by the seat of my pants, but 100% okay with how things were playing out. Yes, I had safeguards in place to protect those I loved in case today broke bad, but nothing remotely as strong as the threat of exposing any of The Fours outside of the three members I knew for certain.

The threat of a library of incriminating videos was so, *so* much better. People had to be panicking on the other side of those video cameras.

"So what is it, Elliott?" I asked, holding up the phone and purposefully ignoring the audio coming out of it. "Do I press pause, or find a camera and show your buddies what you and I are seeing?"

He regarded me with utter contempt and I felt like I was really seeing my old mentor for the first time. "If you know what's on the video, why do you need me to say anything?"

I shrugged. "Maybe I want to finally hear what the truth sounds like when it comes out of your mouth. I have a feeling it will be a whole new experience for me."

"Maybe I don't care what you want."

One of his hands was covertly testing the knot I'd tied around his ankle, so I kicked him in the sternum as the fourth initiate identified himself on the video. Matthew Edwards. I let the video keep speaking for itself and kept my attention on Elliott as he grunted against the force of my kick, curling into the force to absorb some of the hit and cranking his knee yet again in the process.

"Of course you don't care what I want," I said softly. "You always think of yourself first, and that's all I'm asking you to do now." I wiggled the phone between my thumb and forefinger. "Which action serves you best, Elliott? Talking to me, or having me finish tying you up and leaving this video playing for all your friends and allowing them to contemplate what other videos I have in my back pocket?"

If he called my bluff on that one, I'd have nothing. But luckily for me, Elliott was in no position to call my bluff. I didn't have to prove a thing.

"And what?" he mocked. "Tell you that your backwoods friend had the honor of being part of our ceremony that year?"

Oh, he was pushing back and I hated that he could have me seeing red so quickly. "Ah, yes. That high honor that requires drugs to provide blind consent."

"You're really stuck on that, aren't you?" he said with a smile. "Consent. Since when do religious ceremonies require the consent of their sacrifices, Rhea? I mean, you've found God recently, right? Or, at least, that's your story and you're sticking to it. But you've read the Bible. Show me where sacrificial lambs get a say in their role."

"Isaac," I said. "He consented to being a sacrifice."

Even bound on the floor Elliott managed a patronizing laugh. "But Abraham would have tied Isaac up even if Isaac hadn't submitted and sacrificed without consent if it came to it. Because it's the ceremony that matters, Rhea. I don't expect you to understand that. The priest never asks for the sacrificial lamb's consent. He simply chooses the most pleasing sacrifice and performs the rites. The only mistake I made back then was not making your little pet's sacrifice complete that night. I should have spilled her blood on the altar, not had her delivered to the sorority lawn. I don't miscalculate often, but I'll admit that I did that night."

I couldn't breathe, which rendered me speechless as I looked into the serpentine eyes of the man I had defended on so many occasions. Ben had hated him on instinct as had my father. I thought I'd known why they hated him, but now I saw how naive I'd been.

Elliott Church was evil to his core, and I was the last one to see it.

So much for being smart.

Looking into his malicious eyes, I felt something shift inside me, shutting down my sense of right and wrong to the point that anything that harmed Elliott felt right. He was the definition of evil. Removing him from the planet would be a gift to the world. I was sure of it.

Sixty seconds ago, premeditated murder had been off the table. Now it was back on.

Could I rest in peace knowing that I'd let this man live?

I forced my eyes away from his gaze, breathing deeply as I fought to level myself out. He hadn't even started poking at me, and I was already breaking. If I let him keep talking, I didn't know what I was going to do. Neither did The Fours, based on the bets populating the screen. At the moment, 73% of betters thought I wasn't finished inflicting damage on my old boss but only 7% believed I would kill him.

At the moment, I was leaning toward the 7%.

"There's my panther," Elliott cooed, cutting through my thoughts. "I wasn't wrong about you, was I? My only mistake was trying to lure you into your destiny rather than allowing trauma to compel you onto the path you were born to walk."

I didn't want to know what he was talking about, but in that moment I did.

"Show them," he said. "Show them why I picked you, Rhea. Show them how right I was."

Gripping the arms of his chair to keep my hands from doing anything else, I rolled his leather throne away to put distance between us. I had to. Sitting within striking distance opened the door for me to be impulsive and my next move needed to be very, very deliberate. The man was clearly baiting me, and it was working.

I wanted to prove him right. I didn't even know exactly what that meant, but it sounded like a very gratifying thing to do.

Forcing myself to look away from Elliott's unblinking eyes allowed his half-broken computer monitor to catch my eye again. Bets were locking in. On the other side of those cameras, my life-changing moral dilemma was nothing more than a statistical probability of winning or losing money.

Perspective was a wondrous thing.

Bets were still high that my next move would be to torture my former boss and they had all sorts of ideas for me to try out. The thought of Elliott suffering was gratifying, true, but would punishing him really serve me? Would it serve any purpose at all? The man had already proven himself incapable of feeling shame, and physical pain was temporary.

It felt wrong to leave him without doing anything, but doing what I wanted to do would only taint my soul to be a closer shade to his. Killing him would definitely blacken my soul, but what about breaking some fingers or knocking him out? Where was the line where I became the heartless operative Elliott always wanted me to be?

Where was the line?

I leaned back in the chair, looking at the ceiling. *What do I do? What am I supposed to do?*

No answer. There never was. I'd been trying out prayer for the past year and still didn't know how the whole concept of getting answers worked. Either I was asking the wrong questions or totally hearing-impaired when it came to receiving the answers. I'd likely be meeting God later that day, and we were going to have a chat about that.

In the meantime, if God wasn't going to answer my question, I knew someone who could and would.

Picking up the receiver of Elliott's landline phone, I hit the button for his blocked line and dialed a number I knew by heart.

It rang once. Twice. On the third ring, Kay's tentative voice answered. "Hello?"

"It's me," I said, choosing my words carefully.

"Rhea?" she said, her voice choking on my name. "Where are you? What's going on?"

"I can't tell you that," I said. "But I need you to make a decision for me."

"What? I can't do that from here."

"You have to," I said more harshly than I intended to.

"Rhea—"

"What if I told you that I've found the person who planned everything that happened to you freshman year? The man who staged it…who made it all happen?"

Silence.

"What would you have me do with him, Kay?" I pressed. "I

need you to answer that for me because I can't think straight and I've got one shot at this. It's now or never."

"Rhea…" she breathed.

"I'm serious," I said softly. "Anything, Kay. Name it and it's yours."

Again, no answer. I waited her out this time. "Anything?" she said at last.

"Anything," I repeated.

She took a shaky breath. "Then let it go, Rhea."

Her reply shocked me into silence.

"Don't let anything distract you from surviving today," she said with urgency. "That's literally all I care about right now. Whoever this guy is, all he can do is get in the way of you making your way through this. So if the choice is mine, let him go and focus on you. The past can't be changed. Today is what matters. All I want is for you to come home alive, okay?"

Her plea almost broke me. It was so sincere. And yet, I couldn't tell her that by the end of the day I would likely be labeled a terrorist.

If I even hinted at that, she'd be killed. So would Ty. So would my dad and Dahl. I couldn't say a thing.

"Take care of *you!*" she said urgently. "That's it. Focus on that. You hear me?"

My throat was tight with unexpected emotion, but I managed to clear it enough to say. "I hear you."

"Good," she said, her voice sounding suddenly strong. "Now go take care of business. And, remember, no matter what happens, I love you. We all love you."

"Love you back," I said, my voice little more than a rasp as I hovered my finger over the hang-up button. "Gotta go."

I didn't say goodbye, and I didn't let her say it either. I just hung up and looked over at Elliott.

"Well, you heard the lady," I said.

It was really tempting to kick him in his smug face, but I'd promised Kay I'd do anything and she'd said to let him go.

So I did—walking out of his office before stealing a set of keys for the motorcycle I would use to make my way back to the Third Street Promenade and find the Queen of Hearts…whatever that meant.

CHAPTER 12

20/20 hindsight hit me pretty quickly after walking out Elliott's door. Gunning the engine of my stolen motorcycle's engine back to Santa Monica, I realized I may have overplayed my hand.

Okay, there was no maybe about it; I'd definitely overplayed. Thousands of outrageously powerful men now believed I had a library of incriminating videos I didn't have.

It seemed like a good boast to make at the time, but it was a miracle a tranq dart hadn't taken me down already. The Fours had to be desperate to find out where my fictional videos were and the conditions I'd set up to trigger their release.

How was I not already strapped to a board and having water poured onto my face through a rag? Was there a debate on their side about what should be done with me at this point? That seemed impossible, but it was the only explanation for why I was still upright.

I needed to find the Queen of Hearts, and fast.

There was a 100% chance Team Anton wanted to use me as a pawn and throw me under the bus to serve their own purposes, but the alternative of standing on my own at this point was bleak. I'd sealed my fate with my visit to Elliott. The Fours definitely wanted me dead now, but they were going to want to talk to me first.

I didn't come to a complete stop once on the entire trip back to Santa Monica, feeling sniper scopes aimed at my back the entire time. Maybe it was my imagination, but I didn't think so. But if it wasn't, why weren't they pulling the trigger? My would-be assassins could definitely hit a moving target, and yet I wasn't hit yet.

Why not?

Don't think about it. Keep moving, I urged myself.

Still, my heart pounded wildly up until I pulled onto the ramp for the I-10 to head back over to the pier. Maybe I was safer on the freeway; maybe I wasn't. I felt safer, which helped me focus as I performed the jerk move of bypassing gridlock traffic by driving on the dotted lines separating the lanes.

A glance at my wristband showed Anton heading for the Third Street Promenade, which was good for me. Anton and me heading the same direction would give The Fours a sense of control. A sense of control meant they didn't need to act hastily, which was almost certainly why I was still upright.

Why shoot me in public when they could pick me up in the time and place of their choosing? After all, there were big bets on the line and no one liked to spoil the party.

That was my best guess as to why I had yet to experience gladiator-interruptus.

Whatever the case, I couldn't think about it. What would be would be. My only choice was whether I wanted to put myself at the mercy of the supposedly sympathetic Team Anton or the decidedly unsympathetic Fours.

For better or worse, I was choosing Team Anton…if I could get to him.

My internal sense of security disappeared again about a mile before I went down the off ramp leading to the Promenade and stayed with me for the rest of the journey. But there was nothing to be done but keep moving and find the Queen of Hearts.

Whoever she was.

I should have asked. Had Anton been talking about a cosplay thing or a deck of cards or…what? The Promenade was a pretty eclectic place for a description that vague. There were the cookie cutter franchise stores, yes, but the musicians and street vendors were a bit more colorful and unpredictable. Although it was more likely they would be dressed like a leprechaun today than an Alice in Wonderland character. I didn't know what to look for, which meant I had to look at everything. It was something I knew how to do well, but not something I was used to doing while being hunted.

Hunted or not, I had one pass to spot the Queen of Hearts, or red flags would go off like crazy in the invisible coliseum around me.

Illegally parking the motorcycle, I moved onto the Promenade on foot. Tourists abounded, proudly parading about with new purchases and carrying on conversations at twice the volume required. There were a lot of ways to tell locals apart from tourists, and enthusiasm was one of them. Nonverbal patterns like what they looked at and how long they looked were another or the pace with which they walked. A hundred different "tells" let me see who I was dealing with as I gave the area a look over.

Not a lot of locals out today. That was good for me. It made unfriendlies and more fluid energies on the ground level even easier to spot.

A quick glance at my wrist told me that Anton was on the opposite end of the Promenade and holding. Digitally it looked like we were on a crash course to each other, which was both bad and good. It meant The Fours thought they knew what was happening, but it also might put them into action to grab me before Anton and I could face off again. All I could hope was that this Queen of Hearts was closer to me than it was to Anton and that she was obvious enough to catch on a first pass. Because if I missed her…

"You've trained for this. You can do it," I reminded myself, belatedly remembering The Fours could hear me. I replayed my words in my mind and decided they were harmless. They probably thought I was psyching myself up to take on Anton after my pep talk from Kay to do whatever I had to do to survive.

Please let them think that, I thought as I moved to the center of the walkway. Choosing one side of the walking street meant a skewed view the other half. I would see the most from the center. It would also give any sniper in the area an obscenely clear shot of me, but if they really did shoot me then I would go down in the middle of the street and cause a scene. Then it would be harder to frame me for a bombing later that night. The Fours wouldn't want that.

Sometimes the safest place to be was the place of highest vulnerability. Key word being: sometimes. I was about to find out if I was standing in the middle of one of those sometimes.

Taking one last deep breath, I took the white-noise filters off of my mind, opening my eyes and ears to everything around me in equal measure. A woman off to my right was excited that she'd gotten 30% off last year's purse design. A few steps behind her a father twirled his keys around his fingers and yelled for his family to keep up. Hundreds of separate realities were happening all around me, and my ears needed to listen for something out of sync while my eyes searched for the symbol that didn't belong in this highly manicured space.

Ivy-covered dinosaurs spewing water? They belonged. Umbrella-covered patio seating belonged, so did the palm trees. I filtered them out. The street musician strumming his guitar and playing a harmonica for tips belonged, as did all of the store fronts. I filtered them out as well, slowly giving myself less and less to focus on. With no red hearts in sight and no audio that didn't belong, I started my way down the Promenade.

The irony that I was using a skill Elliott had spent hundreds of hours teaching me was not lost on me as I made my way down the street, forcing my mind to focus only on the red and unexpected. The first full block passed with no sight of anything resembling a red heart, but half way through block two my eyes locked onto something that fit the bill.

Maybe.

Off to my left, a street magician was entertaining about a dozen tourists with the old ball-and-cups trick. Five kids stood closest to him, watching as he threw the sponge ball under one cup before switching them around again and again as the kids watched. Then he'd ask them where the ball was.

Their guess was wrong, of course. No matter which cup they chose, the ball was never there. But that wasn't what interested me. The playing card tucked into the ribbon on the magician's hat did: the queen of hearts.

Was this my guy?

If so, what in the world was I supposed to do? Anton had said to find the queen of hearts. He hadn't mentioned anything about what I was supposed to do once I did. I couldn't just stand there and stare at him, waiting for some obvious clue. I had to keep moving, and that meant moving toward him.

As I approached, the magician threw a ball into the air, catching it with one of the cups. He immediately turned the cup upside-down and nothing fell out. The cup was empty. The kids were gobsmacked, begging for the magician to do it again.

He did so as I pushed past the semi-circle of parents and into the grouping of children.

"Do you think I can make all the cups and balls disappear before your very eyes?" the magician asked as I drew close.

"Yeah!" the kids replied in a chorus.

The magician glanced at me for the first time, the look in his eyes somehow sending the message: *Keep walking.*

I did.

"Are you ready?" he asked the kids.

"Yeah!"

"Then watch carefully," the magician said mysteriously. "Abracadabra!"

A flash of light momentarily blinded me an instant before the sun and street disappeared and were replaced with damp and dark. I had no idea what had just happened. All I knew was that I was no longer on the Third Street Promenade, and I wasn't alone.

CHAPTER 13

My senses told me I was now underground as my eyes adjusted to the darker lighting. A man's outline stood in front of me, not much taller than I was. Even in shadow, nothing about him was threatening as he brought his index finger up to his lips in a hushing gesture without making a sound. When I nodded my understanding, he made another gesture with his hand and a small patch of light appeared on his chest. Without a word, he held a 3X5 up a card into the light so I could see it.

Rule 1: No talking, the card said. *They hear everything.*

I knew that much. He held up a second card.

Nod when you have completed reading each card. Once you nod, I will destroy the card you just read.

To demonstrate, he brought a container of water into view of the light and dropped the first card into it. Within two seconds the paper dissolved into nothing—the paper and the words on it gone. When I nodded that I understood, the man dropped the second card in the water and placed it on a box off to the side before reaching into his pocket to get more cards.

You can call me Jack, the next card read. *I am here to stop the bomb tonight.*

I nodded and the card went into the water.

Full disclosure: I have also been hired to save Anton. Both my primary and secondary tasks will be easier with your assistance.

My trust issues prickled at the back of my neck, but I'd made my choice back at Elliott's office. I was in with these guys, for better or worse. I nodded.

I am willing to extend my escape plan for Anton to include you IF you work with us to stop the bomb.

Hope. Part of me hated that this man was dangling it in front of me while another part of me was desperate to cling to his supposed lifeline. I tried to ignore both impulses as I signaled for the new card.

You likely have questions about the bomb. For the moment, we don't have many answers. We'll know more about the time and place when The Fours reveal the target of tonight's attack and start accepting bets.

Again, maybe that was true, maybe it wasn't. Either way, I nodded.

Helping us will require you to go off grid.

Part of me had been expecting this, but I wasn't sure how it could be pulled off. I sent him a questioning look, which he was clearly expecting as he dunked the card and brought up the next.

Right now, Anton is in position to have his wristband cut and go off radar. This means that you will be blind to his whereabouts from here on out, even if The Fours find alternate means to track him.

Alternate means? No, Jack had things backward. The Fours had a lock on Anton's blood. That's how they were tracking us, not the wristband. Anton could cut off his and I'd still know exactly where he was. He just wouldn't see me anymore.

I was tempted to speak up and say something when Jack flipped to the next card.

Within thirty minutes of cutting the wristband, his blood will be untraceable. What you need to decide right now is if you want to go through the same process with him. (FYI: It will suck.)

How in the world were we supposed to stay safe for the thirty minutes it would allegedly take to detox our blood? There were risks, and then there was jumping into an abyss with no safety net in sight.

Jack was asking me to do the latter.

He didn't wait for me to nod before moving to the next card. *If you're in, do everything written on these cards in the order I show them to you.*

He fanned a second card out from behind the first. *No questions. Just do as you're told.*

I'd met the guy sixty seconds ago and he was asking me to put my life in his hands, no questions asked? I could count on one hand the number of people I trusted with my life, and he wanted me to make him one them right out of the gate.

Refuse to complete any of the steps I am about to present you with, and I will disappear. This is a one-time offer.

Now that my eyes were adjusted, I could look into the man's steady hazel eyes and get a read on him. He was no novice, that was obvious. Everything about him was casual and composed, as if what was happening between us was routine for him. He'd just made me disappear off a busy tourist street, yet he had the body language of someone waiting for an elevator. Ready for the next move, but relaxed. He had this entire situation between us under control. None of my five senses could confirm this hunch for sure, but my sixth sense had no doubts whatsoever. This guy was standing arm's distance from me because he was certain I couldn't harm him. He had every base covered.

I don't know how long I stood there feeling powerless before Jack made a tick-tock sound with his tongue to remind me that he was waiting for a response from me.

Do what he said, or don't do what he said. Those were my options, but there was really only one choice to be made. Holding his gaze, I looked into those unblinking eyes of his and gave him a small nod.

The card went into the water and a new one came up that read, *Inject this. This will neutralize the tracking agent in your blood. You will feel sick for about 20-40 minutes while it works.*

This guy wanted me to stab myself and inject myself with an unknown substance?

What's in it? I mouthed to him.

He shook his head and held up a new card. *Trust me.*

That was a big ask in a long line of huge asks.

He held the syringe between us, his eyes watching me as closely as I was watching him. It was my move. Inject myself, be sick for a bit—if that's all it really would do to me—then cut my wristband. It was the equivalent of jumping off a skyscraper with a garbage bag as a parachute when it came to courting death.

But if there was a chance of not dying a terrorist, I had to try.

Taking the syringe away from Jack, I removed the cap and gave the casing a few flicks to get any air out with a test squirt before sliding the point into a vein. One slow squeeze later, it was done. Whatever had been in that syringe was now in my body.

Another card came up. *It will take a moment to reach your heart and spread through your body.*

New card. *Keep moving. An elevated heart rate will help you not pass out.*

Great. Just great. He held up more cards.

If you need to vomit, do so discretely.

Try to keep to the shadows so cameras can't see your face.

A panel behind him slid open, revealing access to an underground tunnel system. Well, this was just getting better and better.

Follow the path of the flashing lights. They will lead you to a secondary location in twenty minutes. I'll meet you there. That's where we'll cut your wristband off.

I flipped my wrist over, pulling the band to the side as best I could to show him the post that went through my entire wrist. He nodded his head that he was aware of the feature, which was good to know. Cutting off the band would require some minor surgery to close everything back up.

He held up another card. *Remember, the tunnels have cameras. They'll see you, and we want that so they feel in control. We just don't want them to see you looking sick.*

I nodded.

Symptoms you can expect to experience in the next twenty minutes include: Chills, fever, rapid breathing, nausea, pale skin, red splotches, confusion, and dizziness. Ignore them and follow the blinking lights.

Sure. Ignore all the symptoms. That sounded like a plan.

New card. *Start running.*

I kept my snarky responses to myself and moved into the tunnel system. A tiny light flickered in front of me. That was my cue. I was all-in now, and there was nothing to do but start running.

CHAPTER 14

I felt like death in running shoes. Whatever I'd pumped into my vein hit me like literal poison, making me sweat an oozing, slippery sheen that coated my skin with some substance that had the viscosity of oil.

Eyes down, I kept putting one foot in front of the other as I moved through the tunnels, going in any which way the blinking lights told me to go. My body shook as my stomach clamped and searched for something to toss up.

Either I was dying or my blood really was being cleansed of the tracking agent.

For the moment, death seemed like the better option. I wasn't sure if I could pop out the other side of this as a fully functioning human—especially with a hole in my wrist.

Jack had said I would only be running for about twenty minutes, but my sense of time was shot and it felt like hours before one final turn brought me into a trucking dock. I wasn't sure where I was and I didn't care. Breathing and staying on my feet required 99% of my energy and the remaining 1% was looking for my stopping point.

All I saw were trucks. Lots and lots of delivery trucks.

Hopefully, my next move would be to pass out in one of them.

My hands shook as I grabbed the rail overlooking the loading dock. The moment my feet planted, my body lurched with a dry heave. Nothing came out, but my stomach tried its best. My clothes were wet in the grossest way. A layer of slime created a layer between me and my clothes, giving the red splotches covering my body a nice sheen.

"I am not okay," I muttered as I fought to put 2% of my energy into figuring out where I was supposed to go next.

No blinking lights beckoned me anymore, but that could very well be because I kept looking at the ground.

Not sure what else to do, I glanced at my watch and noticed that I was within 100 yards of Anton's location. He was in the parking garage too.

Well, if he wanted to kill me here, he could have at it because I was a sitting duck at this point. Death would be a relief. Not even thoughts of Ty or my dad or Kay could spur me into rallying. I had exactly one move left in me and that was to maybe lie down without falling flat on my face. If I accomplished that much, I'd consider it a win.

"Keep moving," I muttered under my breath before realizing all The Fours would hear it. Oh, well. Too bad. Maybe they would just think I was tired. Most of them probably would be after a twenty-minute sprint.

A light flashed in my peripheral vision when I staggered down the ramp leading to the trucks. I moved toward it.

Here it was: my moment of truth. Had I just fallen into a trap, or was I really going to spend the rest of my day trying to stop a bomb?

The answer lay inside the back end of a refrigerator truck.

I threw caution to the wind as I approached the rear of the truck and unlatched the back. Hesitation would change nothing and only made me look suspicious to The Fours, so I popped the back open a few feet, rolled myself in and pulled the door down behind me.

Fluorescent lights lit up the enclosed space and I recognized Jack's frame before getting my first good look at his face. It was different than it had been back in the tunnels—like he'd been wearing a mask before and removed it in the time it took us to meet again. The man I was looking at now had neutral looks that were neither attractive nor unattractive, with no distinguishing marks. He'd be a nightmare to try to describe to a sketch artist and I had a suspicion that wasn't an accident.

Again, Jack held one finger to his lips in a hushing gesture, indicating we could still be heard. I didn't have the energy to respond.

He squatted down next to me and held up a card so that I could read it. *Now it's time to remove the wristband.*

He really wasn't going to kill me? This was the perfect opportunity, but this Jack guy seemed to be sticking to his word. Huh. Maybe I'd live long enough to go on a bomb hunt after all.

Maybe. If this poison didn't kill me.

New card. *Nod if you consent.*

The moment the wristband was cut I would be a marked woman. No going back. I would have a price on my head with dozens of bounty hunters in position to strike and collect. He could cut the band and leave me right where I was for the bounty hunters to give Anton cover to escape.

There was only one choice to make. Even if Anton and Jack cut my band and left me to be hunted by the wolves while they made a break for it, the possibility that he might not do that was still my best move.

The bomb threat was real, as was the likelihood that I would be blamed for it. The second people saw my face they would believe whatever headline was attached to it. With the current political climate, there were easy sells and then there were pre-packaged slam dunks, like blaming a person of Middle Eastern descent for a bomb.

Unplugged from The Fours, I had a chance at stopping the bomb—with or without this guy's help. Plugged in, I had zero chance.

Holding out my hand, I stayed still as Jack aligned a device to my band before making a light click with his tongue. He held position, waiting for a signal I couldn't perceive before I felt a painful pinch all around my wrist. I nearly cried out before biting my lip and swallowing it back.

I imagined there would be more blood when removing the band and the post, but the post hadn't disrupted any veins or arteries, so the bleeding was minimal as Jack slid the rod out of my wrist and bound the injury with a wrap that both soothed the nerves in my wrist and stopped the bleeding. I stared at the new bandage, marveling that my wrist somehow felt better than it had all day.

Jack brought me back to the business at hand when he gave me an earbud and waited for me to tuck it in my ear. At the same time, the truck's engine grumbled to life, and the floor near his feet opened up. He gestured for me to go into the hole in the truck floor so I dragged myself over to it and found a ladder leading down into the cement floor of the bay.

Before I climbed down, he held up one last card. *Climb down ten rungs, then wait for the next truck to pull in over you. When the hatch above you re-opens, climb in. That will be your final recovery spot. You and Anton will do that phase together.*

Since no follow-up questions were allowed, all I could do was exactly what he said. And since doing that hadn't gotten me killed yet, I figured I might as well finish this little game of his.

Rubbing my hands on my pants, I tried to get the slimy sweat off of them before climbing down the ladder. Sure enough, as soon as I counted to ten, the hatch above me slapped closed, the world went dark and I heard The truck pull away. My heart raced in the tight space and I was feeling the beginning of some vertigo, but I focused on holding to the rungs and holding still until the hatch opened again.

It took a minute, maybe two, before I heard the engine of an industrial truck overhead followed by the slide of a metal flooring above me and light.

I climbed up the ladder, half expecting a helpful hand to pull me into the truck before realizing that Anton was the only one in the truck and he was all but passed out on the floor.

As bad as I felt, he looked worse.

"Harm him and I will end you," a female voice said in my earbud.

Whoa. I had not been expecting that. Another woman? Jack definitely wasn't affiliated with The Fours if he had female support.

"Now get up that ladder," the female barked. *"I need to get you two on the move."*

Only my head and torso were in the truck so far, but I made the push to get my legs to join the party as well. The moment I did, the ladder retracted and the floor closed behind me. Then the truck moved forward.

"Okay, Rhea, you are officially in a clean space," the woman said. *"No one outside of the truck but me can see or hear you unless I open the channel. You are also blocked from any type of detection because this truck broadcasts a false interior to anyone trying to x-ray or wifi a view inside. But maybe best of all, the insulation in this truck will block the traceable materials in your blood for the last twenty or thirty minutes you need to fully process it out of your body. So while I know you might feel like a run-over toad right now, you are technically the safest you are going to be for the rest of the day. So enjoy the next few minutes. Your vacation ends when the green dot on the wall disappears. That means your blood is no longer traceable and it's time to get going."*

My brain was a little too overwhelmed to process all the information she was throwing at me real-time, but I heard it as I curled up into a fetal position a few feet away from Anton.

The man had the right idea with the whole passing out thing.

"Who are you?" I muttered before I even knew I had the energy to speak.

"I'm your eyes in the sky for the next few hours, and I'll tell you only what you need to know to help me."

Something in the woman's tone got a smile out of me. She sounded like a queen who had been forced to stand in for her butler. Regal and primly put out.

"Nice to meet you, Eyes," I said, as the vibration of the moving truck lulled me into relaxing.

I had no idea where the truck was going, and I didn't care. The miracle was that The Fours didn't know where I was going either. No doubt the frenzy had already begun in looking for me and Anton. Maybe we'd be blown up by a rocket launcher as we drove down the street. It was a possibility, but not one I was too worried about because the woman on the other side of my earpiece—the disgruntled queen—liked Anton. She might even love him, based on the edge in her voice as she threatened me about harming him.

Whoever Miss Eyes in the Sky was, she wasn't about to let anything happen to Anton Petrov, yet I had a sneaking suspicion that she wouldn't lose a wink of sleep over anything that might happen to me.

I glanced at Anton and saw he was conscious, but not happy about it. That made two of us. And for the next five minutes we both just lay there, waiting for things to get better.

CHAPTER 15

My fever broke ten minutes later, causing my sweat to chill against my skin. I wished I had a hoodie or something to cover me up against the chill. Up until now I'd been doing so much running that lack of sleeves hadn't really been an issue. But lying on the floor of a refrigerator truck with toxic sweat cooling on my skin changed things up a bit. I was cold.

Next to me, Anton's teeth chattered and his eyes were looking a bit bloodshot.

"You okay?" I asked, still not fully trusting him, but knowing that he wasn't faking his current misery.

Anton nodded, his body shaking against his own internal chill. "Been worse."

I hugged my legs to my chest, rocking a bit. I was certain I'd been worse too…I just couldn't remember exactly when or where at that particular moment.

Whether it was luck or because I was so much smaller than him that had me recovering faster, I didn't care. I just appreciated the fact that I was the one looking over him rather than him looking over me. The knowledge that I could easily kill him if I wanted to itched at the back of my neck, but I ignored it. I didn't want to kill Anton. That's what The Fours wanted me to do. And

The Fours were not the boss of me, nor did they seem to be the boss of my Eyes in the Sky, who hadn't had much to say since initial introductions. But I already knew that she was in all of this for Anton. Maybe she was his girlfriend or wife or something. It didn't matter and I wouldn't ask. What mattered was that she would throw me under the bus if she thought it would save her man.

That was the main thing I needed to remember when listening to her…if she ever decided to speak to me again.

The good news was that I had enough energy to think about this. My thoughts no longer extended to wondering whether or not I was going to puke. I was not only upright, but bigger picture things were beginning to process again. On the wall, the green dot representing me grew dimmer and dimmer while the blue dot representing Anton still looked pretty solid. Anton was definitely going to take longer to go through this debugging process than I was.

Better for him to be the weak link than me.

I was rubbing my arms against the cool of the truck when Anton sat up and joined me.

"I'm impressed," he said in a gruff voice. "You didn't even try to kill me once while I was out."

"Hardly sporting," I replied.

His eyebrows twitched upward in surprise before he smiled a genuine smile. "Well, good to have you on the team. We can use you."

I studied him, trying to get a read on how honest he was being with me. After all, I had no doubt they wanted to use me, but for how long, and to what end? That's what I didn't know.

"How are you feeling?" he asked.

"Like I've been through a blender," I replied. "How about you?"

"Like a bug on a windshield," he said, rubbing his temples.

"And it looks like you're going to go clear before I am."

"You have more blood to process," I pointed out.

"Yeah," he said, still rubbing at his headache.

It was so weird to sit next to him so casually after the day we'd had so far.

"I'm good," he said out of nowhere, and it took me a moment to realize that he wasn't talking to me. Miss Eyes in the Sky—or "Eyes" as I was coming to think of her—had him on a private channel. Then he added, "No, that won't be necessary."

I had a feeling the unheard comment he was responding to was about me.

Shaking his head at something he heard that I hadn't, Anton pointed over toward a chest and looked at me. "Since you look confident about being upright, do you want to go grab the two bags over there?"

"On it," I said, pushing up to my feet yet being careful not to give Anton my full back as I moved to the chest he'd pointed out. Inside it were two gym bags.

"One's for me, one's for you," he said. "They should be labeled based on sizing. Bring them over and I'll explain while we recover."

"Save your energy," Eyes said in my ear as I walked over with both packs. *"I'll talk her through it."*

Anton didn't argue as I handed him the pack with his name on it.

Eyes got straight down to business. *"In the bag with your name on it, you'll find a change of clothes, a utility belt, and a few other tools you'll be needing to help us out for the rest of the night."*

Unzipping the bag, I found anti-bacterial wipes and form-fitting camouflage clothing that passed as casual wear.

"The wipes are there in case you want to clean up now. Use them or don't, but if you want to wipe off the sweat from your

detox, that's what they're there for. You'll notice that there's a curtain you can pull down the center of the truck to give yourself a little privacy."

I would definitely be using the wipes…and the curtain.

"The clothes are your size," she said with confidence. *"They're not military, but the colors are urban camouflage that will help you blend in as you move around. They will also alter your heat signature to make identifying you more difficult. What we need to talk about now are the items on the belt."*

I reached into the pack and pulled out the clothes and wipes to get to the belt.

"On the left side, you have a utility knife, a single-use EMP, a flashlight. At the small of your back, you have medical foam to treat any major injuries you might get along the way. I'll talk you through using the foam real-time if it comes to it. On the right side of the belt, you have a remote power source, a breathing apparatus that will give you fifteen minutes of oxygen, an adrenaline shot, and last, but not least, one flash and one smoke grenade. The flash has a silver pin and the smoke has a black."

I'd been introduced to most of these items over the years, but I'd never needed anything she was mentioning in the field—except for the knife. The only thing I hadn't seen at all before was the medical foam, and I would be more than happy if that never became relevant.

"You'll also find a purse-style messenger bag in there with a rope, four carabiners, and some gloves. The bag goes with the outfit."

It totally did. I was going to look a bit like a New Yorker in the middle of LA, but the ensemble was a solid hip-grunge look that didn't hurt my feelings one bit. The woman on the other side of the earpiece may not like me, but she had taste, even when it came to camo clothes and messenger bags.

"Last of all, there are two meal bars that are a couple

thousand calories each. Eat them both. Your body needs everything in them to recover from your purge. If you skimp, you will pass out within the hour and I will let the bounty hunters paint the sidewalk with you."

This woman should write Hallmark cards. She had a gift with words.

"Familiarize yourself with the items on the belt, and I'll be back in a few minutes to answer any questions."

The earpiece went silent.

I looked over at Anton. "I don't think your girlfriend likes me much."

Despite looking like death, Anton threw his head back and laughed. "Wow. You'd better hope she didn't hear you say that, or you won't have just the wrath of Elliott to worry about."

I arched an eyebrow. "Not your girlfriend?"

His eyes dropped. "Definitely not."

Interesting. He didn't make eye contact when he said that. "Good to know. I think I'm going to start getting changed. This sweat is changing from slime to crust."

Anton dragged his finger across his forearm, leaving a visible streak. "I'm still at the slimy phase. The changing room is all yours."

The shifting of the truck made my movements a little less than graceful as I crossed to the curtain and pulled it closed between us. Even though Anton said that he and Miss Eyes weren't together, I had the distinct impression that she had a camera in the back of that truck making sure I didn't do anything to draw Anton's eye as I stripped, scrubbed, and redressed.

If Eyes and Anton weren't dating, what were they to each other?

There were a thousand better things to think about in that moment, but for some reason, the relationship between the guy in front of me and the woman talking to me was the most interesting.

She was acting just like Ty would if he were on the other side of the earpiece knowing that a guy was about to change in front of me.

Ty trusted me, yes, but that didn't mean that he wasn't proactive about limiting my opportunities to prove my faithfulness. Knowing that I was changing with only a curtain between Anton and me would get Ty's fists clenching for sure, and I liked it that way.

Imagining Ty in the place of Eyes in the Sky made me smile. It also helped me humanize her a bit. She wasn't an omniscient voice. She was a woman who was in this to save Anton. Maybe she was in love with him and maybe she just loved him like a brother or something. But there was love in the mix, and knowing that helped me understand her.

I was valuable to Eyes to the extent that I improved Anton's chances of survival. Anything she told me would serve that end. If I remembered that, I had a shot of getting her to pull a favor or two on my behalf.

A bumpy section of road had me wobbling around as I scrubbed down as best I could before stepping into my new clothes. As promised, they fit perfectly and the tactical gloves actually went with the outfit on a fashion level. I didn't have to wait to put them on until I was actually climbing or rappelling with the rope.

"What time is it?" I asked Anton.

Eyes replied. *"It's 4:32 local time and the current detox estimates don't have the two of you leaving that truck for another twenty-five minutes,"* she said. *"Rhea's system will be cleared within the next ten minutes and Anton's in the next twenty to twenty-five."*

Well, wasn't Eyes in a helpful mood. "Where are we?"

"That doesn't matter at the moment," she said. *"The truck you're in has a false back with deliverable product by the rear*

doors. This truck is about to make a faux delivery to permanently remove this truck from suspicion of transporting the two of you. The betting for tonight's terror attack opens at 5:00, so we're waiting on that to determine where we will drop you so we can make our next move."

In other words: Shut up and speak when you are spoken to.

Got it.

When I stepped out from behind the curtain in my new attire, Anton was still sitting on the floor recovering. He looked up at me, a wry smile curling one side of his mouth.

"I have to say," he said. "I wasn't expecting you to be this tough. I knew you were mentally tough, but you're a step above where I thought you'd be physically."

"I'll take that as a compliment," I said, testing the mobility of my wrist with the bandage. It felt fine as I grabbed one of the meal bars Eyes had mentioned and pulled back the wrapper.

Anton was staring at me, but I couldn't tell if it was because he meant to or if it just took too much energy to look somewhere else. Choosing not to care, I took a bite of the nutrition bar and forced myself to chew despite the taste. This definitely wasn't something people ate by accident. Every instinct told me to spit it out even as I kept chewing with a grimace on my face.

"So…I hear you stirred the pot with Elliott," Anton said, eyeing me cautiously. "Word is that you've gotten a lot of spectators scurrying into damage-control measures."

"Good," I said around the protein bar in my mouth.

Anton looked skeptical. "Maybe good, maybe quite bad. Time will tell if you bought yourself a buffer or doubled the price on your head."

I was too ravenous to be nervous. "You don't know yet?"

He smiled. "I've kind of been dying for the past little bit. I'm behind on the status updates."

"Of course," I said, wondering if Eyes would cut in on the

conversation and fill us in. But my earpiece stayed silent.

His smile faded as he continued to study me. "You know, Jack thought there was less than a 15% chance that you'd follow Mark's flags to the right location, even with your skills. We were all very impressed when you walked straight there."

My jaw stopped chewing. "You knew about the flags?"

He watched me for a moment, then nodded. "We had the glass in the window above the dumpster replaced six weeks ago after a production team 'accidentally' broke it. It had to be breakaway glass to avoid impaling one of us after we fell."

Me. He meant it had been meant to protect *me* when I fell. Well, I hadn't. It had been him.

Small victories.

"We had thirty-six Plan B's in place in case you veered off Plan A, and you didn't make us use one of them. You did exactly what I hoped you'd do, to the letter."

Well, that didn't sound like a compliment.

Anton smiled. "You've been a series of pleasant surprises on a horrific day, Rhea. No matter what happens, I want to thank you for that."

Uh...how was I supposed to respond to that? "You're welcome?"

He laughed before looking at me thoughtfully. "All that said, I still don't get how you got into this whole mess."

Yeah? That made two of us.

"I walked right into this disaster," he mused as his eyes fought the fatigue of his continuing detox. "It's my own fault, but what happened with you? You're a woman. I mean, I get that Elliott did what he did and all that, but he never brought you into this world, did he?"

I shook my head. "Never."

"So why are you here?"

My question exactly. "All I know is that The Fours have

wanted me dead ever since I resigned from my job with Elliott. I thought I was a PI quitting my day job. Turns out, not so much."

Anton shook his head. "But they must have let you into the inner circle somehow. There must be a reason they've brought you onto the playing field."

"You studied me for six months," I shot back. "Did you see anything in my file that warrants all of this?"

"Not really," he said, squeezing his arm muscles in a self-massage. "You have test results they'd never want used against them, but that seems a weak reason to proactively kill you. The only red flag I saw in your file was just how quickly you quit after the Martel case. One day you were a happy productive employee and the next you were running away and hiding in Utah, of all places. What was that all about?"

"That…was about getting my heart broken," I admitted, thinking of Ben. He wasn't my ex; he wasn't the one who got away; he was…Ben. Just Ben. My childhood best friend, my co-dreamer for a time, and the perfect example of a fantasy destined for heartbreak.

"Ben Stone," he said with a nod. "I saw him in your file, but you two weren't even dating at the time."

"You don't have to date someone to have your heart broken by them."

"True enough," he said, a brief internal shadow moving across his expression. "But you're saying that's the reason you quit with Elliott and ran off to join a cult?"

"A religion," I corrected.

He arched an amused brow. "If you say so. But I have to say that was the red flag I saw. There is nothing in your file that supports you being susceptible to a faith-based conversion. Your tests profile you as agnostic, at best."

Had everyone seen my test results except me? "Well, not everything can be spelled out on a computer printout."

"But it can be close," he said, even as I noticed some of his sweat was finally drying out. He was on the mend. "And, c'mon…Mormon? Of all the religions you could choose, that's the least believable. Was it cover? Did you really learn something during the Martel case and use a 'spiritual awakening' as an excuse to get away from The Fours?"

"Believe it or not, no," I said, feeling more than a little defensive. "I just…felt something."

"Felt something?" he echoed, his eyebrows the model of incredulity.

I nodded, noting that my core body temperature was finally returning to normal. Whatever was in my brick of a meal bar was hitting my body in a good way, which probably meant I should get back to eating it as we spoke.

"Ever since my mom died when I was a kid, I haven't really let myself feel much," I confessed. "It's like I locked myself down. But when those missionaries told me that this life wasn't the end and I'd see my mom again, I…felt something. I don't know how to explain it, but for the first time since my mom died, I felt like maybe she wasn't really gone after all. I felt like maybe I would see her again. I just…felt. And I wanted to follow that feeling."

"That, I get," he said, flexing his hands to get the circulation going. "I've been trained to turn off feelings since I was born."

"And have you ever had a feeling come out of nowhere and sucker punch you?"

He hesitated before nodding. "Yeah. I've had a haymaker or two shake me up for a bit."

I could see it in his eyes that he understood. "And that's basically what happened to me. I was shaken up, and the feelings had me breaking off one of my oldest friendships and running away to Utah to learn more. That's where I met my husband."

Ty. Mentioning him derailed me a bit, blurring the lines between where I was and where I had hoped to be by this time today: back in his arms. Would I see him again after this? That morning, I'd really thought my chances were high that I would. I'd thought that The Fours would have some sort of final task or case for me, and once I was done I was done. I could go home.

But things weren't shaping up that way.

I couldn't think about Ty right then. I couldn't think about anything outside of Anton's group, The Fours, and the bomb.

One step at a time.

Pushing Ty to the back of my mind, I finished my thought. "Looking back, I don't understand any of it better than you seem to, but it's what happened. I felt something, became obsessed with understanding what I was feeling, then I fell in love. Those are the crimes that landed me here."

Anton shook his head. "That is some seriously bad luck, Rhea."

"Tell me about it," I said, starting on bar number two. "What about you? What landed you here?"

"Oh, I just screwed up," he said. "I've been in this world all my life and I crossed a line. I was coming up against men in the field that were beating me, and I wanted to know what they knew. So I tried to have two masters—kind of like working for Apple and Microsoft at the same time without permission. *No bueno.* Now both masters want me dead. That's my story in a nutshell."

"The Fours have competition?"

Anton laughed. "Of course they do. And that competition has competition."

Interesting. It made sense, but I hadn't considered that angle before. The Fours just seemed so huge and untouchable. "So are The Fours your original bosses or the ones you cheated with?"

"The ones I cheated on," he said, standing up to stretch his legs. He was feeling better, which matched the blue dot fading on the display of the truck. My dot was gone.

I was a free agent. I could run.

But if I did, they would kill Ty and my dad and maybe even Kay.

So I couldn't run.

But I could try to stop a bomb.

"Eat up," Anton said, walking over to the curtain. "We need you."

Then he closed the curtain between us and started getting down to business.

CHAPTER 16

Jack climbed up through the truck's floor when we made our fake delivery—the one that would allegedly remove our vehicle from suspicion. Anton had already downed both of his meal bars while I'd made it half way through the second before hitting a wall. I was feeling sick all over again until Jack's face distracted me.

"Pershing Square," he said, looking at Anton.

Anton nodded, understanding Jack's meaning before I did. "On-site or mobile?"

"Still working on that."

Were they talking about the bomb? If so, the target was Pershing Square in downtown LA, which made sense. The St. Patrick's Street Festival was in full swing. There would be a lot of people there.

"Who's the target?" Anton asked.

"Vadim," Jack said. "They have intel that says Vadim will bring his family there sometime between seven and nine o'clock. He's the target."

I had no idea who that was, but the flat line of Anton's lips told me that he wasn't happy with the news.

Jack kept going. "Bets are heavily skewed that the bomb is mobile, which makes sense. Pershing Square is big enough that it would be hard to guarantee that Vadim stands exactly where they want him to stand."

"But it's not a suicide bomber because they want to frame Rhea or me for the act," Anton said.

"Exactly," Jack agreed, glancing my way for the first time. "Where would you set the bomb if you were placing bets, Rhea?"

Sure. Give me the hard question. I went with the first thought that came to mind. "Probably a vendor that can get into events or a vehicle that can drive in and out of the space."

Jack nodded. "That's at the top of our list, too."

Anton still looked tense. "Do we have independent confirmation that Vadim is in the city?"

"We're looking into it," Jack said.

Interesting. Anton should have been a guy with no personal attachments, but it was clear he cared about this guy's well-being. This was personal. "Am I allowed to ask who Vadim is?"

Jack and Anton shared a look before Jack turned back to me. "He's someone The Fours have wanted to kill for a long time. Let's just leave it at that, since we're short on time."

"No one knows what he looks like," Anton added. "That's what makes him such a hard target to verify."

I held eye contact with him and raised an eyebrow. "No one?"

His eyes narrowed appreciatively. "I used to know. He's changed since then."

Ah, plastic surgery. "But there must be a way to narrow things down."

Anton nodded. "He has two kids. And a wife."

And they'd be in Pershing Square too. That's what they'd be looking for: the family members.

"The Fours feel confident that they've identified him," Jack said. "But we just learned about it, so we're playing catch-up at the moment. All we can really do is run an analysis on all the people who come to the square and identify his family real-time."

"I should be there," Anton said firmly.

"It's too risky," Jack said.

"You can give me a disguise."

"No."

"No."

The second voice came through my earpiece. Eyes was back in the conversation and she wasn't happy.

"If anyone is going to recognize him, it's me," Anton argued.

"Meanwhile, everyone and their dog are going to recognize you."

"Not with one of Jack's disguises."

Jack shook his head while Eyes spoke for him. *"I'm going to give you five seconds to spit out that stupid pill you just swallowed."*

"Jack can—" Anton started to argue before Eyes drowned him out.

"We can change your face and your height all you want, but The Fours have half a dozen other ways to identify you."

"All of which we can bypass."

"Not under our current time restrictions," Eyes replied. *"There's no way I'm draining you, tossing a mask on you, and sending you out into a field of bounty hunters. If you haven't noticed, you're kind of a big guy, Petrov. You stand out."*

She referred to him by his last name, not his first. Interesting.

"But Vadim knows me," Anton said. "He'll trust me."

"More likely he'll watch you die via sniper," she snapped. *"We're not putting you on the ground."*

"It's our best move," Anton argued.

"It's suicide."

For two people who weren't a couple, they sure did argue like one. It felt so personal that I almost forgot that I wasn't really trusting these people yet. They were still an unknown quantity in all of this, but they certainly weren't opting for the ominous and intimidating vibe. The thing I'd have to worry about with them would be growing too complacent.

"Every move we make from here on out is going to include a whole lot of risk," Anton argued. "Every camera is just as dangerous as the next, no matter where I am. Might as well be where I'm most useful."

"Argue all you want, but we both know you don't get a vote in this."

"It's my life," he snapped. "I should get a vote."

"Sorry, Petrov. You gave up that right a long time ago. You'll do as you're told."

Whoa. That turned south real fast.

"I'm the one who is going to identify Vadim, and once we've located him, no one will be warning him about anything. Our priority is to stop the bomb, not save Vadim's life."

"We can do both," Anton argued.

Jack placed his hand on Anton's shoulder. "We do both when we stop the bomb."

Only then did it strike me that Eyes wasn't the support staff in all of this. She was a boss—maybe *the* boss. I couldn't tell since she and Jack hadn't disagreed yet. But while they both cared about Anton, it was equally as clear that they both outranked him.

Curiouser and curiouser.

"So what do we know about the bomb?" I asked, trying to get the conversation back on some sort of track.

Jack looked relieved at the question. "It definitely has a remote trigger, but it also has a fixed timer. The wagers regarding Vadim's death are good until 9:00 pm. That's when the bomb will go off whether he is in the square or not." His jaw clenched with contempt before he added. "Approximately 17% of betters are wagering that Vadim won't show at all. They win if the default timer on the bomb goes off before he reaches the square."

Unbelievable. The fact that thousands of men around the world were betting on all of this like a game when actual lives were at stake made me hate them more than I already did.

"So what's the plan?" I asked.

Jack looked my way. "We locate the bomb; we locate the remote trigger; we render both useless."

Easy as 1-2-3, apparently.

"Petrov will go underground and stay there until we locate the bomb."

We locate the bomb. As in me. I could read between the lines. "And I'll be on the street?"

"It's why we saved you," Eyes said with zero guilt.

She'd just declared going into the square as suicide for Anton, forbidding him from even talking about the option. Now she was making the same course of action my marching orders. She'd saved me because she wanted someone disposable who allowed her to tuck her precious Petrov somewhere safe.

The woman was definitely in love, and I was in a whole lot of trouble. "Do I get a new face or something?"

"You would have if you hadn't made that impulsive visit to your old boss," Eyes said. *"As it is, we're in a bit of a time crunch now. We're already nearing the window of Vadim's possible arrival time, so there's no time for hair and makeup."*

Across from me, Jack nodded. "Sorry about that. But I do have a blind spot set up for you to enter the middle of the square. That will make sure you start out off-camera."

That was a small favor, and we both knew it. There would be overhead drones and plenty of other ways for The Fours to find me no matter how well I hid myself. But again, that's why they had saved me; they needed someone on the ground level and they didn't want it to be Anton.

Mystery solved.

"Rhea, you and I will be working together to identify a remote trigger man. Jack and Petrov will find the bomb and work to

disarm it."

Yet only one of us would be standing directly in the crosshairs of bounty hunters. Nice.

The message was clear: I was that guy in the red shirt on Star Trek who was on the scene for the sole purpose of drawing fire. My survival depended solely on me.

"Hey, Eyes in the Sky," I said. "Are you able to see all the same things The Fours are seeing?"

"I am."

"Is there any way for me to see what you're seeing before I head out there? You know, in case it helps me live longer?"

"We're already into the window of—"

Jack pulled a tablet out of his jacket and handed it to me. "We have time for her take a quick look."

I took the tablet while mentally noting that the unassuming Jack was at the top of the food chain in this group. Good to know.

CHAPTER 17

In the game of cat-and-mouse, it's comforting to imagine yourself as the cat—or to at least pretend that you will have moments of being the cat.

I was past such delusions. I was the mouse in a sea of cats.

For the moment, I was safe in a hole—literally—but not for long.

Just over ten feet above my head, more than a thousand people milled about in Pershing Square. I could hear the echoes of a live band playing in the subterranean tunnels along with the occasional bark of laughter.

The good news in all of this was that I'd have a large crowd to blend into. The bad news was that they were all in range of a bomb.

Eyes claimed she and I were looking for a remote trigger man but we both knew my true role was to be the bait. I was the distraction intended to pull focus while Jack and Anton did the real work.

Pull focus and buy time…even if I died doing it. That was my job.

No one had said as much because they were counting on my sense of self-preservation to fill in the blanks. And while I didn't like that Team Anton was being obtuse with me, I didn't blame them. They didn't have time for me to throw a fit, nor would doing so accomplish anything. It also wouldn't change the fact that I had no regrets about joining their team.

If we stopped the bomb, I couldn't die a terrorist. I might still die, but not on The Fours terms, and that was a win.

A game of tag, I thought to myself, trying to keep my jitters at a minimum by running in place at the foot of the ladder that would take me to ground level once Eyes gave me my cue. *Just think of it like a game of tag...a training exercise. Get to them without them getting to me.*

My mind and body knew that wasn't what was going to happen, but tricking myself was worth a try.

Rolling the tension out of my neck, I looked up the ladder. I might have ten seconds in the square before being detected, or ten minutes. None of us would know until everything actually started happening, but my best hope at delaying the discovery was to try to mask my body signature in groups of other people.

"We're ready for you to get into position, Rhea," Eyes said me in that detached tone of hers.

"Copy that," I said. *Just trying to wrap my brain around my own mortality here. No big deal.*

Pulling my attention back into the moment, I grabbed the first rung and started up the ladder to ground level.

"I have sixteen potential spotters identified at the moment," she said. *"We'll start with the closest and move out."*

"Copy that," I said, climbing until I reached the panel that would take me to the ground level. The panel looked boarded up, but as Jack promised, it moved easily when I pushed it to the side and came up inside a dark space with a door. "I'm up."

"Wait for my mark to exit. I'll find you a good group."

I took a calming breath, hoping this waiting game wouldn't be long enough for nerves to build.

"Okay, I have a group heading your way. Teenage boys. Their

energy level is about at a four. Low key."

Eyes might be leading me to my death, but at least she was being super helpful about it.

"I'll count you down from three. Three...tw—"

"Stop!" Jack said over her in my earpiece. *"Hold position. There's been a change."*

"What change?" Eyes asked.

"Check channel 367," Jack replied.

Obviously, he wasn't talking to me, so I stayed still in the dark, listening to my heart pound in my ears. There was silence in my earpiece for several beats before Eyes swore.

"The good news?" Jack said. *"We now know the bomb is in a vehicle."*

"What?" I asked, reminding everyone that I couldn't see what they were seeing. "What changed?"

"The Fours are holding a vote to see if they want to switch targets," Jack said. *"The choices are Vadim or the hotel your loved ones are staying at."*

For a moment my world froze. Breathing stopped and I'm pretty sure my heart stopped with it.

"Yeah, that changes things," I said, yanking the trapdoor beneath me open again when the world came back up to speed. Without asking permission, I climbed back down the ladder and moved fully back into a safe zone. "How do the votes look so far?"

Eyes answered this time. *"It looks like you have some fans who want to draw you out of hiding and see you in action again. That's what it looks like."*

Yep. My impulsive visit to Elliott's office had been a mistake. But there was no going back now. The only thing I could do now was make certain that the safe zone I'd created for the people I loved stayed safe. I knew the hotel room could take a hit from a bomb, but if that same bomb resulted in the hotel burning down with them in it, then all bets were off.

"Let's give the fans what they want, shall we?" I said, running back down the tunnel.

CHAPTER 18

"We need to talk about this," Jack said in my earpiece as I made my way from Pershing Square back to the original rendezvous point.

"Has anything really changed except the venue?" I asked. "I'm still the bait, and it's your job to find and disarm the bomb. It should be easier if they're forced to move, right?"

"Definitely," Jack replied. *"Our job will be much easier if they move, but—"*

"Then you worry about that and I'll worry about my family. How about that?"

"You're thinking emotionally, Rhea," Jack said gently. *"There are a lot of elements to factor in here. We can't just have you running into that hotel. The second they have all their targets in one spot, they might let things blow, and that doesn't work for any of us."*

He was right.

"What we need to do is wait for voting to close to make sure we're heading to the right target zone," he said. *"Until then, we hold positions."*

I heard his words in both ears, first in my earpiece then in a delay as his voice echoed down the final hall leading to our meeting spot. When I turned the last corner, Anton stood with Jack, both men looking anxious.

"You're insane if you think I'm not going to the hotel right now," I said. "We both know which way they're going to vote."

"So do the bounty hunters," Eyes said helpfully. *"Eight have already relocated."*

Which meant something was definitely going to go down there, even if it wasn't a bomb.

"We all know that you'll be walking right into a trap," Jack said. "Your profile is pretty clear that you're not the kind of person who can let your friends and family die. They know you're going to show, especially with those you love the most all in one spot."

"I knew targeting them was a possibility today," I replied. "Better to have them all in one spot than scattered around the city."

Jack arched his brow as if he disagreed with me but stopped himself before he said as much. "I don't like it."

"Are the bets about blowing up the hotel, or about me?" I asked.

"They mostly focus on your capture or mode of death," Eyes said. *"There is hesitancy when it comes to blowing up the hotel itself. Some aren't too keen on picking that particular fight with a member of the competition."*

Which had been my hope when I chose the hotel to begin with. My friend had assured me none of The Fours owned a stake in it.

"Half of The Fours want you dead and half want you for a pet," Eyes added. *"But they all want you to be interrogated. The bounty is currently three times as high for getting you to talk before you die. It doesn't make it certain that a sniper won't take you out from afar, but it raises your chances for bought time. There is a financial incentive to catch you alive."*

Okay, maybe my bluff at Elliott's wasn't all bad.

"Any bets focusing on me?" Anton asked.

"Those are mostly focused on when and where you'll show

your face again. Right now everyone cares more about the player who beat up and hogtied one of their own while claiming to have a library of incriminating videos."

I couldn't tell if she was mad or impressed at what I'd done but decided not to care either way. I was about to launch into a speech about how things were going to be when Jack's calm voice spoke before me.

"What does victory look like to you in all this, Rhea?" Everything about him was calm as he spoke. That was a neat trick, considering the circumstances.

"Victory looks like zero casualties from that bomb tonight."

"And, specifically, the lives of your friends and family," Jack clarified. "Am I right?"

"Plus everyone else," I said, thinking of my mother's side of the family. It didn't matter who died if we failed—loved one or stranger. My mom's side of the family would be impacted either way. "So if your primary goal in all of this really was to stop that bomb from going off, then congratulations. We're on the same page."

Jack studied me for a moment. "Even if you die?"

My throat suddenly felt very thick. "Obviously I'm going to try to avoid that, but yes. Even if I die. As long as we get that bomb out of there and it doesn't kill any innocents along the way, I'll call that a win."

Jack didn't blink. He didn't even move as he processed what I'd said.

"Tick-tock, Jack," Eyes said after several beats of silence.

The woman really had the tact of sandpaper.

"Every moment here is a moment wasted," I said. "The bomb is going to move and we all need to be there when it does."

"That's not certain," Eyes said, although Jack looked like he was going to nod.

"I'm certain," I said, looking at Jack and Anton. "So how

about this? I head to the hotel and one of you two heads there with me. That way you have a person in each spot, just in case."

Anton looked at Jack, clearly deferring to whatever the man would say. Even Eyes stayed silent as she waited for Jack to speak, and I got the distinct sense that in my ignorance I was bossing around a man most people didn't trifle with.

Without a word, Jack pulled his tablet back out and swiped at the screen a few times. Anton and Eyes stayed silent as he looked at whatever he was looking at, and I followed suit. Everyone knew where I stood on the matter. Rambling wouldn't help my cause. I was going to go to the hotel no matter what. At this point, it was just a question of whether or not I would be alone.

Rather than growing tense in the silence, part of me found comfort in the way Jack closed his eyes and visibly thought things through. Unlike me, all impulsiveness had been trained out of him. He acted; he didn't react. That was the process I was watching him go through as we all waited for him to make up his mind.

He's assimilating new information and choosing his best new move. That's different than reacting.

It was a weird little epiphany to have in the middle of everything, but I was starting to understand why this guy was in charge.

I glanced at Anton, who stood with the mental clarity of a soldier awaiting orders. Whatever Jack said would be done. No arguments. I could kick and scream all I wanted and neither Eyes nor Anton would give me a second thought. They'd follow Jack, and I needed to be ready for that.

Jack's eyes opened again, focusing on his tablet before he made a few swipes and looked up. "We go to the hotel."

Anton nodded, but Eyes needed a little but more than that.

"The reason being?"

"Look who's starting to check out."

"Oh."

I didn't need to hear more to know what he was talking about. When I'd left that morning, several millionaires, a handful of billionaires, and one trillionaire had been staying in the hotel. If they were clearing out, then that was that.

"They won't put the bomb in the parking garage," Jack said to Eyes, tucking his tablet back into his pocket. "This bomb was built to go off in an open space, not demolish a building, so they're going to need a ground-level detonation point, like the roundabout up front. That's going to make our lives hard with all the surveillance. I need you to get a handle on all the cameras in the area."

"I'm on it."

Jack looked at Anton then me. "Let's move."

Without another word, we both followed his lead.

CHAPTER 13

Once again, we were taking a ride in the back of a truck, only this time Jack was along for the ride and the truck was stocked like an armory. Anton looked right at home as he selected guns for himself.

"I'd offer one," he said to me, his eyes flashing with a hint of humor. "But I don't have any tranq guns here, and we both know that you're a bit sluggish with the real thing."

"It's fine," I said. Not taking a gun had less to do with having a sluggish trigger finger at this point than not wanting to have any genuine footage of me with a gun. I wasn't going to make selling whatever story they came up with easy for them.

Across from me, Jack looked like he was meditating.

"So what's the final act in all of this?" I asked. "Assuming we all survive long enough to make it to the exit strategy."

"You die," Jack said, without opening his eyes. "Both of you do—legally at least."

I arched a brow. "And The Fours are going to buy that?"

"Not all of them," Jack said, looking at me. "They won't want to because they won't see it happen firsthand. But they'll have bodies that will be identified as you and zero trace that you still walk the earth. Over time, you will move off their radars, but you will never be able to have any contact with your life as Rhea

Jensen again. You will have to become someone new. So, yes, one way or the other, Rhea Jensen dies today."

My knee-jerk reaction was to fight him on his conclusion. Twenty-four hours ago I would have. But after what I'd seen that day, I knew he was right.

One way or another, I was going to die that night and the realization hit me like a battering ram.

"Breathe," Anton coached me with a bit of sympathy. "It sucks. I know. I'm sorry."

I'd been cold several times that day, but I'd never been truly numb. Anton wanted me to breathe, but my lungs seemed to have forgotten how.

"It took me a while to adapt to the thought," Anton said, his voice gentle as he cradled a sniper rifle. "At first, all I could think of was the life I was losing."

Yeah. I was pretty much sitting right in the middle of that. In my mind, all I could see was Ty and that smile he whipped out whenever he wanted to crack me. The visual made the numb go away, replacing it with the sensation of broken glass coursing through my chest.

A life without Ty? Did I want that? A life where he thought I was dead and moved on to someone new? Both my brain and my stomach recoiled at the thought.

"I wanted so badly for there to be a way to stay connected to my old life," Anton continued, eyes dropping. "And the horrible thing is, I got my wish."

That didn't make sense. "That's horrible?"

His steady eyes looked me in the eye as he nodded. "I watched my best friend die three months ago. As he bled out in my arms, he told me to use his body today—to keep his death a secret and to step into his shoes after all this is over."

My mouth fell open in shock, and Anton studied me for a moment before reaching into his breast pocket to pull out a picture.

He looked at it, visibly debating, then handed it to me. It showed two men, side-by-side. One was Anton, and the man next to him had a broad smile, a Hollywood face, and sleeve of tattoos up both arms.

"If I live through this," Anton said. "I'll have six months of reconstructive surgery that will make me look like my dead best friend. It will let me stay in the world I know, but…"

He'd have the face and life of the best friend who died in his arms.

I thought of Kay, wondering if I could do the same—if I could become her in every way—in order to stay close to Ty. Could I wake up to Kay's face every day and go home to her family on the holidays? Could I look all her friends in the eye and lie in every way as I absorbed her identity?

No. No, I couldn't.

"A fresh start isn't the worst thing, Rhea," Anton said, taking the photo back.

"But you both have a whole lot of mental bridges you need to cross before you get to that one," Jack warned. "We have a bomb and a hotel full of potential casualties. That's the priority here."

He was right. It was.

"How are plans solidifying with The Fours?" he asked, and we all waited for Eyes to respond.

"Still in flux, although favorites are starting to rise to the top."

"Keep us updated."

"Of course."

"What we know," Jack continued, "is that the bomb will be moved to the hotel and that The Fours will do something to lure Rhea there. Whatever the lure is, it will have to be irresistible."

"Which means threatening the lives of the people she has stowed away there."

"Which they can't do without turning that place into a raging inferno," I said. "That safe house is ridiculous in its precautions. A tank couldn't shoot its way in, and nothing they do will open the doors."

"That means going big on their side," Jack said. "They'll have to show their hand a bit."

"They won't like that," Anton said. "Shadows work best for them."

"So we force them into the light," Jack said. "We call their bluff. Whatever it is, we shine a spotlight on it, big and bright."

Anton shook his head. "That's just as likely to blow up in our faces as in theirs."

"Only if we fail," Jack said. "Spotlights pull focus. Whatever they do, they're going to want everyone looking at it. Our job is to get them to fall for their own trick."

In concept, I got what he was talking about. But in practice? I had no idea how he was planning on pulling off something like that. Then again, I was looking at the guy who had made me disappear from a tourist-filled street as if it was the most commonplace thing in the world. Based on that alone, it would be a mistake to underestimate his strategic mind.

"Whatever their lure, it's got to be newsworthy," I said. "The suite my family is staying in is no joke. There's no guarantee anyone inside will die even if the entire hotel burns down. The Fours have to know this. I couldn't hide the fact that I was keeping those closest to me in the suite today, so I'm sure they did some recon on it. The place is a stronghold."

"So I'm gathering," Eyes said. *"The schematics are vague at best. Can you give us a rundown of the security features?"*

"No."

Did I trust this woman with the lives in that suite? Not a chance. And the tone of my voice seemed to communicate as much because my answer was met with a moment of tense silence on the other side of the earpiece. I knew it wasn't my imagination because Jack and Anton shared a look.

"Fine," Eyes said. *"Then you're on your own for controlling whatever happens inside the suite."*

"Fine with me." If Eyes wanted to take offense at my protective instincts then she could have at it. She was all territorial about Anton and I wasn't judging.

"Step one is setting the scene," Jack said, bypassing the tension. "As soon as they're set, they're going to make a move to catch Rhea's attention wherever she is in the city. We need to anticipate this move and play it to our advantage while appearing to give them exactly what they want."

Miraculously, in my imaginings of all the things that could happen today, this scenario was something I had considered as being highly likely. I hadn't known what would be asked of me, but it made sense that The Fours would threaten those I loved if I refused. I hadn't imagined this exact scenario, of course. But I was oddly prepared for it.

"Is voting closed for choosing the target yet?" Jack asked Eyes.

"Affirmative. The hotel is confirmed as the target and they're going to burn it to the ground."

Jack considered that. "They're deviating from their plan. It's way too late in the game for that. This weakens them."

"In theory, yes," Eyes said. *"But I'm not seeing a weak spot in their adjusted plans yet. It's not all that difficult to bomb a hotel and pin it on a pawn."*

"But the hotel owners will not be cooperating," Jack replied. "The Fours are adapting their plan on a property they don't own, which will create obstacles. Those obstacles are our opportunities."

He was right. It didn't make tactical sense to switch targets in the eleventh hour. "Why would they give up their home court advantage like this? It feels wrong."

Jack rubbed his thumb against his fingers. "Money. We are dealing with men of extreme hubris who adore accumulating money. They are switching venues because they see an opportunity to amass wealth while punishing you for making them look like they have a chink in their armor. Egos can be very fragile things."

"Congratulations, Rhea," Anton said, checking the extra magazines for his gun. "They want you dead more than they want Vadim dead. That's no small thing."

"That's what she gets for kicking them in the hubris," Eyes said. Was that a…joke? *"But they have the manpower to plug the gap of a tactical hole in their adapted plans. There's a handful of us and a whole lot of them. They have brute force on their side."*

"But they can only put so many men on the scene without tipping their hands," Jack said. "We need to remember that we're going to be exposed at the hotel because *they* are exposed at the hotel. They are dealing with the same vulnerabilities we are."

"And Vadim is off the playing board?" Anton said to Eyes.

"He is no longer the target of the bomb," Eyes said, and I sensed that she had just side-stepped the actual answer before pressing forward. *"The bomb has a built-in default timer set for 9:00 p.m. That countdown has already been set into motion and cannot be canceled. From discussions I'm hearing right now, they can trigger the bomb remotely to go off at the time of their choosing before 9:00, or simply let it time out. When the clock runs out or if the power to the countdown clock is interrupted, the bomb will detonate."*

"So no cutting wires and no EMPs to disarm it?" Anton asked.

"Correct," Eyes said. *"Time, triggers, and tampering all set off our girl."*

The bomb was suddenly a girl? I wasn't sure how I felt about that.

Also, where in the world was Eyes getting this information? Exactly how plugged in was she?

"So we need a matching vehicle to transport the bomb away from the hotel and get it somewhere before the default timer blows?" Anton said.

"During which time they will use their remote trigger to blow you up, Petrov. That's not an option."

"What if we put the receiver in a Faraday cage?" I asked.

"We don't have the time, materials, or opportunity to build one," Jack said.

"We can use tin foil," I said, knowing it would work. I'd become a bit of an expert at blocking signals over the past few weeks trying to get a few moments alone with Ty. "Wrap the receiver with tin foil really well, and they lose their remote trigger."

"Tin foil?" Eyes balked. *"I am not trusting your lives to tin foil."*

"No, she's right," Jack said. "There can be absolutely no holes in the coverage to allow the signal through, but tin foil will actually work."

"Which solves one problem," Eyes said. *"But plans are evolving fast and solidifying. Latest update is that the main bomb will be parked out front while men are being tasked to strategically place charges inside the building to go off with the main bomb. The internal charges are being placed to block escape, maximize casualties, and guarantee the place burns down."*

"Can we deactivate those charges with the EMPs we have on us?" Anton asked.

"You...could," Eyes said, sounding surprised. *"Yes. That would work. You would just need to disarm all of them before anyone hits the trigger or the timer runs out. The EMP would also need to be out of range of the actual bomb, so it wouldn't trigger the tamper response."*

"If you guys can do all that, I can pull focus while you do," I said.

Jack, Anton, and I all looked at each other, and the two men looked as surprised as I felt.

"Did we just trip into a plan?" Anton asked.

Jack nodded. "I think we did. Rhea pulls focus while staying out of the bomb's range, Anton disarms and removes the charges inside the hotel, and I make the main bomb disappear, as originally planned. All the while, our Eyes in the Sky keeps us safe by controlling what the cameras do and don't see. The Fours will be tapping into the feeds and will have no reason to believe any of the footage is being manipulated real-time since they have no idea that there are any players on the board other than Rhea and Anton. As long as we don't screw up, they'll trust what they see and keep trusting it until we've done what we need to do."

I studied Jack, my mind stuck on one thing, in particular, he'd said. "You're going to make the bomb disappear?"

He nodded. "At least long enough to move it. But this development that it can't be defused isn't one we factored into our original plans."

"We're going to need some place to detonate it within the city," Anton said. "We don't have time to get it out to anywhere remote."

"And the specifications of the bomb show that it has a blast radius of 60 meters in all directions. We're going to need a football stadium or something."

I couldn't help but smile. "I know just the place."

CHAPTER 20

I didn't know how much time I had. Ten minutes? Thirty minutes? One minute?

How long did it take to transport a bomb and wire a hotel to blow when you had a literal army at your beck and call? That was how much time I had.

Standing below an outdated trash chute of the hotel, I pulled back a hidden panel and pressed a button to release the rope that would pull me up to a suite several stories above. Paranoia was many things, including a mother of invention. The suite had been designed with multiple entrances and exits that were all off grid. This secret entrance was the only one I'd been shown, but it was the only one I needed.

Today might be a tragedy in the making, but the miracle of it was that I would be able to see the people most important to me one last time before it was over.

When the rope descended into view with a loop for my foot, I stepped into it, gripped the rope, and slapped the panel shut again. The rope immediately reversed, pulling me back up to its coiled source as I made myself small and did my best not to graze against the sides of the metal chute on my way up.

"Whatever you just did, it was all in a blind spot," Eyes said in my ear. *"I have no idea where you are."*

"That's good," I whispered. "That means I didn't burn my exit."

"And since your comm won't work in the suite, I've hacked into the lights of the hotel sign visible from the northwest windows. Stay in that area, because when that sign goes dark, we need you to move into position."

"Understood." She was being oddly…well, nice wasn't the word, but she wasn't being rude. I wasn't sure what to do with that. It made Eyes feel like a friend, and I knew she wasn't. If I died tonight, she would move on and not blink. She wasn't my friend.

I had to remember that.

A pinhole of light beneath my feet was all I could see when the rope jerked to a halt. Reaching out, I felt around until my hand landed on a latch that opened into an empty storage cupboard. One scoot and a slide later, and I was in the suite.

An unexpected wave of emotion washed over me as I stood and shut the cupboard door behind me. I stopped to compose myself. Ty was somewhere on the other side of that door. So was Kay and my dad. This morning hadn't been the last time I would see them.

Right now was. This was it. This was the last time.

The reality of that fact buried me like a flood from nowhere. Whether I lived or died tonight, I could never make contact with the people I loved again.

"Don't think about that right now," I whispered to myself before taking several calming breaths. "You can cry about that later. Right now you need to stop wasting time and do what needs to be done."

Saying the words out loud helped, giving me the kick I needed to walk out of the storage room and into the suite's hallway. Off to my left I could hear a TV on and chatter of a police scanner. I followed the noise, finding everyone I'd left that morning in the same room. My dad sat in an armchair looking like he was losing a battle with a nap. Across the room, Kay sat in front of a laptop listening to dispatch with one ear as she scrolled through news stories online. Ty was sitting on the couch in front of the TV, but he wasn't watching it. His eyes were firmly locked on the floor as he leaned his elbows on his knees.

Across the room, Dahl stood at the surveillance desk, splitting his attention between what was showing on the monitors and what he saw outside the one-way windows. I could have hugged Dahl in that moment. He was doing for me what I couldn't do for myself and I loved him for it.

But his were not the arms I wanted around me in that moment.

"Ty," I whispered. I didn't mean to whisper, but the emotion in my voice choked the volume back. At least it didn't crack.

Ty was on his feet in a second, as was Kay. My dad's eyes blinked open as Ty crossed the room in what felt like a single step and pulled me so close I could barely breathe. I held him right back, pressing my face against his shirt and inhaling his scent as I let him surround me with his warmth.

I could have stayed like that all night, if given the choice. But I did not have a choice, so after one last squeeze I pulled away from my husband.

"You're back!" Kay said as she ran to me, but I looked at her and shook my head before she could take her celebration too far. Her smile faltered and her pace slowed as she looked me over.

"What's happening?" Dahl said from the other side of the room. "Why are you here if it's not over?"

My dad was standing, but he looked like he was going to be physically ill. When Ty stepped back to take a look at me, I took my dad's hand in mine and gave it a squeeze as I spoke. "I'm here because I don't get to come back from today. We need to have a talk."

I felt my dad's fingers tighten around mine like a vice as Kay's defiant blue eyes locked onto me—the eyes that had inexplicably trusted me since the first day the two of us had met back in freshman year.

Well, she had trusted wrong. Kay couldn't have chosen a worse best friend back then if she'd tried. Through everything that had happened the first year we'd met, she'd seen me as a savior…her champion. As it turned out, I was the only reason she'd needed a champion to begin with.

I hadn't saved Kay from anything. Rather, her friendship with me had subjected her to all the horrors she wished she could erase from her life.

How could I tell her that?

My mind raced, trying to think of the best way to share what I had learned, only to realize I couldn't tell her about Elliott. I couldn't tell anyone.

The lives of every person in the room and anyone they held in confidence depended almost entirely on them remaining non-threats to The Fours after today. They couldn't know anything.

Ty, Kay, and Dahl already knew too much. They knew not to talk about it, but could they keep their poker faces if I told them about what Elliott had orchestrated?

I couldn't chance it. Maybe more to the point, I didn't *want* to chance it. There was already so much room for things to go wrong with everyone I loved. To tell them what I knew and forbid them to ever talk about it out loud ever again would be cruel. People needed to process things, and I couldn't risk The Fours overhearing a conversation between Kay and Ty about Elliott or the initiation ceremony down the road.

I had to keep things vague. It's just how things had to be…which only made it harder to look into Kay's trusting eyes and accept the hug she was pulling me into. I owed her a thousand apologies and twice as many explanations, and she was going to get neither from me.

I was a horrible friend. Downright horrible.

Still, I accepted the hug, not anticipating how hard it would be to hold back tears once I was wrapped up in it.

The day I'd met Kay, she'd been the kindest and most naive person I'd ever met. Guileless. Earnest. Pure. What Elliott had put her through had changed Kay's demeanor forever, hardening her and changing the lenses she saw life through from a shade of rose to shades of grey. And he'd done it all to get me under his thumb.

Kay deserved to know that.

She never would.

I poured all my unspoken apologies for everything she'd endured on my behalf into our hug. I owed this woman for so much, not the least of which was the fact that I hadn't become a murderer earlier that day. Because of Kay, I hadn't killed Elliott. When I'd gone off the rails, she'd pulled me back into my own skin.

I owed her for that; I owed her for way more than that, but all I could do in that moment was hug her back. Her arms pressed my nose into the new perfume she'd bought on one of our recent shopping trips where we were pretending everything was normal. *Versace Crystal Noire*. It was a good fit for her. No doubt I'd think of her if I ever smelled it again.

"Rhea," my dad said from next to me. "What is happening?"

Right. Reality. Hugs were nice and all, but life was still happening real-time.

I pulled away from Kay and caught the look in her eye. Part of me expected to see her holding back tears, like I was, but the gaze I met was much more determined than that. I knew the look. Kay was ready to fight. She was ready to listen to whatever it was I had to say and expose any cracks in my logic before wedging a Plan B into the conversation.

That meant whatever I said needed to be crack-free.

"Right now they're cooking up something to frame me for," I said to the group. "In all likelihood, it will be that I'm a suicide bomber who attacked this hotel and burned it down."

Defiance changed to disbelief in Kay's eyes as Ty gripped my hand. "What?"

"Your plan of action stays the same," I said, looking at Dahl while keeping my hand in Ty's, where it felt at home. "You all stay right here, bomb or not. We're going to do our best to stop the attack, but if it is successful your chance of survival is still higher if you stay in here. Leaving the suite turns you into leverage. You will be killed, and I will likely be framed for your deaths."

Dahl nodded as if everything I'd just said made sense while Ty, Kay, and my dad reacted like normal people and freaked out.

"Rhea," my dad said, stepping in. "What can we do? I have to help you!"

I stepped away from Ty and wrapped my arms around my dad. "You help me by staying safe," I said as I felt the shake of a sob against me. "Both today and all the days that follow, which means not telling the truth of what you know about today to anyone. They will kill you for it."

"No," he said with force. "I can't do that."

"You have to, Dad," I said, doing my best to blink back tears before pulling away and looking at everyone. "You all do. Whatever narrative they come up with to explain what happens in the next few hours, you leave it be. Don't confirm it, but leave it be. Don't grant interviews and don't talk about anything that's happened the past few months. Say nothing. That's what you can do for me. There's no point in you all dying for no reason."

Kay was immediately in my face. "The truth is a reason."

"A truth that will barely be heard and disappear right along with you," I said. "They are going to be watching you all very closely for years to come. Don't talk about today. Don't write anything down. Don't communicate with *anyone* about it. Friends.

Family. Media. No one. I'm serious here."

Ty's hand tightened around mine and all I wanted to do was step back into his arms and let him hold me like nothing else existed. "There has to be another way."

Looking at him was a mistake. The devastation in Ty's eyes cracked through my bravado without warning and suddenly there were visible tears in my eyes. I blinked them back and took a breath that did nothing to help whatever brave facade I had going on. "There's not."

"There is," Kay said with resolve.

I had to put a stop to all this optimism.

Releasing Ty's hand, I took a steadying breath. "Dahl, I need you to keep an eye on the northwest corner and tell me if the hotel's sign goes dark. That's my cue to exit."

He nodded, again saying nothing. Bless him.

"Use us, Rhea," Kay said, looking like she didn't know what to do with her hands. "We can help you."

I shook my head. "I wish you could, Kay. I really do. But…"

But what? What could I say? How could I make them understand?

I don't know how long I floundered with my response, only that I was saved from fumbling for a response when Kay pulled me into another hug. I pretty much crash landed into it, pressing my face into her shirt as my first tears slipped loose.

She was my best friend—the best friend a person could ask for—and I'd never get to talk to her again. This was it. No matter what happened next, this was the last time we would meet like this. Whatever words I said in the next few minutes would be her last memories of our friendship, and I really didn't want those moments to be full of fear and The Fours, even though they kind of had to be.

"I love you, you know that?" I said over her shoulder.

Her arms tightened around me. "This isn't goodbye."

I pulled away. "It is, Kay. It really is."

"No," she said, swiping tears from her eyes as she grew resolute. "We haven't tried everything yet."

I looked from her to my dad to Ty. They all seemed to think Kay was the voice of reason in the room. But when I looked at Dahl, I knew he believed me. He was on my side, and would have my back after I had to leave again. God bless him.

"Look," I said as calmly as possible. "This day doesn't end without me dead—"

Three mouths opened to object and I held up my hand to stop them.

"Whether I actually die or just convince The Fours that I'm dead doesn't change the fact that after today, Rhea Jensen will be legally deceased." I looked Ty in the eye. "Legally, you will be a widower. There will be a funeral. You'll have to bury me, and you'll have to move on, Ty."

My voice cracked at that last part. Dammit. I'd been trying really hard for stoic. But the thought of Ty moving on? I just couldn't make eye contact with those images in my mind.

"Rhea..." he said, stepping closer. I didn't push him away.

"I can't reappear in your life in any way, Ty," I said, touching his perfect face. Man, I loved his face and those eyes that always looked like they had a joke behind them. Except now. All the humor was gone, leaving him stricken. Because of me. I'd done this to him. I was *doing* this to him, and I had to keep doing it. He had to understand. "This organization is huge and it's international. Thousands upon thousands of influential billionaires. People who own governments. People whose hobbies include arranging death matches between people who quit their jobs."

My dad looked ready to kill. "So this comes back to Elliott? He's the one who got you pulled into this?"

I had to state the obvious and put it to bed, or they would talk about it endlessly later and get themselves into trouble.

"Yes, but Elliott's not even a drop in this bucket, Dad. You have to understand that. These people would kill Elliott with almost as little thought as they'll kill me. These are people who are willing to blow up a hotel full of people just to get me to show my face again. These are men with armies and unlimited funds with no aversion for killing or collateral damage." I looked back at Kay. "There is nothing our little Scooby gang can do that will even scratch them before they wipe us out and walk away whistling. Those are the facts. It's not me giving up. It's me accepting reality."

The room fell silent. That was good. It meant they had heard me. They were accepting my words, which only made them more real.

"I love you all," I said, not caring when my voice broke again. "I had to come tell you that and to beg you to keep yourselves safe in the wake of everything that happens. If you have a moment where you even think about trying to take these guys down, I want you to think about your families." I looked at Ty, those gorgeous blue eyes of his shimmering with blinked back tears as he looked back. "Your sister. Your niece. These are the people who will disappear first if you make waves. These men will crash a commercial plane just to kill one person on board. They'll do whatever they want, and it won't bring me back. It will just cause more pain. I need you to remember that and stay safe."

At the mention of his sister and his niece, Ty faltered. He knew I wasn't joking, just like I knew he'd do anything to protect them. Even forget me.

My heart lurched at the thought. Was it possible for hearts to vomit? Because that described the sensation in my chest perfectly. And if I hadn't been looking directly into my husband's eyes as the pain of losing him washed over me, I might have been able to power through it.

It didn't work out that way.

"You have to move on, Ty," I said, hoping my words communicated what my body language could not as I reached up and traced his jaw with my fingers.

One of Ty's blinks came too late to stop a tear from trailing down his cheek and suddenly we were kissing. I don't know who pulled the other in or if we both did it at the same time. I just knew it wasn't gentle.

Behind me, Kay made a small sound of surprise and my dad cleared his throat. Two seconds ago I would have guessed that the vibe in the room couldn't have gotten more awkward, but apparently I'd been wrong.

Ty pulled away and gripped my hand, still looking at me as he spoke to everyone else. "Give us a minute," he said, then dragged me toward the bedroom.

I followed, moving quickly and pulling him closer as I kicked the door closed behind me. "I love you," I said right before our lips found each other again. My heart felt like a sponge full of boiling hot water that burned and spread through my body until the heat was leaking out of my eyes.

He let his mouth and hands speak without words for several moments before a shiver ran through him and he cradled my face in his hands. My lips felt cooler the moment he pulled away and I tried to lean in again. He stopped me.

"You and me?" he said. "This isn't the end. Tell me you know that."

I shook my head. "You need to let me go, Ty. Not today," I said, my eyes dropping to his lips. "Definitely not today, and preferably not tomorrow, but eventually. You need to move on. You have my *permission* to move on."

His response was a slow kiss that somehow had me crying like an idiot until a small sob shook me.

"This," he said softly, pressing his forehead to mine as our lips pulled apart, "does not happen twice in a lifetime. I'm yours,

Rhea."

"And I'm yours," I said, tracing his bottom lip with my finger. "But you've got to leave us in the past. For you."

"Does that mean you're going to let go?" he asked. "That you're going to move on?"

Of course it didn't, but I wasn't built like Ty. I didn't need people like he did. He was my exception. For me, it was him or nothing; but Ty was much more of an extrovert. He needed people. He needed to flirt, and he was really good at it—good enough that he landed me, despite all my defensive maneuvers.

As much as I hated to admit it, the man I loved would disappear and be replaced by a stranger if he didn't move on. Ty couldn't be alone. Not like me.

But I couldn't say any of that. I had to let him go, and I had to pave the way for him letting me go by speaking in the language he understood best: humor. Or at least my best attempt at it.

"When I find someone sexier and funnier than you? Sure. I'll move on," I said with feigned flippancy.

He blinked in surprise, then smiled for the first time that day. "Not possible."

"No? I guess you'll find out when I send you a picture."

"Since when are you the one who cracks jokes to break up tension?"

I ran my fingertips along his stubble, memorizing the feel of it. "I hear that married couples rub off on each other. Must be your influence. Which reminds me," I said, trying for a smile. "Try not to be bitter and distant while I'm gone. That's my thing."

His hands were in my hair, his eyes looking like they were trying to memorize the color of it when he replied. "Hey, one of us has got to carry the baton on that if you're going to pick up the reins on being funny."

I looked into his eyes, seeing the pain there and trying not to get swallowed up in it. "Or maybe we should just stick to our strengths moving forward. We're going to need them."

I saw the shift in his eyes and felt it in his touch when he finally accepted that this was really goodbye. He didn't say anything for a bit. Neither did I. I just waited.

"Well, I guess if I meet someone really hot…" he finally said with just a hint of playfulness as his hand traced down my body.

"Of course," I agreed. "She'd have to be hot."

He nodded, looking like he was picturing it. "And super smart to back the looks up."

"Intelligence is also a requirement," I said, leaning an inch closer.

I was still here. I wasn't gone yet, and even the joke of him thinking of someone else had me fighting for his attention as I played along.

"And endlessly interesting," he said before his lips grazed mine. "And obnoxiously competitive."

"She'd have to be to keep you in your place," I said before our lips met again much too briefly.

"And able to compete with me in all things physical."

"Compete *and* beat," I clarified, trying to keep things playful despite the lopsided beating of my heart. It felt like a flat tire still trying to go full speed.

"I'll let your replacement win at jumping jacks and jump rope," he said against my lips. "The rest is all me."

His next kiss was all gentleness and no brevity. I'd kissed Ty thousands of times, but never like this. It was a connection that was less body and more…what? What was it when you didn't know where you ended and someone else began, like two clouds colliding and merging in the sky?

Whatever it was, the euphoria and the freedom of it was slowly pushing everything else out of my mind and I didn't even try to stop it. I leaned in, embracing the illusion of escape for as long as it would have me.

CHAPTER 21

"Rhea?" Dahl's voice called through the door. "We need you out here."

"Be right there." I slid from the bed without hesitation, gathering up my clothes and accidentally grabbing Ty's shirt in the process. On impulse, I held it to my nose and inhaled.

"I need that," he said.

"Too bad," I said, tossing it out of his reach. "I'm taking it with me."

"Yeah? Does that mean I get your shirt?"

I shook my head, putting on the shirt in question. "I need it for tactical reasons."

He watched me. "Rhea?"

"Yeah."

"I love you, too."

The pain came back in a wave forceful enough to crush me if I let it. I didn't. "After what we just did? You'd better."

He actually chuckled in reply, which did my heart good. I needed to see him happy. I needed to know that one of us was still capable of it.

The room felt oddly silent as I finished dressing while Ty stayed on the bed watching me. I could practically hear the gears in his head turning, but whatever was happening in that copper-topped head of his, he wasn't sharing it. When I was finally dressed, I walked over to the bed and dropped one last kiss to his lips.

"Get dressed and meet me out there."

He nodded, again saying nothing as I turned and scooped up his shirt on the way out. I hadn't been kidding about taking it. If I survived the day, I needed *something* of his to hold on to.

When I returned to the main room, Kay was pacing in front of the coffee table while my dad and Dahl stood near the window, just a few feet away from a black-clad figure playing Spider-man on the other side of the armored glass. Dahl pointed at the device the man was using to etch the beginnings of a circle into the window pane.

"That tool can cut diamonds," he said without preamble. "I don't know what these windows are made of, but if we let him keep doing what he's doing, he's going to get through."

This was my cue to leave. Whether the lights across the street were still on or not, it was time to go.

"Do you know if this place has any defensive measures to knock him off?" Dahl asked. "An electric pulse or something?"

I thought of the thirteen-story drop. If the man fell he would die, which gave me pause. I'd started this day by praying I could make it through without anyone dying. So far, no one had. Making the first kill seemed like a great way to cancel out my prayer and get blood flowing.

Maybe it was superstition, but I didn't want to draw first blood. How could I ask God to protect the people I loved if I was willing to do harm to the loved ones of others?

Even after the day I'd had, I still didn't have an answer to that question that made me feel good about making a man fall thirteen stories to his death.

"He knows what he's risking by being out there," Dahl said as if reading my thoughts. "He's the one declaring war. I have no qualms about ending it."

Sometimes I forgot that Dahl wasn't trained to be a cop first. Before he'd put on a badge, he'd been special ops and, unlike me, he did not have a sluggish trigger finger. Neither did Kay, although she'd only ever shot animals while hunting.

Be like Kay. Be like Dahl, I coached myself.

The sign on the northwest hotel blinked off.

"That's my cue," I said, turning to face Kay and my dad. I looked for Ty. He hadn't joined us yet.

"Our man has a rope anchored to the adjacent roof," Dahl said. "I think he's going to plant an explosive device to create a breach, then slide down the rope to make a getaway."

"Your instincts are good," I said, my mind calculating the time the man would need to create the hole, based on his current progress. "The breach will be so the fire has an inlet after the bomb blows. Creating a breach makes it more likely you all will be smoked out or killed in the fire."

Dahl walked past me to the bar area and picked up one of the many rifles he laid there after we checked in. "So how do I open these windows?"

"I don't know," I said, walking over to grab one of the handguns. Something told me I was going to need an extra, so I tucked the second handgun in the back of my pants for the time being. "I don't even know if they open."

"I'll find out," Dahl said, starting to pull panels open on the wall to search for anything that might be helpful.

"And I'll go get his attention," I said.

"How?" Kay asked, looking pale.

"By stealing his landing spot," I said to Kay before clapping my hand on Dahl's arm and looking him in the eye. "I owe you the world, man. Whatever happens here, thank you."

He nodded as I turned and pulled my dad into my arms.

"I'm waiting for you to tell me this is all a joke," he said against my shoulder.

"Not a joke," I said, holding tight. "But I love you forever, okay? Whatever happens tonight, I'm never far. Even if you don't see me, I'll be watching you."

I wanted it to be the truth so badly that I chose to believe my own lie. I pressed a kiss to his cheek before turning to Kay. The tears running down her cheeks caught me off guard.

"Tag," I said, throwing my arms around her as I threw out the catchphrase we had used since college when doing the other a favor. "You're it."

"Don't say that," she said, crushing me in her arms. "Not when you're going where I can't follow."

Her words felt like a punch to the heart, and I pulled away. "Don't worry. I'll be stalking you, too, one way or another."

Just then Ty stepped out of the room. He'd found another shirt to make himself presentable, but he did not look like he wanted to be there. He looked broken.

I walked up to him and dropped one last kiss to his lips, trying for a light tone as I spoke. "I told you that you should have let me be the one that got away. You totally could have skipped all this."

His eyes locked on mine. "Not for the world."

My heart puddled a bit in spite of everything.

"And Rhea?" he said.

"Yeah?"

"We are going to see each other again." He tapped his fingers over my heart. "I feel it. Here. So don't get too comfortable without me."

Denial. The fact that I wanted to believe him told me I was still standing in the middle of it, too. There was no time to argue with him and I didn't want to. I wanted him to be right, so I forced myself to smile. "Well, see you later then."

"Later," he agreed.

I gave everyone one last look, then ran back to the garbage chute.

CHAPTER 22

No one could hear me cry as the wire rope lowered me back down the old trash chute. I think that's what finally got me to break.

No one could see me and no one could hear me—maybe for the last time in my entire life.

It felt like someone had ripped my heart out of my body, torn it in half, then put it back where it belonged like I wouldn't know the difference.

Seeing Ty again had been a tactical error…as had seeing Kay and my dad and Dahl. Leaving them twice in one day—the first time with hope and the second time with no hope whatsoever— might just kill me before the stupid rope unraveled enough to get my feet back on the ground and put me back into the insane cat-and-mouse game my life had become.

I was never going to see my friends and family again.

Ever.

No matter what happened tonight, reuniting was off the table. The weight of that realization had me wanting to pound against the trash chute in futility, or cut at the steel rope until it dulled my knife, or scream until a hotel guest called security to report wailing in the vents.

Something. *Anything.*

But freaking out wasn't practical and there was no time to mourn, because…bomb.

Bounty hunters, and bombs, and unknowing civilians, oh my!

Yeah, I was totally up for trading shoes with Dorothy in Oz at the moment. I would take a tin man and flying monkeys any day over The Fours. In a final moment of whimsy, I actually gave switching places with her a shot. But three clicks of my heels later, I was still dangling from a rope with Eyes' voice back in my ear.

"…Rhea, are you there? We really need you to—"

Nope. Definitely not in Oz.

"Here," I said over her as swiped the wetness off my face. "I've got the signal back."

"Where are you?"

"Still dropping down to ground level."

Did my voice sound normal, or did it have that cry warble going on? In general, I didn't like anyone knowing that I was crying, but Eyes was at the top of that very long list at the moment. If she sensed weakness in me, she might just execute me herself.

I cleared my throat and fought for normal. "What did I miss?"

"I don't see you," she said in confusion.

"My paranoid friend will be so pleased that his secret entrance is still secret. What did I miss?"

"The bomb is a few blocks away from the hotel. As we speak, they're starting to set chargers to blow along with it," she said. *"It's pretty much what we predicted. The original bomb will be the shock and awe, and the charges they're setting are to ensure the building burns."*

"I need to get the guy outside the window of the safe house," I said, watching the dot of light from the hotel's basement below me grow larger and larger while wishing my ride had a fast mode.

"Yes," she agreed. *"That charge will be problematic. Once it's placed, I don't know that we have a way to interfere with it without*

blowing it."

"I saw the man's escape route. That's where I'm heading."

"*And you won't be alone,*" she said. "*The operative setting the charge has a bounty hunter covering his exit point. If you go across the street, you will have to engage.*"

"Then that's what I'll do," I said, willing myself not to just drop the rest of the way down to the ground so I could get moving.

"*He's an assassin, Rhea. You need to kill him,*" Eyes said, her voice cold. "*No clamming up this time. No hesitating. You get the drop and you take the shot. Don't think. Do.*"

I wanted to tell her I had it covered, but we both knew that was a lie. I thought of Dahl and his willingness to let the guy setting the charge drop thirteen floors.

"I hear you," I said.

"*Not good enough,*" she lectured. "*I don't need you to hear, Rhea. I need you to execute.*"

Literally. She wanted me to execute, and I could tell by the tone in her voice that she was a woman who had ordered hits like this before and been obeyed. She was no novice, and it burned her to be working with one.

I thought of the two guns in my bag with Ty's shirt, both unfired. The thought of firing them—of taking them out of my bag and aiming and shooting—still felt so incredibly wrong. Here I was fighting for my right to live, yet I was supposed to sneak up on someone and unceremoniously rob them of their life?

It didn't make sense, especially when a new person would just be tasked to come after me again and again by my real enemy.

Why hadn't I brought a tranq gun to the safe house? Then my problems would be solved.

Eyes annoyed voice cut through my thoughts. "*Rhea, we're going to need a confirmation that you will take care of the bounty hunter and the operative. Petrov and Jack will be busy with their respective duties. They can't cover you on this.*"

"Headed there now," I said.

"That's not what I asked," she replied just as my feet cleared the bottom of the chute. Ten more feet and I was on my way.

"I'll make sure the charge doesn't blow," I said. "Do you have eyes on the bounty hunter?"

"Yes, I have three views of him, all real-time. I can guide you."

"Is there a way for me to get up there without drawing focus? They must be watching for me."

"They actually aren't that concerned about you yet," Eyes said. *"But yes, they are watching. It's a busy area, though, and that will buy a few more minutes of invisibility. You have the businesses on the street level with the condos and apartments above. Wear the hat in your bag and act like a resident as you go to the top level. Then take the stairs to the roof. They'll definitely see you by then, but that gives them thirty-second notice that you're definitely not a resident, rather than several minutes."*

"Copy that," I said.

"Also, leave your gun in the bag as long as possible. It's less likely to draw attention there."

"No problem," I said, finally touching down on the ground. I stepped out of the harness and sent it back up the chute before shouldering the bag and moving to the exit.

"No running, in case I have to remind you," she said just as I picked up my pace. *"Walk like a normal person. Go with the flow."*

It wasn't an unnecessary tip, considering how anxious I was. "En route."

"Just saw you emerge from the dead zone, so I've got you. I'll let you know if I see anything suspicious closing in."

So this was how Anton had been operating all day? Pretty handy. Although I needed to remind myself that I'd still gotten the drop on him back in the Arts District. I had no idea how, except for the fact that Anton had already confessed that he'd underestimated me physically. But it was a reminder not to lean on Eyes too much. Sometimes you had to trust the voice in your ear and other times you had to trust instinct.

It killed me not to jaywalk once I hit the street. Instead, I walked to the corner like all the other law abiding citizens and meandered to the other side. I took note of the businesses I passed, two restaurants, one already packed pub, a gift shop, and several mostly empty clothing stores. The dinner rush had started, creating a moderate bustle on the sidewalk. I blended in.

"You need a keycard to get past the second set of doors," Eyes said. *"Pretend to flash something over the scanner when you reach the front door. I'll unlock it for you."*

That was a nice trick. The people who paid six- and seven-figures to live in the building probably appreciated the immaculate security. Still, I did as instructed. I didn't have keys or anything to put in my hands, so I pretended I had something in my pocket and raised my hip scanner level. The security light switched from red to green.

"Do the same thing inside the elevator," Eyes instructed. *"Push the button for the top floor first, then fake scan. And keep your chin down. You're showing too much face."*

Her running commentary helped me focus, as did her clipped tone. Doing as I was told, I got into the elevator alone and started the ride to the top floor.

"Only the lobby and the elevators have cameras," Eyes informed me. *"But The Fours currently do have a full wifi look at the building and are watching it for red flags. Keep things casual as long as you can. I'll let you know when it's time to step on the gas."*

I didn't reply. There were probably no microphones around me, but it was better to be safe than sorry. When the doors opened, I walked out with a confident stride.

"Take a right then an immediate left," she said, and I did it. *"Now go all the way to the end. The stairs for roof access are on the opposite side of the building. The last lock on the door leading to the roof is a standard deadbolt. I trust you can handle that."*

"No problem" I muttered, reaching for my wristband. If there was one thing I could do as well as anyone on Team Anton, it was pick a lock—not that Eyes was going to be too impressed by that, all things considered.

I made the walk to the other side of the building in silence and took Eyes' shared silence as a good sign. No news was good news. When I reached the emergency exit, I pushed through and headed up to the roof like it was the most natural thing in the world. One long set of stairs led to the roof exit and, as Eyes promised, there was no keypad protecting it. Just a deadbolt that required a key on either side.

"This is the part where you start moving as fast as you can," Eyes said.

I took the stairs two at a time then started on the lock.

"They know you're there," Eyes said a beat later. *"The bounty hunter is moving from the roofline to set up a shot at your door. You have maybe three seconds before he's ready for you at your nine o'clock."*

Without answering, I pushed the door open and surged around the corner to my right to take cover, putting the cube-shaped roof exit between me and bullets on the otherwise flat roof.

"Rhea, this is the part where you take out your gun."

Oh, yeah. That. I slid my hand into the bag, gripping the gun I'd pulled from the wall earlier that morning. Nine bullets in the clip, one in the chamber.

"He's holding position. You have seconds before he starts angling into your position. Also, bets are coming in. The payout is double if he kills you on a live camera feed, which would require getting you to the edge of the roof. The maximum payday is to

bring you in for interrogation. He will want that, if possible."

I was pretty sure Eyes ordered off a menu with more passion than she spoke about my life, but in a way it was a good thing. It kept me focused.

"Move clockwise around the next corner to stay in his blind spot."

I didn't hesitate. I moved.

"Now do I need to keep holding your hand, or do you have this?"

My ego said to tell her I was fine. My will to live had less pride. "Just let me know if either man makes a big move."

"Copy that. I'll keep the training wheels engaged."

Man, if the day ever came where I met Eyes, I was going to high five her right in the face.

Wrapping my finger around the gun's trigger, I moved further along the wall until I had sight of the man setting the charge on the window across the street. I could cut the rope leading back to where I was, but doing so would likely leave enough slack to simply let the man rappel to the ground level after succeeding in his task. I needed to do something that would require him to abort.

For some reason, that realization was the moment where everything I needed to do next to succeed became very real.

Eyes' passé tone had kept me calm until the moment I saw that first man at work on the window separating him from everyone I loved most. Seeing that, and knowing it was his intent to kill, kicked my brain into a new gear that my brain had been avoiding all day.

Before I was fully aware of what I was doing, I leveled the gun at where the rope was anchored and fired. I didn't care if I hit it, only that I had the undivided attention of both men for a fraction of a second as I reached around the corner and fired a second bullet in the direction of the sniper.

I knew where they were; they knew where I was. It was game

on.

"That was stupid," Eyes said and I ignored her.

People had been underestimating me all day, and I needed that trend to continue. Stupid is as stupid does, and there was no way these guys were going to be anything less than precise professionals unless they thought they were engaging stupid. Overconfidence was my friend, and I needed an opening. Only an impulsive move on their part would give me that.

I shot off another round in the general direction of the bounty hunter just to piss him off.

"A little to the right."

I adjusted and fired.

"Lower."

I fired again before looking back to the man clinging to the side of the hotel like Spider-man and leveled my sites on him. I squeezed off a round that hit to the left of the man.

"You didn't adjust for wind."

I knew that.

"Both men are wearing Kevlar. Aim for the head."

Bulletproof vests? I could work with that. The many hours of shooting out in the desert with Kay played in the back of my mind as I adjusted my aim on Spider-man and fired again. The man flinched.

"Congratulations. You shot him right in the center of his vest, where it's least effective," Eyes said with more than a trace of annoyance. *"Take the head shot, Rhea."*

But my gun was already aimed back toward the bounty hunter, where I blindly fired off another round.

"Two more bullets."

If she was counting, they were counting. That was good for me.

"You're going to get a gas grenade in about ten seconds. He's putting on his mask now."

I trained my gun back up on Spider-man, making sure my aim was as true as I could make it, then squeezed the trigger three times.

Bang-Bang-Click.

I was on empty and everyone knew it.

I dropped the gun and reached into my bag to grip the second one. I didn't pull it out, though. The gun's outline would clearly show up in wifi imaging once I pulled it out, but with my hand in the bag they would maybe only see the bag.

"Another vest shot and a butt shot," Eyes said, thoroughly unimpressed. *"And fyi, the oxygen on your belt won't help you with this gas once it's deployed."*

I'd forgotten I even had the respirator. But now that she reminded me about the belt, I remembered the two grenades—flash and smoke. I could use them.

"Tell me when he tosses it," I whispered.

"Well, you're out of bullets now. He may not need to go that route anymore."

I crossed my fingers for that. Most gases were pretty aggressive and there was a decent chance some of it might get to the street level and cause problems there. The Fours would want to avoid that. Tonight was a night to control the headlines. News of a rogue gas in downtown LA hitting the airwaves before a bomb would dilute the impact of the bomb and raise questions about correlations.

Tactically speaking, taking me out with a bullet was preferable to gassing me out.

"Lucky you. The gas mask is coming back off," Eyes said as if listening to my inner train of thought.

This was my opening. They thought I was out of bullets and they wanted to take me alive for interrogation.

I grabbed the flash grenade, pulled the pin and made the toss.

"He saw that," Eyes said as I covered my eyes and mentally

reviewed the path between me and the sniper's position.

"Rhea, he's—"

Eyes panicked tone was upstaged by the small scrape of a pebble against cement behind me. It served as my only warning that my man wasn't where I thought he was. Somehow, the bounty hunter had made it from his staked out position to sneak up behind me quicker than it took Eyes to open her mouth.

Instinct screamed to run, but I'd long past trained myself out of reactions like that. I moved toward the sound, releasing the gun in my bag when my eyes spotted his knife. He didn't swing the knife at me, but stabbed, my reflexes parrying the strike out of the way as I punched at his face. He adjusted his weight to make my fist fly harmlessly past him, leaving me to hit nothing but air as his free fist struck me right in the solar plexus. I breathed through the impact, concentrating on getting the knife out of his hand. But the man worked with knives a whole lot more than I did. Taking the blade from him would be about as easy as taking one of his fingers. Still, as the flash grenade went to work behind me, I managed to hang with him for all of five seconds while only receiving surface cuts. When sheer luck saved me from a stab between the ribs, I pushed away to put distance between us.

With several feet between us, the man and I circled each other, sizing each other up as the flash grenade strobed on the other side of a 10X10 brick cube, minimizing any advantage it could have given me if I'd held onto it a second or two longer. It was mainly just a strobe that gave me intermittent glimpses at the man's face. He had a European look about him—maybe Russian—and I wondered if Anton knew him. Eyes had made the claim that she knew this guy would want to turn me in for triple the money, which spoke to the possibility that this man just might have a history with Team Jack.

I didn't have time to ask, though.

"You're a wily one, aren't you?" the man said in accented

English. "I like wily."

Well, then, he was going to love what I did next.

I went for a strike, leaving my torso wide open for a shot from him. My hope was that he would underestimate me and take the bait, and he did. When his blade struck forward toward my liver, I countered with a move I'd practiced thousands of times with Dahl. I batted the knife off course as I moved in, getting my hips beneath his and his shoulders over mine before executing a standard hip throw.

The assassin flew over my shoulders, landing hard. His head cracked into the roof, dazing him enough to get the knife clattering out of his hand. But he recovered quickly. I stomped down at his face, trying to buy an opening to go for the gun on his hip, but my heel stomped into the roof as he rolled into my leg, nearly taking me down until I stepped over him.

It was now or never for the knife. It took only two steps to get to it, grip it, and turn, but that was enough for my bounty hunter to unclip his gun and have it leveled at me by the time I turned to face him. He fired without hesitation.

I expected to be blown back like people are in the movies. Instead, I only felt my leg twitch a moment before it felt like it was being burned by a hot iron. Then it buckled.

"That should make you a little less unpredictable," he muttered, holstering his gun again before casually walking over to me. I moved to get back up and faltered. One look down told me that he had shot me right through the meat of my thigh. The bullet had gone in the front and out the back, leaving me with a leg that didn't work exactly how I was used to. Oh, and a hole that was now leaking blood at an alarming rate. The bullet had left me with that, too.

The assassin moved forward with confidence as I processed my new state. "When was the last time you went skydiving, Ms. Jensen? Because we're about to see how well you fly."

I had the knife, but it didn't matter. One swat to the back of my hand from the assassin sent it flying before he grabbed me by the collar and started dragging me to the edge of the roof.

I punched at his hand…his elbow—anywhere I could reach—but I was in panic mode and nothing was really landing. Liquid heat saturated my pants and my leg seemed to be growing more and more uncooperative.

"Where's the best camera for a drop?" he asked, and I knew he wasn't talking to me. He was talking to someone just like I was talking to Eyes. I used the moment to stomp my good foot down the front of his knee, stripping his knee cap. It had to have hurt, but he made no sound and barely even flinched, even though his next step revealed he was injured.

Emboldened, I went for his elbow again, trying to break his hold on me and earning a punch that had my ears ringing and my sight shattering for a moment.

Without another word, the bounty hunter gathered my hair in his fist, yanking me off my feet and dragging me toward the front of the building. I tried to get another hit on his now-bad leg, but his grip on my hair put too much distance between us. Short of cutting off my hair—

Knife! I had a utility knife on my belt.

I fumbled for it even as the edge of the roof drew closer. I had seconds. I had…the knife! I didn't have time to cut my hair off, but I had the knife.

The drop was nine stories with foot traffic below. I would die on impact. The bigger question was whether I would take someone with me if I touched down.

"Wait," I called out, as I tried to figure out how to work the blade open out of his line of sight. Was there some sort of safety release or something? I should have played with it more and talked less in the back of that trailer. "Not here. We can find other cameras."

There was no reason for him to listen to me and he didn't.

I sprawled my legs, my left leg spurting blood at the move. The goal was to make myself heavier or more cumbersome, but the man wasn't lacking in the strength department. Not even with a bad knee. He easily swung me up to the edge of the building.

"Can you see us?" he asked the night sky. "Can you see her face?"

I kneed at the back of his leg and barely got a bob out of him. When I grabbed for his groin, I found a cup. He barely paid attention to me as he reached into his pocket and pulled out his cell phone. Two swipes later he had a flashlight shining bright and he aimed it right at my face.

"Can you see her face now?" he called out. "This is Freelancer 57. I'm now accepting bids to deliver her to a location of your choosing. Anything less than $15 million, and she drops."

Freelancer 57's grip tightened on my hair and I swung my feet forward to brace them against the edge of the building while I punched at his wrist. It was like punching a lead pipe.

It was now or never for the knife, which meant looking at it. He'd see it, but it was my last hope.

"I don't want to hear a bid unless it's over $15 million," he repeated loudly before kicking the foot of my shot leg over the edge of the building.

I brought the knife up behind his shoulder, immediately spotting the release mechanism. If I cut the tendons of the arm holding me, I would drop.

"She's a pain in the ass," he yelled as I brought the blade into play and assessed my situation. "There's a surcharge for that."

I tried to get my bad foot back on the safe side of the ledge, but it no longer bent on command. I was about as secure as a flag hanging from one hook. For the moment, I was still in position to land on the roof if he dropped me, but a little push from him would switch up my balance quick enough and I'd drop.

"Going once," the bounty hunter called out to our invisible audience. "Going twice…"

Hanging from my hair with one foot precariously anchored into the ledge, I saw The Four's verdict in the bounty hunter's eyes before his lips smiled.

"You're done, Ms. Jensen," he said as I hammered the blade into the back of his forearm and dropped butt-first into the ledge—one leg on the safe side, the other starting the nine-story drop. I rolled my shoulders to force gravity to make me land on the roof with one leg sticking up lamely above me.

My vision fractured from the impact of my head against the roof, but I ignored it as I fought to get distance between me and the bounty hunter before he could grab me again. When I was sure I was out of reach, I turned to face him, expecting incoming. So…why was he laying on the ground?

I felt the answer before I saw it.

Then I saw it.

A hole. A pool of blood. Vacant eyes. The bounty hunter had dropped me because he was dead.

Had there been a gunshot? If so, I hadn't heard it. But the Freelancer 57 had definitely been shot. He probably hadn't even felt a thing.

Mark, was my first thought, followed by Dahl and Kay.

I glanced over to where Spider-man should have been and saw nothing but the hotel. I checked for open windows or any other places where Kay or Dahl could have taken a shot from the suite and didn't see anything.

So where had the bullet come from?

It occurred to me that the shooter could have been any of the other freelancers who just wanted to stop their competition from collecting the bounty. Whoever had killed Freelancer 57 could be aiming at me right at that very moment.

I rolled to my stomach, army-crawling to cover and hating the feel of dirt and rocks grinding their way up into my leg wound. The adrenaline of the moment was keeping me from fully feeling the gaping hole, but I knew I was bleeding out. I needed to get off the roof and get my leg wrapped, stat.

There was no time to process anything. I was a sitting duck on that roof now that everyone in The Fours network knew exactly where I was. I needed to get far away and do it fast, without leaving a blood trail. And there was only one way to do that. I needed to break into one of the apartments.

CHAPTER 23

It was prime time, which meant people were cooking. TVs were on. Residents of the apartment complex were unwinding after a day spent at work. I pressed my ear to each door as I passed, searching for a door with silence on the other side, all the while hoping that no one would step into the hallway and spot me. I'd taken my shirt off and tied it as tightly around my gunshot wound as possible. Yes, I was trying to stop the blood, but I was also trying not to leave a blood trail straight to someone's door.

So far I wasn't doing so good with that, and with every passing heartbeat the situation only got worse. Blood saturated my pants all the way down to the hem, which I had tucked into my socks. *Squish* sounds seemed to echo down the hallway with every step and my shoe was just a few ounces away from overflowing.

I needed an empty apartment. Now.

"Seventh door on your left," Eyes said in my ear. *"And fyi, I know where you are because they know where you are. We're all looking at a wifi view of the apartments and your limping makes you stick out like a neon sign."*

Great. Just great.

"How much time do I have?" I asked, doubling my speed as I headed for the seventh door.

"Honestly? I have no idea. The bounty hunters don't have cameras on them, so I don't know their locations unless they make themselves known."

I was almost to the seventh door. "But that's good for me, right? They won't want to kill me in here. Too many cameras catching them coming in and no cameras broadcasting out. Just the wifi outlines as proof of a kill, which earns them less."

"Not actual cameras yet," she warned. *"We don't know what kind of TV is in that apartment, though, or what other electronic devices. There may be plenty of cameras in there."*

Just the kind of silver lining I'd been looking at all day.

"I'll keep you updated, but move fast," Eyes said.

As if that didn't go without saying.

The blood on my hands marked everything I touched. By the time I picked the lock, the door was well decorated with my DNA. Even if an assassin couldn't track my wifi profile in the building, I might as well put out a sign broadcasting my location.

Shutting the door behind me, I locked it and turned on the lights. I was definitely in a guy's apartment. Sparse decorations, more than a day's trash hanging around on countertops, and a large screen TV with gaming systems attached.

I hobbled over to the entertainment center and glanced behind it. Six cords were plugged into a power strip. Hoping it would do some good, I yanked the power strip out of the outlet and went looking for the bathroom.

"We have eyes in the bedroom," Eyes told me. *"He has a laptop open. If you need to go in there, close it."*

"Copy that," I said as my shoe started overflowing.

It was a one-bedroom apartment and the door straight ahead was clearly the bedroom, which made the door on my left the bathroom. I pushed through the door, turning on the light and immediately stripping down. I toed out of my shoes, throwing them into the bathtub. Next off was the tactical belt which I placed on the counter before carefully peeling off my pants.

My hands shook and part of me reeled at the sight of the leaking hole in my leg.

"Don't speak aloud to me," Eyes said in my ear. *"They have audio. They'll hear everything you say and know you're not on your own."*

At that moment, I couldn't have spoken if I'd wanted to. I'd never seen a hole my body, not to mention a potentially fatal hole. It could have been seconds or minutes that I stared at my blood-drenched leg, trying to wrap my head around the reality of my situation.

I was in trouble. Big trouble.

"Nope," Eyes said authoritatively in my ear. *"No going into shock, Rhea. Get into that shower and rinse off as much blood as you can. Then I'm going to walk you through using the medical foam Jack gave you. It will plug the hole and numb the pain. It won't fix you, but it will buy you time."*

Plug the hole? Did that mean I'd just be bleeding internally rather than externally? How was that any better?

Still, her words woke me up and had me reaching for the water nozzle.

Rinse off. I could do that. Or could I?

Staring at my leg had flipped a switch in my mind. Gone was the numbness. Replacing it was a stabbing, sharp pain that screamed at every slight movement below my waist. My hands weren't the only thing shaking now. My leg was visibly quaking and sending tremors through the rest of me.

I stared at the side of the tub. The bathroom had a shower-bathtub combo and no matter how I navigated it, I couldn't find a way to step over the top of the tub. My left leg just couldn't hold the weight on either side.

My mind felt a little sluggish, so it took me a moment to come up with the solution of sitting on the edge of the tub and swinging my legs in. Then I put all my weight on my right leg and stood up in the stream of water. It was a bit too hot, stinging my skin wherever the stream of water hit, but I couldn't worry about that. I just needed to get my left leg clean.

"That's good enough," Eyes said after what felt like two seconds. *"Now go to your utility belt."*

Right. Just go to my utility belt.

Sitting on the edge of the tub, I turned off the water and reached out as far as I could until my fingertips touched the belt. When I jerked it my way, it came. Thank heavens.

"Your wound doesn't need to be clean to apply the foam," Eyes said. *"Don't worry that the wound is still bleeding. I just want to minimize the amount of water the foam is exposed to after you apply it."*

"Okay," I said softly, figuring that was a vague enough acknowledgment to pass as a personal pep talk if anyone heard it.

"The syringes you're looking for are the two in the very center of the belt, one blue, one white."

I saw syringes and reached out to dry my hands on the closest towel before grabbing them.

"Blue first," Eyes said. *"Do half of the contents on each side of the wound, so you get both the entrance and exit wound. One side with both syringes, then the other. Press the nose into the wound as much as you can."*

She made it all seem so easy—like pushing a syringe into a hole in your leg was the most natural thing in the world while your body was shaking like you were in the middle of an earthquake.

"Time, Rhea," Eyes warned me. *"I don't see any bounty hunters heading into the building for you, but every minute you delay allows another one to arrive and catch you on the way out. There's no time for hesitation here. You are completely compromised."*

I stabbed the syringe into the front hole in my leg, dry heaving as pain shot through me. I rode the reaction out then pressed the plunger half way down.

I was a quarter of the way there.

Repeating the same thing with the white syringe, I realized I was crying and bit the impulse back. The Fours had audio. Any sign of weakness would only encourage them.

The chemical reaction was immediate—the two liquids expanding and turning firm. I could literally feel the bleeding stop within me, but I wasn't sure that was a good thing. Muscles needed circulation, didn't they?

Whatever. I couldn't think about that right now.

Repeating the same process on the back of my leg, I noticed that the foam wasn't just stopping the bleeding, it was numbing it like a local anesthetic. I slapped my leg, feeling nothing, and realized that I was dealing with medical-grade stuff. My leg was literally ready for surgery. That was great for relieving pain but not so good for mobility. A numb leg was a dead leg.

"If the foam is firm then you can rinse your leg again if you need to," Eyes said. *"You're going to need to steal some clothes, and it would be best if they weren't bloody. Lose the shoes. They're soaked and will leave a trail."*

Everything she was saying might have been obvious, but in my current state of mind, I needed to hear it.

Pushing up with my right leg, I used a towel to wipe blood off my leg before testing it. My left leg didn't want to walk, but I had to find a way to force it. That was pretty much non-negotiable in all of this. I couldn't hop around for the rest of the night. I did plenty of hopping on my way to the bedroom, though. A queen bed with iffy sheets sat against the far wall and dirty clothes were piled at the foot of the bed. The computer Eyes had been talking about was sitting on a makeshift desk to my right and I slapped it shut.

No more eyes and maybe no more audio…although the latter was too much to hope for.

I moved to the closet, praying for clean clothing options, and saw that the guy who lived here was definitely a good six inches taller than me. He wasn't overweight, though, which was a small favor. His waist might be several inches bigger than mine, but it could have just as easily been twelve or twenty inches bigger.

I needed two looks: one to get out the door and one to swap into the moment I hit a blind spot.

Assuming you get that far.

Stop. I had to stop thinking like that.

I needed two looks…and a working leg…and shoes that were definitely not in this closet. I had t-shirts, jeans, gym shorts, about a dozen ball caps, and size 9 men's sneakers to choose from. I wore size 5 in women's.

I looked through the shirts, choosing the smallest one. I'd wear my own shirt out, then change into the t-shirt and a hat outside. My big problem was pants and shoes. If ever there was a "make it work" moment, I was standing smack dab in the middle of it.

"C'mon, dude," I muttered. "You live in LA. Don't you ever have girls over?"

Based on the state of his bedroom, no girl stuck around for long. The sheets hadn't seen a washer in at least a couple of weeks.

Time was slipping by like water through my fingers. There had to be dozens of bounty hunters in position around the building by this point. Realizing that had me testing out my left leg again. Now that the anesthetic had set in, I could feel how localized it really was. I could feel my foot and almost everything below my knee. There was just a dead zone between my knee and my hip on the front and the back of my thigh. Weirdly, I could still feel both my inner and outer thigh.

I pressed the blade of my foot into the ground and pressed into it. It felt unstable, but it held. I could use that. But not yet.

Grabbing the only pair of skinny jeans the guy owned, I did a one-legged hop over to the bed and rolled back onto it to slide the pants over my hips before rolling up the hems. I'd use the utility belt to hold them up until I found something better. Same with shoes. A pair of Converse were the smallest design he had and they would just have to do until I could swap them out.

"It's time to get out, Rhea," Eyes said in my ear. *"You are beyond out of time."*

I finished tying the shoes, keeping my limp exaggerated as I headed to the kitchen to look for a sack to carry the extra shirt and hat. It killed me that I had left the bag with Ty's shirt up on the roof.

I couldn't think about that.

A Taco Bell bag with sauce packets and extra napkins sat on the counter and I dumped it out before my eyes moved to the fridge.

Where there was this much junk food, there had to be soda. I hadn't touched the stuff in years, but I had just bled out several pints of blood. My blood sugar had to be crazy low and I couldn't chance passing out as I made a break for it.

I hopped to the fridge. It held condiments, beer, and a cardboard 12-pack of Coke. I grabbed one and chugged it. The liquid felt like a toxic high, and only when I was finished did I realize that my utility belt was still in the bathroom.

Hopping back down the hall, I returned to the bathroom and saw it with fresh eyes. The entire room was a bloody mess, all thanks to me. Blood on the floor. Blood on the wall. Blood on the counter and toilet. Bloody shoes in the tub and soaked pants on the floor.

I grabbed the belt, strapping it around my sagging pants and looking at myself in the mirror. I looked…pretty butch, which gave me an idea even as I fought the urge to clean up the bathroom a little.

Catching my own eyes in the mirror, I looked into my eyes and whispered, "Move."

But I didn't move. I kept imagining the guy who would come home to this.

On an impulse, I put some toothpaste on my finger and wrote *SORRY* on the mirror before pulling out a few $100 bills and tucking them behind the sink faucet.

Like that made things better.

Who was I kidding?

Whoever lived here was going to freak out when they got home. But just like the man lying up on the roof, I didn't have time to worry about what I was leaving behind. I had to just keep pushing forward.

There was a bomb scheduled to go off at 9:00 p.m.—or earlier. That gave me a maximum of an hour to finish what I'd started three hours ago.

I didn't have time to clean the bathroom I'd turned into a war zone.

I had to go.

Sticking to my hop-limp, I headed to the front door and let myself out. "Where to?" I whispered to Eyes.

She didn't answer immediately. *"Honestly, Rhea, I don't know what to tell you."*

That was encouraging.

"Everyone knows exactly where you are and your injury makes you pop out like a rabbit on a golf course. Every exit is covered now. I see at least seven lurkers who are overtly hovering. You're surrounded."

"Then I need the busiest exit," I said. "Is there a group of people near the building anywhere? Any busy stores on the main level? I need a really large group."

"It's St. Patrick's Day. The pub on the main level is definitely the most populated area."

"How do I get there?" I asked. "Which exit?"

"Can you do the stairs?"

"If I have to."

"The stairwells are clear," she replied. *"Take them down to the main level. You'll be about half a block closer to the pub from that direction."*

"Copy that," I said, hop-limping down to the end of the hall and pushing into the stairwell.

I used my hands on the railings to swing down each flight, landing hard on my right leg each time. It was only nine flights. I could handle it.

"Everyone is moving to your position, Rhea," Eyes said, her tone grave. *"One freelancer is dressed as a cop. They're going to pounce the moment you exit."*

I stopped on the second floor, considering that before pushing out of the stairwell and back toward the apartments.

"Tell me when I'm over the pub," I said.

"About 100 feet," she replied. *"On your left."*

I gimped my way down the hall, barely touching my injured leg to the ground as I went. "Tell me when I'm hot."

"Still cool...warmer...warmer...two more doors... next door."

I stopped right where she told me, knocking politely on the door. I heard a TV on the other side and smiled for the peephole. The resident peeked through before tentatively opening the door. It was a girl in her early twenties.

"Yes?" she said, looking at me nervously.

"I'm really sorry," I said, pushing the door the rest of the way open. "I really need your window."

She squealed in fear, backing away from me like the intruder I was.

"I swear I'll be out of your life in five seconds," I said, moving straight to her window. "Really sorry about this."

The window was already open to let in the cool evening air and I popped it the rest of the way with one push of my hand.

"Sorry, again," I called back before using my hands to lift my left leg through the window first and following it with the rest of my body. Luckily, I was out of the window before the girl's brain processed the scenario enough to start throwing things at me or screaming. It was one of the few perks of being a small woman. You were slightly less intimidating when you forced your way into someone's home.

My stomach sank as I took in the drop-off beneath me. It had to be over fifteen feet. Maybe twenty? It was always harder to tell when you were looking down in the dark. There was no canopy between me and the ground. Just me, air, then sidewalk. Oh, and one good leg.

Also, there was definitely one bounty hunter about fifty feet away and closing in. And as much as I hated it, this was my best move. I had to jump.

CHAPTER 24

I had no time to think and limited space to land on the patio beneath me. A forward jump with a front roll was out. It would put me too far away from the entrance and my leg was way too unpredictable in supporting a forward-roll after impact. It might just crumble beneath me the second it touched and leave me to splat like a bag of graceless rice. My only hope was to roll backward, so I quickly grabbed the window ledge and lowered myself until I was hanging out of the window back-first.

"Whoa," someone called out from below me. "Is she for real?"

Good. They saw me. Maybe that meant they would clear a landing spot.

"Back up," I called out right before I pushed away from the building and let myself free fall.

"Dude!" the same guy yelled. "Move! Move!"

I led with my right foot, waiting until I felt it touch ground before tucking in for a back roll over my shoulder and pushing up into a handstand so I could land my right foot first again. I brushed into someone as I pushed out of the roll, but they moved out of the way before we collided. Small favors.

"Sorry," I muttered, ignoring the sting of impact that went from my right hip up to my left shoulder. It felt like I'd been run over crossways by a car, but at least my technique had been good enough to avoid smacking my head during the roll. An unhappy back was better than trying to work around a concussion.

"Are you okay?" someone asked, but I had no time to answer. Back hunched and still limping, I ran into the pub.

A glance showed that it was standing room only inside the pub. That was good for me. Large groups stood around TV screens watching some March Madness game. Noise, congestion, chaos, and alcohol all in one spot. It was as ideal a scenario as I could have realistically hoped for.

Limping past the entrance, I pushed my way into the loud crowd. The patrons were drunk, or close to it, and more focused on the screen than someone pushing past them.

"Can you see me?" I asked Eyes.

"See you? In that swarm? No," she replied. *"But I know exactly where you are. You're in the middle of all those tall guys. There are security cameras everywhere. The second you come out, I'll see you."*

"Copy that," I said, pulling out the extra t-shirt and hat I'd borrowed from apartment guy before noticing a soccer jacket one of the guys had hung over the back of a chair. That would do much better than changing my shirt in the middle of a bunch of dudes. "Let me know if you see them spot me."

I donned the cap to block my face before stealing the jacket to finish my look—hair covered by the jacket to hide its length.

"Ten feet away and at your six, Rhea," Eyes said. *"You have serious incoming."*

I tested my left leg, pressing into the blade of my foot to let my outer thigh know that it was time for it to step up. It was time to stop limping. It was time to act casual. It was time to walk like a normal human on a leg that was fifty percent numb.

Feeling through the pockets of the jacket I'd stolen, I searched for a phone. When I didn't find one, I checked the pockets of guys around me and found one on my third try.

Keeping my movements casual, I walked out of the group with the smoothest gait I could manage while pretending to text on "my" phone. I didn't look up. I didn't glance around. I'd told Eyes to tell me if they spotted me, and so far she was silent.

I had to trust her.

"He's in your grouping," she warned in my ear. *"I don't see you, but he's probably close enough for you to touch."*

She couldn't see me, which meant she was looking in the wrong place. That was very good for me. I kept my eyes on the phone and my thumbs moving like I was texting as I moved toward the entrance.

"Seriously, dude!" a guy was saying outside. "Did that just happen? Tell me I'm not the only one who just saw that."

According to the pain in my back, *that* had *definitely* just happened. But, like any self-absorbed urbanite, I didn't give the raving man a passing glance as I walked back out of the pub while keeping my eyes locked on the phone.

A man brushed up against me, going in as I walked out, and neither of us apologized at the contact.

He was one of them.

The adrenaline spike of knowing that had the pain in my back disappearing in an instant as I turned right and started down the street.

"You have three bounty hunters in the pub and the one dressed as a cop is positioning himself between your two exits. It's time to get serious, Rhea."

I didn't answer. I didn't dare. I was surrounded by cell phones on the street, all of which were live mics looking for my voice signature. The pub had been chaos. I could talk in there and blend into the din, but not out here. I couldn't speak again until I reached a safe location.

"Rhea? Do you copy?"

I was nearly to the street corner, and if Eyes hadn't spotted me then The Fours hadn't either.

Even gait, I coached myself as I continued my fake texting. They were looking for a limp. They were looking for a girl in a black top. They were looking for a heat signature that had been mine before I lost a few pints of blood. Being shot was going to mess with me for the rest of the night, but for the moment it might be the one thing that was saving my life as I made my way a block-and-a-half to a local gay bar.

No men allowed.

I was dealing with The Fours—a boys' club. I highly doubted they had any female assassins. In fact, I was about to bet my life on it.

"Okay, I don't know where you went, but good on you. For the moment, everyone is stumped."

I had to stay calm. I had to stay casual. I couldn't run—not that I could've had I wanted to at that point. If it came down to a footrace, I was sunk. Casual was my friend. Normal was my friend, which was why I tucked the phone in my back pocket after one last fake text. No one texted all the time.

Still, I kept my chin down and the collar on the soccer jacket up. Doing any more than that would pull focus.

The toe of my oversized shoe caught on an uneven portion of sidewalk, nearly causing me to trip. I caught myself but hated the attention I knew it pulled on all the cameras pointed my direction. Finding my stride again, I held my breath and waited for Eyes to tell me that my cover was blown.

"At least one of the bounty hunters doesn't think you're in the pub anymore," Eyes said. *"If you are, keep doing what you're doing. The others might give up, too."*

I was just starting to feel smug when I realized I didn't have an ID to get me into the gay bar I was walking to. That was a problem I had about two hundred feet to figure out how to skirt.

Reaching into my pocket, I grabbed one of my remaining hundreds and palmed it. There was no line out the door, which made sense. It was early.

"ID," the muscular doorman said as I approached.

I held up the hundred, hoping that was enough.

He looked at the bill then at my face before focusing back on the hundred. His hand reached out and plucked it out of my hand. "You're good to go."

For once I was catching a break. Thank heaven!

I walked in, taking the first full breath in hours. There were maybe two dozen women in the bar and all of them looked my way as I walked in. Hmm. I'd forgotten that would be part of the dynamic in here. Someone was bound to talk to me, and anyone who spoke with me was potentially someone The Fours would target down the line.

Anxiety hit me anew a moment before I realized I was smelling food. This place served food—or at least it served nachos—and my stomach roared at the realization. I headed straight for the bar where the female bartender looked me up and down.

"Hey there, honey," she said with a hint of flirt. "What can I get you?"

"Orange juice," I said in a whisper that hopefully disguised my voice enough not to flag the system in case any microphones picked me up. "How long for nachos?"

"Right now?" she said, gesturing around. "Five minutes. Or we've got pizza ready."

"Perfect," I whispered, finding a twenty. "Two slices. Three if they're small."

"Coming up," she said grabbing the bill and quickly making change.

"Bathroom?" I asked, not picking up my change.

"Around the corner, on the left," she replied.

I gave her a nod of thanks and left the phone I "borrowed" on the bar before following her directions. I was hoping for one of those private bathrooms rather than a row of stalls, but it was early enough that it didn't really matter. The bathroom was empty and I kept it that way by locking it behind me.

"Eyes?" I said, once I knew there were no secondary cameras or microphones picking me up.

"Where are you?" she said. *"And how did you do whatever you just did?"*

"Later," I said, putting all my weight into the door. I didn't dare sit. I might not get up again. My leg was growing more numb by the moment. "I don't know how much time I have before I'm found again."

I didn't say it out loud, but a gut feeling told me I'd just made my last getaway. The next time I landed on the radar of The Fours, that would be that. I had exactly zero more tricks left up my sleeve.

"How are Jack and Anton doing?" I asked, massaging my numb thigh and trying to find spots where I still had feeling. There was a little bit of sensation on the outside of my hip, then nothing. "Have they made a bomb disappear yet?"

As if that were possible. It couldn't be. And yet—

"They're on schedule," she replied. *"As we speak, the advance team is heading to the detonation location you chose. Right now, you're the wild card. Where are you?"*

"Answering that feels like bad luck," I said, letting my eyelids rest for a moment.

"And the gunshot wound?"

Why did she have to bring it up? If I wanted to make it through the next five minutes, I needed to focus on happier thoughts, not the expanding chill overtaking my leg. "It's a problem. My left leg is completely numb from hip to knee. I could drive a car, but not run or fight."

"They'll find you in a car," Eyes said without hesitation.

"Every traffic camera is looking for you."

Great. Just great.

"I need to get back to Jack and Petrov. You've got ten minutes to figure things out, Rhea, or you're on your own."

"Yeah, yeah," I breathed, eyes closed once again. "Go make a bomb disappear. I'll figure out a way to bypass traffic cameras."

"I'll check back in when the bomb is in our hands," Eyes said, then the comm went silent.

She sounded so unimpressed as she said it, like making bombs disappear under the noses of a near-omniscient crime syndicate was a daily occurrence in their world. Well, if they could do that, then I could find a way to outsmart traffic cameras…after I ate something that gave my brain enough fuel to think.

My hand drifted to the adrenaline shot on my belt. I so badly wanted to take it right then, but it was too soon. I needed it for the finale and would just have to find a way to get there on my own steam.

CHAPTER 25

Pizza and orange juice. If things didn't go my way, that's what the autopsy would show was in my stomach at time of death. I would never have imagined either food to be part of my last meal, but that looked to be the direction of things.

Ty would be proud.

I was eating unsanctioned food at an unscheduled time. Go me! I was finally learning to let go and listen to my body. Although it was kind of hard not to with my body teetering on the edge of functionality.

No level of training could have truly prepared me for the past fourteen hours. I'd been drugged twice, had objects implanted and removed from my body, undergone a blood purge, had a bout with hypothermia, done a triathlon, been in several fights, taken a bullet to the leg, and was currently trying to pass off a dead leg as a functioning one to avoid taking a final bullet.

Oh, and a bomb was going to go off in forty-three minutes. So there was that. But if I was going to make it another hour without passing out, I needed food I could keep down so I could stay upright long enough to take that adrenaline shot when it would truly help me.

Then...whatever was meant to be would be.

If I could have magically transported Ty so that he was sitting next to me, it would have been a nice "told you so" moment. Ty had thought I'd been overtraining these past six months.

Guess I showed him.

I'd just seen him, but the temptation to call him one last time still felt overwhelming. It wasn't a possibility. I knew that.

But a worn out girl could want.

I'd tell him I was sick of always being right—that I didn't want to live in a world where my dark thoughts were real. I liked his world better. I liked his thoughts better, and I wanted him to steal me away to a land where I was always wrong and he was the one who always got to say "I told you so."

Instead, I took a bite of over-cheesed pizza in the real world.

The slice was true bar food, greasy enough to lap up the alcohol in someone's stomach and sober them up. I felt both a little sick and satisfied as it hit my stomach. The orange juice didn't really go with it flavor-wise, but this was all about blood sugar. Orange juice to give me the energy to get me out the door and pizza to keep me going fifteen minutes from now.

"You have a maximum of five minutes until you need to be on the move," Eyes said in my ear.

I didn't reply. Cell phones were everywhere in the bar and could easily pick me up. I'd used a Batman whisper to order from the bartender, but each time I opened my mouth was another opportunity to screw up. Best to stay silent for the last five minutes of my life that wouldn't be utter chaos.

Pizza and orange juice in a gay bar with Tegan and Sara playing over the speakers. If Ty could have seen me in that moment, he would've had a good laugh. But the joke was on him because there was a 100% chance none of the people around me were bounty hunters for The Fours. I was in one of the safest places in the city, thanks to good ol' sexism.

"You're just lucky none of them are hitting on you," Ty's

voice said in my head, surprising me. *"Even mortally wounded, you look pretty hot."*

Then I saw him. Not really. Ty clearly wasn't sitting next to me at the bar, but in my mind Ty was suddenly on the stool to my left, his hand holding mine while Kay sat off to my right.

This was it. I was finally snapping, but I didn't have the energy to fight the hallucinations. So I rolled with them. It took less energy.

"You've got this, Rhea," Ty said, his imaginary hand squeezing mine. *"You can get to the rendezvous point."*

I shook my head, speaking to him in my mind. *"It's not that easy, Ty."*

"But you always knew it wouldn't be," he pressed. *"That's why you kept pushing yourself to train harder and practice longer. You felt what was coming and had the gut feeling that you would have to do things you've never done to survive. And you have. Now you're going to do it again."*

"Getting shot changed things, Ty," I argued in my mind. *"It's fully numb now. I need crutches. As soon as I go on the move, they're going to find me. It will be easy."*

"Only if you make it easy," he challenged.

It was pretty futile to argue with one's imagination, but imaginary Ty was starting to make me mad. What did he know about anything? Well, other than the fact that he was technically a part of my psyche.

Yet since the day I'd met him, Ty had always had a way of getting me to think outside of the box. It was one of the reasons he'd been so hard for me to avoid. I was a better version of myself with him around, both professionally and personally.

But that was real Ty, not the psychotic-break-induced Ty sitting next to me in my head.

On my right, Kay spoke up. *"He's here to remind you of all the things you've trained for to get you through all this, and I'm here to remind you not to be nice about it. No rules, Rhea. The only thing you can do that I won't forgive is die. You have a blank check when it comes to anything else. You hear me? None of this 'What would Jesus do?' crap. Your job is to survive. Got it?"*

Yes, I heard her. I didn't necessarily agree with her, but I was glad to have her imaginary thoughts on the matter.

"Your current problem is that you need to get from here to the blast site without being detected," Kay said. *"We both know you need to do something shady or you won't make it to your final destination. The Fours will kill you en route if you give them an opening. On foot isn't an option. Cars aren't an option."*

"I get it!" I thought, feeling overwhelmed.

"Also," she added, *"let's not forget that you're in a gay bar and currently have no less than six pairs of eyes on you...just throwing that out there."*

Ty's eyebrows jumped up and he looked around with a coy smile curling his lips. *"Well, look at that. She's not wrong."*

"You have to use it, Rhea," Kay said, her expression no-nonsense. *"If there's a way to get one of these women to help you, you have to do it, by flirt or force. It's all fair game."*

I glanced over at imaginary Ty, who was nodding. *"She's right. We definitely didn't train for this, but I think you've got it in the tank."*

Even imaginary Ty could get me to smile in the most stressful situations, it seemed. Still, I wasn't on board. *"It will put them in danger."*

"Not if you do it right," Ty said gently. *"You know what you're looking for."*

"A motorcycle," I said without hesitation.

He nodded. *"And you know how to find out who has one here. In fact, you already have. You did it the moment you walked in."*

I had. One woman had definitely ridden a motorcycle to the bar, and she was sitting in the corner booth.

"You should steal her keys and get going," Kay said.

"Too risky," Ty countered. *"The average turnaround on a table eating out is forty-five minutes and the bomb goes off in about forty. It's too close. If the woman finds her bike missing and reports it, Rhea's done."*

It was fascinating to watch my psyche debate itself like I was some passive participant. I must be in worse shape than I thought.

"By the way," Ty said. *"Keep eating. Whatever you can cram down in the next forty seconds is all you get."*

Well, which did they want from me? Flirting or eating? Because the two didn't really go together.

"And don't forget you're dressed in oversized guy clothes at the moment," Kay reminded. *"You don't look like your usual self, and you need to approach accordingly."*

"True," Ty said, getting into it. *"And since the chick with the bike is butch, too, you should make her look good. She's already with someone. Don't compete with that. Use it. Get her bike in a way that makes her look really good to her date."*

"Or she could just steal it," Kay argued.

"And risk getting reported," Ty countered as I took another bite of pizza.

I was supposed to be out the door and on my way in three-ish minutes.

No one flirted that fast.

If my two options were flirt or force, I'd choose force…pretty much every time.

"She's made up her mind," Kay said as I chugged the last of my orange juice. *"Direct approach."*

"It is kind of her thing," Ty said with a sigh. *"And there really isn't time for finesse, if you think about it."*

"But still," Kay argued, looking a little nervous. *"We can't just let her—"*

"Yes, you can," I said, pushing myself up from the bar stool. I

started out with all my weight on my good leg and slowly tried to distribute some over to the numb one.

It didn't go so well.

"Give it a few stomps and see what you feel," Ty coached me.

I did, realizing that I barely felt my foot now, too.

"You need a brace," Ty said, looking around for something I could use.

"She can't ride a motorcycle with a brace on," Kay argued. *"Also, can I just remind us all that we literally have less than a minute? I'm sure that snobby lady in the earpiece will remind us of that in the next few seconds."*

No doubt.

I tried using muscles to pick my dead leg off of the ground and saw movement. I didn't feel it one bit, but there was definite movement. That meant I could probably take steps without collapsing. The medical foam had shut down feeling, not function.

"I guess the question is how much you trust your body to do what your brain tells it to do," Ty said. *"Looks like you can walk if you trust yourself."*

He was interrupted by Eyes' actual voice in my ear. *"I hope you're on the move. Your clock has officially run out."*

"Told you we'd hear from her soon," Kay drawled, looking like she like she wanted to punch Eyes in the face.

I looked between the two of them. *"Are you two going to stay with me through this, or are you leaving now that I'm done eating."*

Imaginary Ty and Kay shared a look and then shrugged.

"It's your brain," Ty said. *"Your decision."*

"I just need you guys to know I love you."

"We know," Kay said.

"Totally," Ty agreed. *"You're weird about showing it, but we've got you figured out. And we love you back."*

Kay nodded her agreement.

"I know," I said softly, feeling myself eyes start to water up.

"Nope," Kay said. *"None of that. Not even a second of that. That's not why we're here."*

"I know," I agreed and pushed away from the bar. It was go time. It was past go time.

"Trust it," I whispered to myself as I put weight on my dead leg and started for the corner booth, leaving the phone I'd borrowed on the stool behind me where someone would find it.

The first few steps were rough, and my leg dragged a bit. But I pushed forward, only bumping into one chair, before reaching the corner booth. The two women were clearly on a date and still seemed to be in the getting-to-know-you phase where people smiled too much and leaned into every word.

Well, if they ended up staying together, tonight was probably a story they would tell again and again.

When I stopped in front of the table, the woman wearing motorcycle boots smiled up at me. "At last, a server. We'll ha—"

I shook my head and motioned for her to follow me, earning a skeptical look.

I repeated the gesture, wanting to avoid speaking, if at all possible. Their phones were not on the table, but that didn't mean they wouldn't pick up my voice well enough for a computer to identify and pinpoint me.

"Look, honey," the woman said, looking annoyed even as her date took in my ill-fitting clothing. "I don't know what you're about, but—"

"Trust me," I whispered, sending her date an apologetic smile. "I only need to talk to you for a second. It's important."

The two women looked at each other as if silently debating my sanity.

"Follow me to the bathroom," I whispered, placing a hand on the table and leaning in to grab their attention.

The woman laughed. "You must be insane. There's no way

I'm going anywhere with you."

I took a few steps back before bringing my other hand up and showing her I had her wallet. "You will if you want this back."

Her eyes narrowed in recognition before her hands darted to her pockets. "How did you…?"

My back was turned and I was moving as quickly as my leg would let me before she could finish the question. I needed to make it to the bathroom before she caught up to me if I wanted to avoid a scene.

And I really wanted to avoid a scene.

She was behind me, though. I could hear her pushing chairs aside as she cleared the quickest route, but I still made it into the bathroom about ten steps ahead of her. I quickly glanced at all the stalls, but it was still empty. It looked like—I flipped open the wallet and took a look at the ID inside—Lucinda and I were on our own.

"Fifty bucks says she goes by Lucy," Kay said off to my right.

"Not betting against that," Ty said on my left.

Ah, my delusions were still on hand. Lucky me.

Lucy charged in a breath after I came to terms with that fact.

"Look, lady!" she sneered right before I clamped my hand over her mouth and shook my head. She jerked away as I moved to the door and locked it.

"What is your damage?" she snapped. "Give me my wallet back."

Rather than answering, I walked up and gave her a quick frisk that revealed a cell phone in her back pocket. I snagged it and quickly removed the battery.

"Any other electronics on you?" I whispered.

"What's going on?" Eyes asked in my ear. *"Are you mugging someone?"*

"Hopefully bribing someone," I said to Eyes while Lucy blinked in confusion and held out her hand for her wallet while I continued to talk to one of the many people I was aware of who were not actually in the room. "Can you hear me through anything besides our comm? Am I broadcasting?"

"Not yet," Eyes replied.

Good. That was good.

"My wallet, psycho," Lucinda demanded across from me. "Now."

"Look up Lucinda McCormick," I said to Eyes before rattling off her driver's license number. "I need something to bribe her with."

"You've got to be kidding," Eyes groaned.

Across from me, Lucinda appeared to share the same thoughts. "How do you know my driver's license number?"

"Because I'm not a normal person, Lucy," I said, cutting to the chase. "And I need your motorcycle and helmet. Now. You won't get them back, but they will be replaced."

"Uh, that's not happening."

I reached into my pocket for the money that remained from my pickpocketing that morning, handing her all the hundreds I had left. "This is all I have at the moment. I can promise you more and a new bike. But in exchange, I need you to give me your keys and never report it as stolen. This is doing *you* a favor, not me. No one can know I took your bike. Ever. It stays our secret."

"Or," Lucy said, stepping forward like she thought she was making some sort of alpha move. "I can take my wallet back and keep my bike while telling you to go to hell."

I shook my head. "Not a good choice. I'm leaving with your bike, and what I'm proposing to you now is the only version of tonight where you don't end up hurt. Not cooperating with me at this point or reporting this conversation to police will end very, very badly for you, if that's the route you wish to take."

"Got her," Eyes said. *"That bike you're stealing is a black Ducati. She's only had it three months and pretty much owes 100%*

on it right now."

"Can we get her a new one before the end of her date?" I asked. Why not? I was dealing with people who could make a bomb disappear. Maybe they could make a Ducati appear just as easily.

"Oh, I'm definitely calling the po—" She blinked and stepped away as I undid my belt. "What are you doing?"

"Notice how these clothes don't really fit me, Lucy?" I asked as I undid my pants as well. "Notice how they look like they belong on a guy about six inches taller than me and about sixty pounds heavier?" I undid the zipper. "That's because they do."

"Whoa," Lucy said, backing away from me. "You're hot and all, but—"

I pulled the pants down until the medical foam was clearly visible. "I'm going to make things very clear to your right now, Lucy. Are you listening to me?"

Her eyes took in my leg like it was an alien. It kind of looked like one. "I, uh, yeah."

"My leg looks like this because I got shot a few minutes ago, and I got shot because I'm trying to stop something very bad from happening tonight. Terrorist bad."

The look on her face said she was listening, and I went with it.

"If you don't want to see a news story that says hundreds of civilians died tonight in a senseless act of violence, then I'm going to need your Ducati and helmet."

Not true. Getting her bike would determine whether or not I had a chance of surviving this day, not whether the bomb made it to a safe location. That was in Jack's hands.

"Stop sweating the small things," Kay said. *"Your version makes her a hero. Stick with it."*

I pulled my pants back up and refastened them. "Now there are a lot of people out there who want this attack to happen as planned, and they have access to every traffic camera in the city. And they're looking for me. So I'm going to need your bike, your helmet, and your silence. I'd prefer you gave them to me voluntarily, but I'm fine to knock you out and take what I need, too. That's Plan B."

Lucy blinked, more than a little stunned. "Either you're insane, or—"

"It's door number two," I said over her then held up a finger as Eyes spoke again.

"You don't have time for this," she said.

"Tell me something useful," I said to the ceiling.

"We can get her a raise and promotion at work. Regional Manager and $85K per year. Make the offer."

Really? Eyes had that kind of power?

"I'm going to make you an offer, Lucy," I said, staring into the woman's now clearly nervous eyes. "You get $500 right now and I get your keys. A new bike will appear in the parking lot within two hours. On top of that, next time you go to work, you'll be offered the Regional Manager position with an $85,000 per year salary. How does that sound? Like a fair trade for losing a motorcycle for two hours and never talking about this conversation ever again, even in private?"

Lucy looked a bit shell shocked. "That would be a $30,000 raise."

"And it disappears in thirty seconds if you don't hand over your keys."

She hesitated. "How do I know—"

I used what little coordination I had left to get her face down on the bathroom floor with her arm locked behind her back before she could finish the question. "If you don't trust that I will deliver on the promotion and the new bike, trust that handing me your keys saves you from a hospital visit. That's a promise."

"Okay, okay, okay!" she called out.

I pulled her back up and handed over the $500. "Remember,

stay here with your date for two hours—even if you see a news report of an explosion. Don't leave for two hours, and speak of this to no one. Understood?"

Lucy blinked like she had fifty questions that all wanted to come out of her mouth at once. Instead, she mutely slid her key off its key ring and handed it to me.

"Oh, and enjoy your date," I said, opening the door and stepping out. "She looks like a keeper."

I left Lucy standing wide-eyed and confused in the ladies' room. Her date gave me some serious side-eye as I crossed the bar toward the exit, but didn't leave her seat.

Small favors.

"If you're going to pull out of a parking lot on a motorcycle, I need to loop that footage now so it's not backtracked to Lucy," Eyes said as I walked toward the exit.

After everything, the fact that I had to tell her the bar's name felt really, really good. Part of me still wanted to hoard the information, but she was right. I needed her.

Whispering the bar's name under my breath, I stepped out onto the sidewalk and turned toward the parking lot.

"Okay. Parking lot surveillance is looping. Go get your bike."

I used my best non-limp to lead me to the Ducati and eyed the gear shift on the left side. That was my numb leg.

Looked like I would be taking my adrenaline shot a little bit early.

Before climbing aboard, I searched for something to cover the plates.

"I can modify enough traffic cameras to mask your origin point, but I can't cover you the entire way. Just the first mile or so. I'll make it appear like you magically appeared under an overpass."

That was better than I'd been hoping for. I'd take it, just like I'd take the neck warmer stuffed inside the helmet and use it to cover the plate with a solid knot to hold it in place.

I swapped my hat out for the helmet and closed the tinted visor. Yes, it would reduce visibility, but that was a two-way street. I had to use my hands to get my left leg over the seat so I could straddle the bike and gave a test pass of shifting through the gears with less-than-successful results.

Knowing what had to be done, I pulled the adrenaline shot out of my utility belt and stabbed it into my thigh. Side effects of adrenaline included a whole lot of things I wasn't looking forward to, and one thing I needed: circulation that would make my shifting foot work again.

The engine was gunning to life when the shot hit me like a scream. Anger washed over me, making me see red through tinted black. I took a steadying breath and backed the bike out of its parking spot with one push of my legs. The thing glided like a dream.

"Oh, baby, you and I are going to get along," I whispered to it as I put it in first and gave it just enough gas to get to the entrance of the parking lot. "You fit my current mood perfectly."

Then, when I saw the path was clear, I peeled out and raced down the road like a bat out of hell.

CHAPTER 26

Between the adrenaline shot and the Ducati, I got to Elliott's house in record time and minus two imaginary friends. I would miss having Ty and Kay articulating my subconscious thoughts to me, but was glad they wouldn't be around to see this next part.

Jack and Anton were still en route, and Elliott wasn't home. If all my happy thoughts were coming true, he was sitting in a hospital somewhere being shown x-rays of the tragic state of his knee while I stood in his personal temple, surrounded by all the things he truly loved.

Things. That's what Elliott loved. Not people. Things.

Such being the case, the security built into Elliott's house was insane. But I'd been counting on that. I wanted him to know I was there, which meant not caring that I set off alarms while hacking around the door locks with an axe. Even with my bad leg, a few solid swings was all it took.

The alarms could rage all they wanted. Jack's team was cutting off the alert to emergency services and Eyes was somehow ready to intercept all the calls from neighbors who might call to report a disturbance to private security or police.

Jack's team were the technicians and I was the distraction. We'd hammered out the details on my ride over. It wasn't a pretty plan, but it was a plan that just might be enough to work.

Maybe.

Step 1: Get The Fours attention.

"Knock, knock!" I called out, still pretty high as I hoisted the axe I'd used to chop around his doorknob against my shoulder. Even with the adrenaline, my gait was more hobble than strut as I walked over to one of the cameras watching over his entry and looked straight into it. "Anybody home?"

My smile was genuine as I imagined Elliott freaking out while all his buddies started placing bets on what would happen next. Would they help him? Had we raised the stakes high enough to rain the power of The Fours on us in the time it would take for us to finish our plan, or was this just another bet to them?

The next fifteen minutes would answer that question. Either way, I was at peace. If I died here, it would be on my terms— although I was still definitely aiming for not dying.

"You're probably wondering what I'm doing here," I said into the lens. "Well, keep wondering."

Gripping the axe again, I swung it into the camera. It wasn't necessary, but my audience did love drama.

Step 2: Create the blind spot.

Dropping the axe amidst the debris of the now-ruined camera, I took the mini-EMP off of my belt. One flip of a switch was all it took for all the cameras within one hundred yards to flicker and die. No more audio transmitting around the world. Not until they got a satellite or drone over Elliott's house.

Jack's advance team had stayed down the street while I set off the EMP. We needed Eyes to give us the countdown of when we moved back under a camera lens, which meant we needed working earpieces on the scene.

When the house went dark and dead, the advance team finished their trek up the street, pushed through the now-disabled gate with their bumper, and pulled into the roundabout. The cargo in this first van contained the "victims" of the bomb blast that Jack had arranged to double for me and Anton.

Faking death was grim business—the kind that made you a bit ill if you thought about it too long. But it was important to acknowledge the reality of the situation: bodies needed to be found. And the state of those bodies needed to match the alleged cause of death, which meant we needed to create a scenario where it was realistic that both Anton and I would be burned beyond recognition while thousands of people watched real-time and played the video back again and again in the future.

Our deaths needed to not only be likely, but seemingly unavoidable when the bomb went off. We couldn't be hiding in the swimming pool or hot tub when the house exploded. Not only did that make us likely survivors, but our bodies would definitely be intact and recognizable.

No, it had to look like the explosion caught us by surprise—that it went off while we were preparing to take defensive measures. That's why I had pitched the panic room for our staged demise. The room was fully reinforced and had access to a secret exit to the house. If we weakened the Faraday cage around the remote trigger to allow it to detonate prematurely, we could make it look like we were heading for the cover of the rear underground exit, only to be caught unprepared when the bomb went off prematurely.

A probable scenario with the bodies to back it up.

It wasn't a perfect idea, but it had won the popular vote of everyone. So here we were.

Or here I was.

Everyone else was en route…which was good because I was still doing my part.

Step 3: Use the blind spot to get our body doubles into position.

I didn't want to watch Jack's men work, yet part of me felt

compelled to do so—like I owed these cadavers some sort of acknowledgment for what they were about to be forced to endure.

These people are already dead, I reminded myself. *They donated their bodies to a good cause. This is a good cause.*

It still felt odd to watch two masked-men carrying body bags into the house. If they had any qualms about what they were about to do, it was hidden under those masks.

"Where do you need them?" a husky voice asked me.

"There's a safe room in the basement," I said, leading them to the stairs. "The combo to get in was 1-3-4-6 a few years ago. If that's not it anymore—"

"We have options," the masked man said. "Just take us to it."

It was so odd to be working with people so far ahead of me on the learning curve. I'd always felt pretty darn smart, but today had been a constant reminder that in the scope of things, I was still in kindergarten. I might feel smart; I might even feel tough, but I was miles out of my league when it came to real-world competition.

There wasn't a single person I'd met that day who couldn't take me out at will, including these two masked men. Well, except Elliott. I'd beaten him, fair and square.

If I lived through all this, there was a whole lot out there I needed to learn if I wanted to keep on surviving. The realization left me feeling a bit dizzy…or maybe that was the shot wearing off and blood loss setting back in. Either way, I kept my poker face fixed as I led the men to Elliott's safe room and punched in the code I remembered from years ago.

It opened.

It opened?

I was surprised, but the men with me weren't. They marched right in and started unloading their bags with a practiced efficiency. They'd done this before. I didn't know if that was reassuring or terrifying.

The bodies they pulled out had been through more than one lab experiment, but I made a point not to look too hard before getting back up the stairs, leading with my right leg. My left quad barely kept me upright on flat ground, and was useless on the stairs.

When I reached the main floor again, the roar of the engine out front was my only warning before a van crashed through the front door and came to a stop in the main entry.

The bomb had arrived.

Anton opened the driver's side door and stepped out, looking around casually. "Nice place."

"It's meant to be," I replied, leaning against the wall for support as Jack got out the passenger side. "Your men are downstairs with the, uh…"

"Good," Jack said, unfazed. "We have four minutes before drones get overhead. Side bets are going crazy and they're still trying to trigger the bomb via remote trigger."

"That's good," I said. "They have to think they surprised us."

"Exactly. You two get on finding ear plugs and anything that can absorb the punch this thing is going to pack." He sent Anton a worried look. "That safe room might take most of the punch, but if it rocks your brain enough then there's no coming back from that."

"Copy that," Anton said, looking my way. "Where's the bedroom? Bathroom?"

I pointed to the floor above, but didn't have a chance to speak before Jack started restating the obvious for us with the first hint of nervousness I'd ever seen from him.

"You're going to be running out of a burning building," he said, inspecting the vast lobby. "That has to happen while the flames are high to hide your body heat signatures from the drones. Then you need to stay close to the burn until the fire department arrives. Then you need to blend into their movements. You'll likely be deaf from the percussion and dizzy and ill during all of this. Find anything that will help you suppress those states and bring it to the safe room."

Sure. We could do that in the next three minutes.

There was no time to think. I ran to the second floor where Elliott's room and all of the guest rooms were located.

"Mattresses?" I said.

"More the merrier," Anton said.

I opened the door of the first guest room. "He has six on this floor, but I don't think we have time for all that."

"Grab stuff for our ears and heads, along with anything that can serve as a barf bag. I'll get the big stuff."

It was a bit sexist, but the fact was we didn't have time to be all equal-opportunity about things. We had to go with our strengths. I was fast(ish); he was strong. I went for the bathrooms and Anton went for the bedrooms while Jack descended the stairs to do a visual inspection of the scene.

Cotton balls. Bath salts. High-end shaving cream. Towels. It was like trying to find survival supplies in a hotel bathroom's courtesy toiletries. I grabbed the cotton balls for our ears and the towels for our heads before running to the next room to see if I could find anything better.

Nope.

I was headed back down the stairs to head to the kitchen when Jack came up the stairs and Anton appeared at the upper railing and threw two mattresses down into the smashed-up entry below.

"We have two minutes until they have a drone in range," Jack announced as his men loaded Lucy's Ducati into the back of their truck. "My team and I have to be out of here before the drone gets in range to read our heat signatures and track us."

"Go," Anton said. "We've got this."

Jack nodded, resting his hand on Anton's shoulder. "See you on the other side."

"That's an affirmative," Anton said. "Now get out of here."

"Gone," Jack said, then he and his team were out the front door and gone.

Anton turned back to me, all business. "We've got ninety seconds to set that Faraday cage up to fail before they're watching our every move."

"You get the mattresses downstairs," I said. "I've got the Faraday cage."

We both went to work.

Step 4: Make the staged scene survivable.

That was Anton's job.

Step 5: Set up the bomb to go off early, while still allowing enough time to get downstairs.

That was on me.

I hadn't really mentioned it, but I was kind of 50/50 on whether my plan would work. Vinegar damaged the integrity of tin foil. So did lye. So did some toilet bowl and drain cleaners. But I didn't know which, if any of those, Elliott had on hand ... not to mention which I would find in ninety seconds of searching.

There was only one way to find out.

Dropping everything I'd gathered upstairs at the top of the basement entrance, I gimp-hopped to the housekeeper's supply closet and started grabbing anything that looked right.

Clorox? Sure. That ate through stuff.

Toilet bowl cleaner? Definitely.

Stainless steel cleaner? Why not?

Hydrogen Peroxide? Couldn't hurt.

White vinegar? Yes!

When I spotted drain cleaner, a calm confidence swept over me.

I had this.

Anton was screaming "Thirty seconds!" up the stairs as I limped to the van with my cache and dropped them at the base of the bomb.

Holy crap, that thing was intimidating. I didn't have time to study it, though, only to find the wrapped tin foil blocking the signal.

The drain cleaner got first crack because it had lye in it.

"Fifteen seconds until the drone is overhead," Anton called out from the stairwell as I fought with the childproof cap.

Apparently, the cap was also panic-proof.

I took a calming breath before giving it one more try that was met with success. Cap off, I immediately dumped the contents on the target area. When the foil around the trigger hissed and bubbled, I sensed that I had seconds rather than minutes before the tin foil lost its integrity.

"Five seconds!"

Based on what I was seeing, my brain wasn't sure whether Anton was counting down to us being back on camera or to the bomb detonating. In the end, it didn't matter either way. It was time to get my butt downstairs.

I ran—or my version of it—to the basements stairs, barely remembering to pick up the towels and cotton balls before taking the first step down on my bad leg. It crumbled, sending me falling headfirst. I clutched everything in my arms to my chest as I fell, accepting the impact before straightening my body and sliding the rest of the distance to the bottom where my face barely missed hitting a pair of boots.

"You okay?" Anton asked.

"Go!" I rasped. "We have to go-go-go!"

He picked me up like I was nothing, carrying me into the safe room and leaving the door open behind us, as planned. He had angled the mattresses up against the wall, giving us each a small area to crouch between the mattress and the wall. Neither of us spoke again until we were safely behind those gaps.

His eyes dropped to what I was holding in my arms.

"What do we have?" he asked.

"Not much," I said, laying the items between us on the floor. "Cotton balls for the ears and towels for our heads. They'll have to double as barf bags."

He grabbed for the cotton balls first, jamming them in his ears while I did the same.

"How much time do we—"

My body hit something…or maybe something hit my body. Maybe both. I had no idea. My mind didn't have time to process it. There was just a flash of white followed by a silent black void. Then there was nothing.

CHAPTER 27

The world was burning. Silently.

A mattress lay next to me, flames dancing out of it as it glowed like a mute bonfire.

I had no idea where I was, although instinct told me I needed to run somewhere off to my left. But there was only a wall to my left. It wasn't on fire. Yet. It was the only thing that wasn't.

Maybe if I went to sleep everything would be done burning by the time I woke up again.

It sounded like a solid plan, but the primal part of my brain wanted to run—*needed* to run.

But where? I didn't even know where I was, not to mention how I had gotten there. All I saw was a wall and flames. There was nowhere to go.

Passing out was the better option. A silent void was preferable to a blazing inferno any day.

Run!

I looked at the wall again, pushing up on my hands and knees and feeling my left leg wobble beneath me. When I glanced down to see why it wasn't working, I spotted an unconscious man. Reaching out my hand, I gave him a shake to check for signs of life.

"Hey," I rasped.

He didn't budge. I gave it one more shot, slapping my open palm against his face with as much force as I could manage.

"You okay?" I called out…or thought I did. I didn't hear any words leave my mouth as suffocating heat pressed into me from my left.

The man's eyes popped open, glancing at me in confusion before he leapt to his feet and started running.

Follow him, instinct told me, so I did—again confused when my left leg did little to cooperate with what my brain was telling it to do.

Still, I trailed behind as the man moved through a wall of flames to an open door on the other side. Bits and pieces started coming together as I limped down a dark, scalding tunnel behind a man moving triple my speed.

Anton. The man ahead of me was Anton, and I wasn't allowed to puke in the tunnel. I wasn't allowed to leave a trace.

I couldn't smell anything, and the only thing I could feel was the oppressive heat of flames urging me to be still and become their fuel.

Oxygen, something said in my brain. *All the oxygen is burning up. You need to get outside so you can breathe again. Hold your breath until you see sky.*

It was the only thought in my mind that wasn't fragmented, so I listened—pushing forward while holding my breath. I felt cool air before I saw it. It wrapped around me like a blanket and whispered, *Breathe. It's safe now.*

So I did.

More pieces fell into place as I approached the exit, and something in the back on my mind reminded me that I needed to stay close to the flames and hide because…

Because?

My mind stalled until I reached the exit and saw that Anton

was doing exactly what my instincts were telling me to do. He was staying close—painfully close—to the flames as he worked his way around to the front of the house.

He was staying so close to the flames because…

Cameras.

Drones.

Bomb. A bomb had just gone off. That's why the world was on fire.

I'd made it go off.

Anton had been with me, and Jack was waiting for us to make our way to him.

Nothing was safe but Ambulance 62.

I needed to stay close to the house, hide my heat signature in the flames, and only trust Ambulance 62.

Jack.

Eyes in the Sky.

Sky…Ty. Ty was okay.

I was not.

Thoughts and memories started replacing themselves like snapshots of film placed in no logical order. One moment my brain was recalling a random day I went surfing, the next moment I was in a training exercise with Elliott. Then suddenly I was sitting on Kay's childhood bed back in Alabama seven years ago, watching her pull pills of fabric off her ancient comforter as she bit her lip to stop words she wanted to say. Then I was sitting on a porch swing with my dad telling him that Anton and Eyes were desperately in love, but star-crossed and could never be together.

Wait. That never happened.

The good news was that my brain had pieced itself back together enough to discern fact from fiction while still managing to trail Anton on the edge of the flames. He glanced my way a few times, but it was clear he wasn't going to wait for me if I fell behind. At best, he would tell Jack's team where he'd last seen me so they could come collect me if they chose.

I couldn't put my life in their hands like that. I had to keep going.

The audio of the world came back in hiccups of white noise. I still couldn't hear the fire or even the fall of a beam that crumbled from the house. The earth literally shook beneath me at its impact, but it was like watching a Michael Bay movie on mute. Silence made it easier to plow forward into the insanity—the lack of sound making it all seem less dangerous somehow.

Anton paused as we reached the last turn leading to the front of the house. Much too close, flames rose into the sky off to our right as firemen arrived to contain the chaos. I saw their mouths yelling and saw the spray of water aimed at the house, but again heard nothing.

Don't let anyone see you. No physical eyes. No digital eyes.

This thought was paired with a sense that I was getting seriously burned. I wasn't feeling it for some reason, but my skin was in trouble.

I needed Ambulance 62, but everything was too far away. Anton and I would have to leave the cover of flames to reach anything in the front drive.

It was as I was trying to think my way around exposing myself to a drone when something dropped from overhead, crushing me into the ground. Air rushed out of my lungs at the impact, and when I gasped to replace it, my mouth was filled with…foam? The ground was suddenly slippery and air was nowhere to be found. Some of the foam had gotten into my lungs and it was odd that through everything, that was the only part that felt like it was burning.

I tried to clear my face—seeking air—when something hooked around me and started dragging me. Whatever it was, there was no fighting it. It had me and it dragged me in the foam for what felt like forever before I was hoisted up and tossed on a gurney. A man dressed as an EMT strapped me down without hesitation before cutting away the leg of my pants to get a good look at my bullet wound. I spotted Jack sitting between me and the ambulance's other gurney.

Oh, yeah. I'd been shot. That's why my leg didn't work.

The EMT sent Jack a look I didn't like then started to set up an IV.

Jack looked me in the eyes before tapping a finger against his ear. *Can you hear?*

Maybe he said the words, maybe he mouthed them. I couldn't tell. All I could do was shake my head. He nodded and picked up a tablet. As he spoke, words appeared on the screen.

You're going straight into surgery. You're in the danger zone, but your surgeon is amazing. I feel confident that you will make a full recovery.

I had to blink a lot to make the words hold still long enough to read them, but when I finally made it through I looked up at Jack and nodded for him to continue.

I will not be here when you wake up but—

The text started spinning and I squinted my eyes shut to try to find my center. It helped for a second.

—as promised, I have created a new identity for you with all the necessary documents you will need. That said, you cannot return to your own life and cannot show your face anywhere again. The same goes for Anton. As you know, he has already been scheduled for reconstructive surgery.

Yes. Anton Petrov was about to become his best friend. It would take six months of reconstructive surgery and some extensive body tattoos, but in the end, he would be able to return to the world he wanted to live in and be with the people he loved.

I envied him that.

You must leave the country, the tablet read as the EMT prepped a needle to go into my arm. If it was anesthesia then I wasn't going to need a ton. I was an inch away from passing out on my own.

Jack started talking again, but I couldn't read the tablet because it started shaking like crazy…or maybe it was me that was shaking. I couldn't tell until the EMT dropped the IV on a tray and fought to tighten the straps on the gurney. It all played out like a movie in the distance, where I heard and felt nothing even as I knew the arms being pinned to the bed were mine and the strap being pulled tight across my hips was to keep me from harming myself.

People were yelling, I could tell that without hearing. I could feel their voices on my skin like a touch. Then I felt a pinch on my neck several moments before my body started to calm. I didn't feel the change physically as much as I watched the world settle through my own eyes. A moment later, my eyes locked on the ceiling of the ambulance and lost the will to look anywhere else. Then my vision narrowed and narrowed until it went black.

Then there was nothing. Again.

CHAPTER 28

I could smell again.

That was the first thought I had before my ears registered the steady beep of a heart rate monitor. The sterile hospital-like smell registered in my mind, letting me know I had been moved out of the ambulance.

I could smell. I could hear. I could see. The bomb hadn't permanently taken any of my senses away from me.

That was something, at least.

Yet even as I became aware of those senses, I also became aware of the fact that I could not feel anything below my waist. I couldn't bend my knee or wiggle a toe.

Next to me, the heart rate monitor picked up its pace.

"Someone's awake," a female voice said and a moment later I heard the click of a button being pushed.

I squeezed my hand into a fist, feeling my short nails push into my palms, then I tried to curl my toes. Nothing. I felt nothing.

"Hold still," the female voice, presumably a nurse, said. "You just came out of surgery. You were a bit of a mess, but I think we fixed you up. Just don't try to move. Not yet."

My mind heard her words but had yet to connect their meaning to the lack of feeling in my legs. I continued to try to feel something—anything—from the waist down until a door opened off to my left.

"She's half awake," the nurse said, her voice angled away from me. "Not fully aware yet."

Another woman moved in next to me. "Ms. Fischer?"

Who was that? My hands gripped onto cool steel as I tried to reach the straps holding my arms in place.

"Kali," the new woman said a bit more firmly. "We need you to hold still. You just had some pretty serious surgery and you need to rest. We operated on your leg and also started the skin culture to replace the scarring you received in the fire. You'll get your replacement skin a few months from now, but for now, we're treating the burns and the pain."

After a moment of confusion, I realized she was talking to me. She was using the name Kali and talking to me.

I grew still.

"That's better," the second woman said. "We don't want you undoing any of the hard work we just put into you—not if you want to walk again."

Yes, I wanted to walk again. I definitely wanted to walk again.

I went still and forced myself to focus on my surroundings.

One glance around and I knew two things: I wasn't in a traditional hospital, and I wasn't with The Fours. The Fours would never use female nurses or doctors, and no hospital looked like the room I was currently lying in. The ceiling was too low and the space felt more like a pod than a room. Except for the machines hooked up to me, nothing around me looked like it belonged in a hospital. It felt like a small-scale board room.

"Go ahead and go back to sleep, Ms. Fischer," the second woman said to me, her accented voice comforting. "You'll feel better in a few hours."

"Fischer?" I echoed, looking at the woman's patient face. She looked to be in her forties and had Latin features that matched her slight accent.

She smiled. "That's your name now, ma'am. Kali Fischer. I know that's not the name you had before you came to us, but for security reasons, it's the only name we know you by."

I blinked as that registered.

"You are on a plane en route to a secure location, and everyone from here on out will know you only as Kali Fischer, daughter of Anthony and Camila Fischer."

I blinked, barely processing that. "Camila?"

The doctor nodded. "Yes. Your mother is from Argentina and she married an American man, Tony Fischer."

Tears sprang to my eyes before I could blink them back. Tony? My dad's name definitely wasn't Tony. And Argentina? No. Nothing against Argentina, but that's not where my mom was from. It wasn't who I was. Sure, a lot of people assumed my coloring came from Latin America, but it didn't. It hadn't. It had come from my mom, and she had come from the Middle East. I wasn't going to spend the rest of my life pretending my mom was someone she wasn't.

"No," I muttered, my voice cracking. "I'm not—"

"It's okay," the doctor said softly. "You're going to be okay."

I shook my head, a thousand objections going through my head although only one found its way out of my mouth, "I don't even speak Spanish."

"You'll learn," she said softly before holding up a folder in her hands for me to see. "Becoming fluent in Castilian Spanish will be part of your new identity. When you wake up, I'll talk to you about the two locations you have to choose from after your recovery. You can either go into hiding for the rest of your life or Jack has set up a second option for you to keep training in order to improve your skill sets and possibly start working for him to help people like you in the future."

She had to be kidding. Jack wanted me to blindly jump from

the pot to the kettle? From The Fours—whom I knew nothing about—to him—whom I knew equally nothing about? That would be the definition of insanity.

"Do you work for him?" I asked before I was consciously aware of the thought.

A quick smile flickered on her lips. "Yes and no. He calls me when he needs me, which is rarely. I can count on my fingers the number of times Jack has asked for my assistance, but I will come as many times as asked. It is my honor."

Her honor? Was Jack the leader of a cult or something? Normal people didn't talk like that.

"We can talk about everything when you wake up again," she said, pressing the back of her hand against my forehead. "You've had quite the day, young lady. It's time to heal now. We'll be landing in just a bit and then you'll have a safe place to heal up and start anew."

Start anew. The thought made me feel sick. All I could think of was Ty…and my dad…and Kay. They would believe that body in the house was mine. They would think I was dead. Maybe they already did.

I had to let them know I wasn't dead—even if I never got to see them again. They needed to know I was okay.

I tried to sit up, which was futile since I'd been strapped to the bed. "I need to go back."

My doctor pressed me back into the bed. "No, Kali. There is no going back. I'm sorry. Jack wanted me to inform you that 67% of your audience still believes you to be alive and have put a substantial bounty on your head. You are a very wanted woman, and anyone seen with you will likely be interrogated and killed by The Fours. You cannot go back and you cannot contact anyone."

A dream. This all had to be a dream…only it wasn't. Even in my half-delusional state, I knew that.

I was very much awake and this was not a dream.

"We are flying to a private island now," she said softly. "You can either stay there and train to be someone useful to Jack, or you can live out your life in a remote part of South America that has been chosen for you. Again, we'll talk about all that when you're fully awake. But it's important that you realize that you cannot return to your former life under any circumstances. The Fours will know, and they will take a wrecking ball to everything you love to flush you out. Do you understand? The moment they become certain you are still alive is the moment everyone you love becomes collateral damage." A dark cloud seemed to pass over her face. "Trust me on this. It is not worth it to trade your peace of mind for their lives."

She was speaking from experience. I could tell.

"I know the price is high," she said, her hand stroking my hair away from my face. "And I am sorry for your loss but, as you rest, think of this as a beginning, not an end."

She *had* to be kidding!

As if sensing my rejection of her words, the woman kept talking.

"Not many years ago, I also thought my life was over. But it wasn't, and today I got to save yours," she said with a smile. "I was a nurse back then, but Jack didn't need a nurse. He needed a surgeon and saw the skills he needed in me. I may have lost the life I was born to, but the life I have gained is one I am now passionate about. I still mourn those I lost, but on days like today, I cannot imagine ever going back. Perhaps if you accept Jack's offer to continue your training on the island, you may feel the same way someday."

I heard her words, but her face disappeared in a blur of tears as I thought of Ty. He deserved so much better than this. I'd told him that a thousand times, but he'd never believed me.

Why couldn't he have believed me and just let me walk away months ago? No marriage. No nothing. Just cut ties and let me go.

As much as the past few months with him meant to me, it definitely would have been easier for both of us if they'd never existed at all.

I should have walked away. I shouldn't have let myself be swayed. I shouldn't have loved—not when I knew it would end up like this. He'd already had to say goodbye to so many people in his life…his twin sister, his parents, and now me.

Ty's heart was about to break anew, and it was all my fault.

And my dad…he'd barely started dating again with a woman named Meredith. In all the years since my mom died, he'd never dated anyone seriously until her. No one could replace my mother, but Meredith and my dad were a good fit. All I could hope was that whatever news story they created about my passing would somehow bring the two of them closer together rather than push them apart. If Meredith stayed with my dad through all this, he would make it. He would never get over losing me any more than I would get over losing him, but as long as he had love, he would be okay.

I had to believe that.

Then there was Kay. Instinct told me that she might take this the worst of everyone. I had no logical reason for thinking that, but part of me regretted not preparing her more. With Ty, I had said as much as I could and made it clear how badly everything might end, but with Kay I'd often let her optimistic tone lead the way.

I shouldn't have.

She wasn't going to be okay. I felt that to my bones all of a sudden, and there was nothing I could do about it.

I can't go back…not even for a minute, was all I could think as the doctor reached over and adjusted something on my IV. I felt tears slip down the side of my face a moment before all thoughts disappeared into blackness.

Little did I know that drug-induced blackouts were about to become a mainstay in my life.

EPILOGUE

One Year Later

Which was more godly: the wave, or the surfer riding the wave?

I'd had at least a year to answer that question, and I could still argue it both ways.

For example, it could be argued that the immutable laws of nature were the embodiment of God—the rise and fall of the sea, the rush of the wind, the birth of a volcano…any natural phenomenon was evidence of a god.

But was a god something else, perhaps? Was a god more like a surfer, who harnessed existing laws, like a wave, and exercised free will in the midst of an allegedly fixed environment?

Regardless of what God was or wasn't, time was running out for me to choose which I would be: the wave, or the surfer?

The question gnawed in the back of my mind as I tallied my 346th day on a boulder at the mouth of the one beach I had access to. I removed my shoes, wading into the surf and letting gentle waves lap at my ankles as I paced the boundary of my prison— feeling the primal connection of earth and water and flesh as I tried to figure out my role on its stage.

Was I order, or the chaos acting upon order?

It was a question I needed to answer before I left the island.

In my old life, my actions had defined me. Someday they would define me again, but for the moment everyone who interacted with me judged me by my test scores—precious, precious test scores like Elliott always used to talk about.

Turns out, my life had changed forever back when I was a freshman in college; it just took me eight years to realize it. All thanks to an aptitude test I'd taken with dubious consent.

But what was done was done. A system that sought out people like me with "aptitudes" around the world had done exactly what it was supposed to do: it had found me. And now it had me…sort of.

I didn't have my mind fully wrapped around who Jack was yet, but he held sway in my new world. A lot of sway. It didn't make sense that one man could have as much clout as a group like The Fours. The juxtaposition almost felt like a comic book movie putting Captain America up against Hydra. One man against a massive worldwide organization?

We all know Hydra wins in the real world, but the fantasy of them not winning makes for a great myth. A movie. Not real life.

The sheer numbers and the level of infiltration obtained on all levels of society make Hydra—or The Fours, or whatever the group wants to call themselves—an insurmountable enemy that a man like Jack could never rival in a meaningful way.

Could he?

All I knew was that I was in the same facility as militants being trained for The Fours and their peers, and that my instructors were hiding my presence from all the other organizations at Jack's request.

One man had asked that I be trained in secrecy, so an institution located on an uncharted island somewhere was hiding me under a net of camouflage.

That told me that whoever Jack was, he and The Fours held the same amount of sway on an island in the middle of nowhere. And that was something my brain was still working its way around.

If Jack was keeping tabs on me, he would likely be happy to know that I'd been doing well—really well, based on conversations I heard between men who talked outside my window from time-to-time. The other residents seemed to train together, waiting for the day their test scores proved they were ready for the field.

I wasn't allowed to see my scores, but based on bits of conversation I was picking up, there were definitely a few categories where I wasn't at the bottom of the pile…not by a long shot.

It was a small bit of solace in my new, grim life. That, and walks on the beach.

Given how much time I spent attached to machines, it was hard to know what was real and what was simulated most of the time. But there were some things the virtual reality simulations just couldn't get right. The ocean was one of them.

Something about the sound of the surf in the computer program was two-dimensional, flat. And there was a certain aura to the sea that was missing in the virtual world—a saltiness to the air and the intangible sensation that ran up your legs when you walked ankle-deep in the final push of surf.

No, the ocean had yet to be replicated by computers, so it was only when I was touching the true ocean that I knew my day of plugging my brain into a box to prove my mettle was truly over.

From what I could tell, I spent 20% of my awake time undergoing intense physical training to keep my body in ideal shape, and the other 80% in virtual reality simulations aimed to make me into a strategic, heartless assassin.

Well, the joke was on them—whoever *they* were—because I still hadn't killed anyone yet. But I had died 1,372 times in the virtual world.

Not to brag, but I'm pretty sure I held the Assassin's Island record for most VR deaths and least amount of kills.

Zero kills, 1,372 deaths, 12 languages, and 346 sunsets. Those were the numbers I held onto as everything else around me flattened into a blur.

I didn't know much about the conditions of my life anymore. Just basics. My body had never been stronger or more fit; my mind had never been sharper or more ruthless. That was exactly why Jack had sent me to the island: to get to know my enemy on a level that allowed me to compete with it. The other men on the island had come to train to be super soldiers for the same powers who had a bounty out on my head.

Outsmart. Outwit. Outplay. That was the tagline of a reality TV show and now also my life. Without my current training, I literally couldn't survive a day in a first-world country without being spotted and executed. I was a chick who didn't want to kill anyone living in a world run by men who wanted me dead.

How was I supposed to make a life out of that dynamic?

I didn't know, which was why I sought out the ocean both within the VR simulations and outside of them—to experience the difference between something real and something simulated…and to decide which I was anymore.

Was I still me, or just an avatar in a virtual reality scenario?

Or was I both?

I had no idea, but the ocean was the closest thing I had to an answer to any of life's questions anymore—the build and crash of waves coming ashore as the sun dipped toward the horizon at the end of the day. Sometimes the waves were nothing more than a small lap of water pushing onto the sand before pulling away again. Other times the build was immense and its crash enough to take a life.

Such was nature.

Such was life.

Such was…God?

I didn't know anymore.

God had been banned from Assassin Island. I knew that much. There was only the programmer and the programmed, the hunter and the hunted, the mighty and the weak. My handlers drilled that idea into me day after day. My physical survival required learning everything the instructors had to teach me…with each lesson having a higher cost than the last, it seemed. Assassin Island was a hard place to keep your soul, but I was holding on. Or, at least, I thought I was. Maybe I wouldn't know the answer to that until I saw another non-simulated, non-sociopathic human again and had something non-simulated to compare myself against.

Until then, I had the ocean as my touch point to both reality and sanity…although my grasp on both was admittedly iffy. Facing my own mortality countless times in a virtual world over the period of a year really had me waxing philosophical about the meaning of life because…seriously, what was the point? I didn't know anymore—if I'd ever known at all.

Things that made sense in the comfort of a concrete, man-made city started making less sense in the free-for-all zone. It was no wonder PTSD was so prevalent with soldiers returning from combat. The split between who you needed to be to survive a battle environment versus how you needed to behave to fit in a peaceful city simply couldn't coexist. The set of rules that allowed you to thrive in one environment led you to implode in the other. You had to compartmentalize like a freakin' ninja to pull it off.

To survive, you needed to be like the ocean and seamlessly shift with the tides of the day…or a surfer with the skill to stay safe in whatever nature dealt out that day.

Assassin Island was where you learned to be a one-person tsunami that could rise up and swallow targets on demand. It was where you learned to be as thoughtless and heartless as the sea in going through the motions.

It was kind of astounding how alluring it was to give in to that mindset…to become one with the beast and accept the unlimited power it offered.

To be the wave.

But then I thought of Jack.

If The Fours were a giant wave pool, Jack was the guy seamlessly surfing on the waves they generated. He had the skill to move in and out of their turbulence while actually using it to his advantage.

In religious-speak, Jack was a miracle. He was an angel. He was the thing that defied the rules of how things should play out, replacing natural consequences with his own will.

Jack was a guy who knew how to surf in a tsunami and come out unscathed, and I'd piggybacked my way out of my personal apocalypse on his back.

I should be dead. The tsunami The Fours had tried to swallow me up in should have crushed me into the sand, and would have if it hadn't been for Anton and Jack. I hadn't seen either of them since climbing into that ambulance a lifetime ago. If everything worked out to plan, that meant that Anton was now living life in his best friend's shoes.

A life close to Jack was what Anton had chosen for himself. Jack had made the same offer to me, and I still hadn't answered him. It was past time that I did. I owed him that much.

It all came down to one simple question: Was I the wave, or the surfer?

All around the globe—as vast and deep and powerful as the ocean I was currently looking at—were powerful people like The Fours who would do anything to maintain their hold on the world. They moved like the tide, had weather systems, and created insane storms that the average person either fled or could only pray to make it through.

Men like Jack were storm chasers who ran into the storm to save key things that would otherwise be swallowed up. There was no such thing as a serene day at the beach for men like Jack. I sensed that. The question looming over me every day now was whether I wanted to be part of the storm or if I wanted to be a storm chaser?

Did I want to be a force of nature or the one who defied nature?

Because if God was personified in nature, then that meant my mentors were on the right track. But if God was something different than the ebb and flow of the ocean or the circle of life all around me—if God was something higher than all the systems I saw around me every day—then maybe Jack was onto something when he surfed in on a tsunami and altered natural selection by saving people like me.

"If I become a storm chaser, I'm probably going to die young," I said to the ocean. "But I'm on borrowed time anyway, so who cares, right?"

There was no reply, of course. The ocean wasn't much of a talker. Yet another thing it had in common with God.

It was getting time to head back to the compound anyway. They ran the place like a prison, and one of the rules was that no one could be outside the walls after sundown.

I took one last look at the oranges and golds of the fading day before walking back to grab my shoes. I was just picking them up when my wristwatch rang. I froze.

I'd been told there was a phone on my watch, but it had literally never rung before. This was the first time, and the old school rotary ring paired with the name Jack across the display made it clear who was on the other side.

For a heartbeat I stood in stunned shock. Then I recovered and swiped right.

"Jack," I said, my heart pounding in my chest at the thought of talking to him after all this time. So much had changed, and yet so much hadn't. Could he have sensed that I'd just been thinking about him?

"Kali," he replied, sounding like he'd been a little tempted to call me by my real name before thinking better of it. "It's been a while."

"It has." What else could I say? Thanks for the scholarship to Assassin Camp. Training with soul-dead sociopaths every day has been a true joy?

"I need something from you," he said without preamble.

"Name it," I heard myself say and knew that I meant it.

Whatever he needed, I would do it. Thirty seconds ago, I hadn't been so sure I was ready to make that move. But now, in the moment, I knew where I stood. I wanted him to teach me how to ride a tsunami.

I didn't want to be the wave; I was Team Jack, and ready to be a storm chaser.

SHERALYN PRATT graduated from the University of Utah with a BA in Communication. A gypsy at heart, she enjoys traveling and acquiring new skills. These days she can nearly always be found out and about with her dog, who has spend hundreds hours watching her type. Visit Sheralyn online at www.SheralynPratt.com.

Need to know what happens to Rhea/Kali next?

Pick up Pimpernel today!